A WOMAN UNDERGROUND

A
WOMAN
UNDERGROUND

ANDREW KLAVAN

THE MYSTERIOUS PRESS
NEW YORK

A WOMAN UNDERGROUND

Mysterious Press
An Imprint of Penzler Publishers
58 Warren Street
New York, N.Y. 10007

First Mysterious Press edition

Interior design by Maria Fernandez

Library of Congress Control Number: 2024911692

Cloth ISBN: 978-1-61316-553-9
ebook ISBN: 978-1-61316-562-1

10 9 8 7 6 5 4 3 2 1

Printed in the United States of America
Distributed by W. W. Norton & Company

This book is for Neal and Rhonda Edelstein, friends for life.

Some say the world will end in fire,
Some say in ice.
From what I've tasted of desire
I hold with those who favor fire.
But if it had to perish twice,
I think I know enough of hate
To say that for destruction ice
Is also great
And would suffice.

—Robert Frost

PROLOGUE

Something terrible is about to happen.
The thought seemed almost spoken into Miranda's mind, as if by a voice, a spirit voice, not her own. She would have silenced that voice if she could have. She would have unheard the words.

She was standing at the living room window of the house they called the Farmhouse. It was a ramshackle, weather-worn two-story building in an unmown field near the woods outside the city. Its once-white clapboards were stripped raw by wind and rain. Its roof was slumped like the shoulders of a disappointed man. Inside, all around her, hallways seemed to run off haphazardly in different directions. The hallway walls were stained and faded. There were no pictures hung anywhere. In the living room, the furniture was worn and dusty: sagging armchairs and a colorless sofa, which the men had brought in from secondhand shops in town.

To Miranda, the place had become a prison, though it was only fear that held her there. She could have walked away any time. But where would she have gone?

She gazed out the window. She stood and watched as the two men waded away through the high grass. Theo and Moran.

They were dark figures in the gray morning. They moved slowly toward the line of evergreens, tall pines standing stark against the clouds.

Theo was the smaller of the two. His body was stunted and misshapen. His legs were spindly. His hips were weirdly wide. His shoulders were overly broad and his arms overly long and powerful like an ape's. His two vicious Dobermans trotted along beside him.

Evan Moran, on the other hand, was a big and well-made man. Tall, slim-waisted, broad-shouldered. He was fit and taut, and his gait was easy. Miranda could see his face in her mind's eye: cruel but handsome, frightening but thrilling too. A round, rough face with hot eyes under boyishly mussed brown hair. For weeks, those hot eyes had been gazing at her. He didn't try to hide it, not even when Theo was in the room with them. Whenever Miranda glanced back at him, Moran's thin lips would curl up at one corner in a knowing smile, as if she were complicit in the flirtation. She would look away, but she could feel her cheeks grow warm. When Theo wasn't there, Moran would sometimes move to stand beside her, too close. He would look down at her from his greater height and speak her name in a soft growl, a rumble she could feel in her stomach and below. She would shake her head *no*, but she did not mean no and they both knew it.

Something terrible is about to happen, said the voice in her mind. *Soon. Very soon.*

She watched from the window as the two men reached the trees. She watched them enter the forest, side by side. Both were carrying rifles in their right hands. There were deer in the woods. It was October. Hunting season.

When she could no longer see them through the trees, Miranda turned away. She faced the living room. The colorless sofa with its cushions collapsing in on themselves. The colorless easy chairs with the arms soiled. The scarred wooden table beneath the far window. The small dusty mirror on the opposite wall.

She saw herself in the mirror. She was a small woman in her thirties. She was wearing jeans and a black T-shirt. Her face was expressionless and pale. Once she had been beautiful in a delicate, dreamy way. Finespun blond hair. Perfect small features on a porcelain face. Now as she looked in the mirror she saw something that frightened her, sickened her even. It wasn't her age. It wasn't the faint shine of silver in her yellow hair. It wasn't the lines on the slightly bloated cheeks. All those changes were still almost unnoticeable.

What made her queasy was the frantic fire of panic in her crystal blue eyes. She could see it clear across the room. They were the eyes of a woman spinning out of control, trapped in a life spinning out of control. She was no longer in charge of her own destiny.

I am no longer who I am, she thought.

Restless, she moved down one of the haphazard corridors into the kitchen. It was her best room, the room in which she felt she belonged. There were dishes in the stained bronze sink. She had made the two men breakfast before they left. She knew she ought to take the opportunity to clean up while they were gone, but the dread in her stomach sapped her energy. There was still some coffee left in the carafe in the coffee maker. She poured herself a mug of that instead. She didn't drink from the mug. The coffee was surely cold by now. She simply sat at the kitchen table by the window and held the mug's handle for comfort. She stared into space. She tried not to think about where she was or how she had come here, but her mind wandered aimlessly over the past. Her life back in the city. Her life with Theo. Theo and those Dobermans. His angry dogs. His furious soul made flesh.

Had he always been like this? she wondered. So angry? So violent? Had he always been the way he was now? Had she?

Once, not long ago, Moran had found her alone in the kitchen. She was standing at the window, staring blankly as she was staring now. She was still wearing her long nightshirt. The bruise on her neck was plain to see.

Moran stood too close, towering over her. "Miranda," he said in his low growl.

He reached out with one big hand and gently touched the purple bruise with his fingertips.

She drew away. She put her hand up. "Don't," she said.

But there had been a moment's lag before she moved, before she spoke. There had been a moment when she'd let his fingers linger on her. When she finally did move away, she looked up at him. Their eyes met too directly. Too much feeling passed between them.

"You don't have to live with this," Moran said.

"It's all right. It's nothing," she told him.

"It's not all right . . ."

But then they heard the skitter of the dogs, their nails on the wood of the upstairs hallway. Theo was coming downstairs.

Moran hovered over her another long moment. Just to show her he was defiant, he was not afraid. But before Theo came into the room, he moved away from her.

Now, she began to lift the coffee mug from the table. She knew the coffee would be cold but she lifted the mug to her lips anyway.

I am no longer who I am, she thought again.

Then she heard the rifle shots.

There were two, one after another with a dreamy, slow swiftness, the noise rising above the forest and echoing under the high clouds. *Boom* and then *boom*. With the chatter of birds panicking out of the branches and into the gloomy sky. Then a half beat and then a third shot: *boom*. Her hand trembled violently. The cold coffee spilled over the rim of the mug. It dripped down over her spasming hand.

Deer, she thought. They must have brought down a deer. Or missed it. Isn't that what the hunters always said? One shot meant they'd brought the animal down. Two meant they'd wounded it. Three meant the deer had gotten away while they fired after it haplessly. *Deer*, she thought.

She stood up from the table. It took her two tries. Her body was shaky and weak. With ferocious mindlessness, she went about her business. She did not dare to think. She would not allow herself to think. She went to the sink. She emptied her mug into the green-streaked bronze basin. She ran the water from the faucet until it steamed. Then she washed the breakfast dishes, unthinking. For a few moments, she went motionless, paused with a plate in one hand and a sponge in the other. She felt she was going to be sick. But she would not be sick. She refused to be. The feeling passed. She cleaned the dish.

She went upstairs. Up to her bedroom, hers and Theo's. She hated the smell in there. It smelled of the dogs, their fur and their viciousness. She made the bed. Housework always comforted her. But her hands were still shaking. Her body still felt windy and weak.

She paused again. She held one pillow to her face and sniffed it. The pillowcase needed washing, but somehow she didn't have the energy or the heart to start a load of laundry. She didn't know what she had the heart for, if anything.

She was still hugging the pillow to her breast when she caught a movement at the corner of her eye.

She turned her head to look out the small bedroom window. Through the dust on the pane, through the glare of the sun as it pierced the low clouds and stabbed in bright rays between the branches of the evergreens, she saw Moran returning. He had just stepped out of the tree line. He was walking back across the field, through the knee-high grass. He was carrying his rifle. He was alone.

Miranda stood where she was, clutching the pillow, gazing down at Moran as he came toward the house. She did not know how she felt. Too much of what she felt was unspeakable, unforgivable. She couldn't face it, couldn't admit to herself that she felt it. She felt she no longer knew herself at all, in fact. In that moment, in her own mind, she was a shadowy stranger.

Moran stepped up onto the front porch, under the porch roof, out of her sight. She heard the front door open downstairs. She heard the front door slam shut. She heard Moran's boots clomping up the stairs.

She turned to face the empty doorway. Moran stepped into the frame and filled it. He met her frantic eyes with his grim, hot eyes. He stepped over the threshold. He set the rifle against the wall. He shut the bedroom door behind him.

No, no, no, she thought.

He stood over her, large and powerful. She did not look up at him. He drew the pillow from her hands and tossed it onto the bed behind her. He took her into his arms. She looked up then. He kissed her hard and deeply. She closed her eyes as he breathed in the spicy smell of her, vanilla with a hint of coffee. Then her feet left the floor as he lifted her easily, as easily as if she were air. He laid her on the bed and knelt over her. He stripped her jeans off. He lay on top of her and his cruel, handsome face filled her vision.

She no longer knew who she was. She no longer was who she was. Moran covered her face with kisses and her whole body melted into him.

No, no, no, she kept thinking. *No, no, no.*

But she didn't say a word.

PART ONE

THE SCENT OF SOMETHING GONE

I need to tell you how it all went bad. The beginning of it anyway. The first stages of the catastrophe.

There had been so much death since I'd joined the Division. Roy, Madeleine, all the villains whose killings I'd arranged, the assassin I'd put down with my own hand, face-to-face. I had become—just—a different man. You would not have known me, Margaret. I barely knew myself. I barely recognize myself now when I look back. I guess this is the reason I needed therapy in the first place. Because of this man that I became back then. This man I was that haunts me as I am.

Anyway. I had just gone dead inside. Cold as ice. And my chief, my boss, my mentor—the Recruiter—I guess he knew me. He saw what I'd become and he used it, used me, to get the hard cases done. The direct action, as they sometimes called it. Which means exactly what you think it means. Up till then, my work had mostly been a matter of arranging for one bad guy to take out another. Planting evidence that made it look like a terrorist had sold out his brothers, or a dictator had raped his rival's daughter—whatever scenario would end up with the bad guy's car exploding or the wing mysteriously falling off his plane midflight.

But now. Now I was the guy that was sent to personally insert a bullet in the neck of a paramilitary leader or to give a cartel boss flying *lessons by shoving him out of a helicopter. All right, sorry. Don't make that face at me, Margaret. No more details. I'll stop. I'm just trying to say: When you look upon this lovably tweedy associate professor of English literature at a middle-ranked middle western university, you should know that you would not have recognized me as I was back then.*

So. Anyway. One day, I got a message. A strange message. I'd been back home for a while. Back from whatever sandy hell I'd been in, doing whatever hellish things I'd done. I was in my apartment in Alexandria, across the river from the nation's capital and heart of darkness. I was reading Keats. I remember that. Sitting by the fireplace in autumn, reading "To Autumn." What a perfect poem. "Where are the songs of spring? Ay, where are they? Think not of them, thou hast thy music too." The kid was twenty-three years old when he wrote that. It was like he already knew he was walking with death beside him. Walking with easeful death and half in love with it. "Where are the songs of spring? . . . Think not of them . . ."

Where was I? It was late afternoon. Dark clouds at the window. A view of the river. A couple of pedestrians and joggers on the path, not many though, with the rain threatening. And me reading in a chair before the fireplace. And then—just as I read the words "thou hast thy music too"—right on cue, right on the word music, *my phone chimed. I glanced down at it and saw this text: "Walk to Mount Vernon along the river."*

What could I do? I threw on my coat and went out and walked along the river.

It was a long way to Mount Vernon. Ten miles at least. I walked, I don't know, maybe forty-five minutes. After a while, I was out of the city, under a canopy of trees. The road was to the right of me and the river was just visible through the forest to my left. It had started to get dark. I had a cap on but I could feel a light mist of rain on my face. There was traffic on the road, but no more pedestrians or joggers or bikers on the path. The path was empty, except for me. Me and the shadows closing in.

And then—and I can't overstate how startling this was, how eerie it was—it was eerie as hell—suddenly I wasn't alone anymore. The Recruiter was walking beside me. It was like a ghost story. Like a special effect in a film. I was walking alone and then I glanced to my right and he was right next to me. With his hands in the pockets of his long black overcoat and an old-fashioned porkpie hat on his shaved head, a black porkpie with a brown feather on the side of it. And that face of his, that dark face, barely discernible in the surrounding darkness. But I didn't have to discern it. I knew it so well. Deadpan and absolutely unreadable. Staring straight ahead as always.

Well, this was not the usual thing at all. Normally, his secretary simply called and invited me to his office in the brick building in DC. So to be walking along the river in the dark and suddenly have him next to me—it was everything I could do not to let out a high-pitched scream like the last girl in a horror movie: Eek!

Somehow I managed to give a more or less manly sniff and just continued walking in the cold and rain. We went on like that together side by side in silence for what seemed a long time.

"Do you remember Jerry Collins?" the Recruiter said finally.

I did remember him. I had trained with him, first on the beach, then at Cathedral Station in the woods. Jerry was as straight arrow as an arrow gets. About my height, a little taller, classically handsome face, boyish, almost too handsome, with blond hair, blond-white. He didn't drink, didn't smoke, didn't curse. The guy barely even smiled. He had this hesitant smile, like he had to consider first whether God would approve of his smiling at that particular moment before he let go with it. Very religious. Superpatriotic—incredibly patriotic. When they played the anthem at the end of the day and brought the flag down, he stood there, saluting, and you should have seen his face, like a friend was dying. Then, morning colors, so help me, when the flag went back up again? It was like he was a witness at the resurrection.

Awestruck. Like he was watching the stone roll away from the tomb right in front of him.

I can't say I ever got to know him all that well. He wasn't the talkative type. And sometimes when he did talk, he would start reminiscing about Ma and Pa back in Indiana and his two sisters, Mary Jane and Janey Mare or whatever the hell they were called. He would reminisce about them and gaze dreamily into the middle distance. I was never sure whether he was talking about his actual life or about some television show from the 1960s he'd seen in reruns. Anyway, that was Jerry Collins. You couldn't have made him up.

I said, "Sure, chief. I remember him."

"Yes, I can hear that you do. I can hear the underlying mockery you use to mask your anxiety that his sincere faith in the God who made him and for some unknown reason yourself stands as a rebuke to your own nihilistic emptiness and the pseudosophisticated irony that already echoes in your inward darkness as a prophetic reminder of the eternal condemnation to come."

"Really? You can hear that? I only said five words."

"Their tone was rich with meaning. He's gone missing."

"Who has? Collins?"

"He was on a ferry on the Bosporus, then just like that he was gone."

I restrained myself from glancing over my shoulder. I assumed if the Recruiter had thought someone was trailing us, listening in on us, he would have paused in his story long enough to kill him.

"Was he on an assignment?" I asked.

"That seems like a reasonable supposition."

I stared at him. Though there wasn't much point. It was almost night now and we were under the trees, and even if I could have made out his features, I couldn't have read the expression on them because there never was any expression on them. But what did he mean by "a reasonable supposition?" Had he sent Jerry on an assignment or not? And if he hadn't, who had? And why?

I didn't ask my questions aloud. I didn't have to. I don't think I ever had a single thought the Recruiter couldn't read straight out of my brain.

"He was sent to see a trafficker in Istanbul," he said without looking at me.

I nodded at the darkness in front of me. "Sent to see" of course meant Collins was sent to ensure the Turkish trafficker experienced a fatal series of events.

"The trafficker's name is Kemal Balkin," the Recruiter went on. "He's a dealer in girls and boys. Weapons and drugs too, but girls and boys are his central source of income since, as I'm sure by now you must have discerned from your own faithless and therefore willfully meaningless existence, anyone who fails to accept the gifts of the spirit is left with nothing but the degradations of the flesh and idols of temptation."

"Actually, no, I never have noticed that."

"The soon-to-be-damned often live in denial."

"So you sent Collins to see this guy? This Kemal Balkin?"

I phrased the question carefully, trying to get at whether it was, in fact, the Recruiter who had sent him. It wouldn't have surprised me if it was. The Recruiter had a special animosity toward dealers in children. It was some biblical thing having to do with Moloch and Baal and the high places and I don't know what else. Millstones around the neck. I'm not sure. I haven't read the Bible in a while.

But if it was the Recruiter who had sent Collins after Kemal, why were we out here in the dark and the drizzle and the cold, under the trees? Were we hiding from someone? Someone in-house? Did the Division know we were here? Did anyone?

But the Recruiter avoided answering. "We know Jerry made contact at Balkin's villa on Büyükada in the Princes' Islands, but there was no end-of-mission report. We know Jerry boarded a tourist ferry headed for the Dardanelles, or at least his phone did. Then he was gone."

"Gone? As in, just gone? Right in the middle of the strait? You think someone tossed him into the Hellespont?"

"Doubtful. Like I said, it was a tourist ferry. It was crowded with people."

I opened my mouth to respond, but I didn't respond. If Jerry hadn't been murdered, the only other likely scenario was that he had thrown his phone into the water himself or pulled the card out at least so the Division couldn't track him. But it was hard to imagine a patriot saint like Jerry going rogue like that. It didn't compute. It would be like George Washington betraying his country.

"Have you ever been to Mount Vernon?" the Recruiter asked.

I gaped at him. How the hell had he heard me thinking about George Washington? We had just passed a sign that said we were seven miles from his home, so maybe that explained it . . .

I grunted. "No. I've never gone."

"Of course not. How could you bear it? In the ambient heat of even his residual virtue, you would evaporate into an odorous gas."

"What about Balkin?" I asked. "What about the trafficker? Do you know for sure he's still . . . active?"

"Good question."

"You want me to find out."

"I want you to find Jerry Collins."

The misting rain seemed to have stopped. I raised my hand and wiped my face dry. We walked through the dark in silence for another few moments. All my questions hung unspoken between us. Had this been an official Division assignment? Could I report back in the usual way? Or was I going to be operating independently on a mission for the Recruiter alone? In which case, who was the enemy?

"You know," the Recruiter said quietly. "I would hate to have to entertain regrets for what I've turned you into, Poetry Boy. I told myself that since you were already damned by your conformity to a fashionable *but ignorant unbelief, I could at least put what was left of your shriveled raisin of a soul to use in eliminating the enemies of our great and good nation. You'd already refused the precious gift of salvation freely offered in the death of our kick-ass savior Jesus Christ, so you were hardly likely to have your spiritual buttocks roasted in a hotter flame for the sake of a few righteously slaughtered Chinamen."*

I didn't dare glance at him. This was as close to an expression of doubt in the moral purity of our mission as I had ever heard him express. I feared that if I did look at him, if I saw a true measure of remorse in his eyes, my own confidence would crumble on the spot. Whatever faith in myself I had was really just faith in the Recruiter. If he lost his nerve, my carefully nurtured self-image as an all-American superspy would collapse and I'd be left with nothing but the unbearable shame and guilt of any other murderer.

"There'll be a phone in your apartment when you get back," he continued. "I'll be in touch."

I tried to go as deadpan as he was, to hide the fact that I was totally baffled now. What the hell was going on here? Why were we breaking protocol? Who was I working for? Who was I working against?

"His grave is aboveground, you know," the Recruiter said.

"Whose?" I asked. "Oh, you mean George Washington?"

"It's so you can watch him spinning in it."

I snorted, but the remark only strengthened my sense that something was wrong, something at home, in-house. I needed to know more.

"Let me get this straight . . ." I began.

But as I spoke, I turned to where he walked beside me, and he was no longer there. I was suddenly all alone on the path.

I walked on a little way farther in what was now full night. A pall of anxiety descended on me. For the life of me, I could not figure out whether . . .

1

"Have you called Gwendolyn Lord?" Margaret Whitaker asked him. She didn't mean it to sound accusatory, but she knew it did.

Winter stopped talking midsentence, startled. The therapist did not interrupt him often, not when he was in full narrative flow like that. For over a year now, she had allowed him to tell her these stories of his, long stories about his secret past with the Division. It was not the usual way she did therapy, letting the client ramble on in that fashion. But then, Winter was not the usual client, not at all.

She knew his work for the government haunted him. "So much death," as he put it. So much death that he could not move on with his life. He could not break free of his solitude, could not let go of his cloyingly sentimental attachment to his first love, a boyish crush on a girl named Charlotte Shaefer. He was in his late thirties, but he was trapped in his past—in his guilt and his shame—like a beast of old sunk in a tar pit. Margaret sensed that he needed to tell her these stories, to lay out this narrative in full so he could receive . . . well, forgiveness, probably more than anything. Acceptance from her motherly presence. Healing. He needed to feel he'd been cleansed somehow and was worthy to be loved again. More than that. He needed to be loved in fact. To have a woman in his life. A home. A family. He needed to rejoin the human race, in other words, instead of living as he lived, endlessly walking down empty streets in an inner city of shadows.

This time, though—this time, she felt the interruption was warranted—necessary—even though she saw the flash of resentment flare and die in his usually quiet eyes—his melancholy, watchful eyes. He did not like it when she nagged him about Gwendolyn.

Gwendolyn Lord was the first woman who had really reached him recently. It had been a kind of breakthrough. She was a therapist, like Margaret. Which was flattering to Margaret. But it also made her jealous a bit. More than a bit. Part of her countertransference during their work together consisted of the fact that she had fallen head over heels in love with this man. Which was ridiculous. It was a cliché for one thing—going gooey over a client. Plus she was nearly seventy. The whole thing made her feel like a silly old biddy.

Still—he was the sort of man she had always been attracted to. Tweedy, dreamy, ethereal. With longish blond hair framing a face like an angel's—a bespectacled angel. He was lean and fit in jeans and a tweed jacket and a light purple sweater against the cool of the April day. He looked like what he was: an English professor at the university. But from their very first session, she had sensed the violence in him. It was not at all difficult for her to imagine him pushing a gangster out of a helicopter—and that, too, was part of his appeal. The whole idea of him had gotten under her skin.

"Well," she said. "Have you? Called her?"

"You keep asking me that," he said sulkily.

"We haven't talked about her in weeks."

"Mm."

"How long has it been since you last spoke to her?" He didn't answer. They both knew: It was more than five months. "She took a big chance approaching you the way she did. She opened herself to rejection. It wasn't an easy thing for a woman to do. You've humiliated her by not getting in touch. Don't think she doesn't feel it."

Winter was not usually short with her. He loved her back, as Margaret well knew. He loved her as if she were the warm, caring mother he'd never had as a child. Which, OK, was not exactly the sort of love she fantasized about but, this being real life, it would have to do. Now, however, there was an edge to his voice.

"I take it you don't want to hear the rest of this story," he said.

"No, I don't think I do. Not today anyway."

He sulked some more. She waited him out. She steepled her fingers under her chin, swiveling back and forth in her high-backed therapist's chair. Her brown chair in the tan-and-brown office with the tan-and-brown rug on the floor and the tan-and-brown pictures on the wall. Everything here was designed to be dull and neutral so that all the emotion could come directly from the client. In these bland surroundings, Winter always seemed to leap out at her like a great gaudy splotch of colorful life.

"Well, what should we talk about then?" he asked finally.

"Let's see," said Margaret. "Last session, you spent twenty minutes trying to describe Charlotte Shaefer's perfume. Overly sweet, you said, with a hint of strawberry in it. The sort of perfume a twelve-year-old girl might wear. Which makes sense, I guess, because she was so young when you knew her. It was all such a very long time ago that . . ."

"All right, all right, I get the point," he said.

"Why don't we talk about how you're feeling right now? Let's start there."

He shrugged. "I don't know. I feel fine."

Margaret raised her eyebrows.

"What?" he said.

"I think that's the first time you've ever actually lied to me. I don't mean unconsciously. I mean knowingly lied."

He frowned down at his loafers.

"You're depressed again, aren't you?" said Margaret. He didn't answer. "How bad, Cam? On a scale of one to ten?" He didn't answer. "As bad as when you first started coming to me? Worse?"

"I was feeling so much better for a while and then . . ."

"Then you met Gwendolyn, for one thing. You met Gwendolyn and you've been mooning over Charlotte Shaefer ever since. Hiding from the future in the past." But he looked so exposed and beleaguered now, she felt sorry for him. She let her gaze become soft and sympathetic. "It's all part of the process," she told him. "Two steps forward, one step back. It will come right, in the end."

The poor man. He looked at her with the wretched anguish of a child. "Will it?" he asked her desperately.

"Yes, dear," she said. "I'm sure of it."

That was a lie, of course. She could see for herself the state he was in. How bad his depression was. How deep, how dark. A full-fledged crisis of the heart, she thought. With any other client, she would have recommended medication. Insisted on it even, to make sure he wouldn't harm himself. But there was no point with Winter. She'd tried it in the past. He wouldn't agree to it. It had taken him years to break free of the drugs they'd pumped into him when he was in government service. He would not go back to them.

Which meant there was nothing Margaret could do but keep talking to him, keep listening. Which simply might not be enough.

The truth was: She was afraid she was losing him. She was afraid he was losing himself.

2

The problem with going crazy, Winter thought, was that he couldn't be sure whether someone really was trying to kill him or he was just going nuts. That is, he knew the going nuts part was real, but he wasn't sure whether to trust his instinct, his sense that he was being followed, watched, hunted.

Because Margaret was right: He had lied to her, even after she caught him at it. He had confessed to being depressed again, but he had hidden how bad it was, how deep, how dark. He wasn't sleeping at night. When he did sleep, he had bad dreams. During the day, he went about his teaching duties in a fog of lethargy. He had recently begun doing research for a book on second-generation Romanticism, the transition from the concerns of Coleridge and Wordsworth to the concerns of Shelley and Keats. But the work had stalled. He didn't have the energy for it. There were nights when he found himself drinking more whiskey than he wanted to. There were nights when he even found himself watching television, which he considered an act of intellectual suicide.

And always, every hour these last few days, there was that sense of someone haunting him, trailing after him, moving in. Yet when he looked around him, head on a swivel, he saw nothing, no one.

And still—still—there was this tremulous sense in the pit of his stomach that something—someone—someone from his past had returned to claim him, to drag him back into the darkness of that world. Offhand, he could have named maybe a dozen people who would have enjoyed killing him. But were any of them really near, or was it just his depression, and his haunted mind?

A few nights after his session with Margaret, he went to a small dinner party. He was pathetically glad to get the invitation. Glad to get out of his apartment, glad to get away from his own miserable company.

He had been invited to the Sextons'. Or whatever you were supposed to call them when he, Roger, was named Sexton, but his wife, Adele, had kept her maiden name, Reinhold. They were an odd couple, he thought. They were odd together, and it was odd that they were friendly with him. He did not have many friends at the university. There were not many who dared to be his friend. He was considered toxic because of his old-fashioned ideas—specifically, his idea that poetry should be taught as a spiritual communication from the past, not judged by the tedious politics of the present. Winter was done with the politics of the present. He had seen too much of them too close at hand.

Roger Sexton was in the computer sciences, of all things. He was studying and developing artificial intelligence, which Winter cared about not at all. His wife, Adele Reinhold, was a feminist Jane Austen scholar. She wrote books and articles that read to Winter like the impenetrable diatribes of a brainy adolescent, not yet wise enough to see things simply. Winter knew the work of Austen well. He thought Adele's theoretical approach was claptrap.

Their friendship, then, had been a surprise. Winter had hit it off with Roger after they attended a conference together where they joined in a panel discussion about AI and the arts. When he realized Roger was married to Adele, he had faced their first social gathering with dread. But no, at home, in person, he found her delightful. For all her ferocious writings about the "patriarchal consciousness" or whatever other nonsense the bluestockings were currently griping about, it turned out she was an excellent hostess, an affectionate wife, and the indulgent mother of a rambunctiously masculine seven-year-old boy named Arthur, whose antics Winter enjoyed immensely. Even more surprising, she was indulgent of Winter too. She welcomed his curmudgeonly, patriarchal self into her home with genuine warmth, if with a touch of rueful irony.

So he was glad to join them for dinner, and it turned out to be a pleasant evening, pleasant enough to help him forget his paranoia for a while, if paranoia was what it was.

The Sexton house was set out in the residential south end of the city, far enough away from campus to be free of the stagnant air of intellection. It was a comfortably sloppy and homey place, a place fit for a living family. Along with Roger and Adele, Roger's department chairman and project head Devesh Khan was there, along with his Realtor wife, Laura. There was also Wanda Cheney, one of the many university administrators Winter thought should be excised from the budget if not actually put to death. But Wanda managed to be fairly pleasant, and was clearly determined to despise him in silence, which was all Winter asked of anyone.

Along with her other graces, Adele was a gloriously talented cook. Winter overflowed with praise for her lamb curry, and she seemed genuinely pleased by his compliments. She was a sleek, smallish woman of forty, a bit rigid of bearing but with warm, dancing eyes behind gigantic glasses. Winter felt she suspected his low opinion of her work. He thought it hurt her feelings and he was sorry for it. He was happy to have something he could sincerely flatter her for. It seemed to make her happy too.

She was sitting at the foot of the table, with Winter at her right hand. She was teasing him now about Lori Lesser. The dean of student relations had been running a ferocious crusade to either destroy Winter's career or sleep with him or possibly both.

"I'm absolutely sure you're to blame for this sabbatical of hers," Adele said. She gave him a secretive, throaty laugh that he liked.

"What could you mean by that?" he said. "Inoffensive me?"

"I think you've driven her insane. I'm serious. I think she's at some rest home somewhere recovering from you."

"How could that be? Was it something I said? Something about William Hazlitt's prose style maybe?"

"Oh, stop. You're a contrarian masculinist beast, and you torture her on purpose. She has a tremendous crush on you and has been trying to get you fired for months."

"But does that make sense really?"

"Well. You know what women are."

This last she said leaning toward him confidentially. It was just the right measure of harmless hostess-like flirtation, and it was a tremendous pleasure to him, lonely as he was, hyperalert, in his loneliness, to the womanliness of women. He wondered if she sensed this about him—his solitude, his melancholy, his agitation. If she did, he thought, it was incredibly kind of her to have him here, to give him this bit of herself, knowing what he was and how he felt about her work. He was grateful to her.

Between dinner and dessert, Roger and Devesh, loose with wine, grew absurdly chauvinistic about their projects, as Winter felt computer people were prone to do. Roger was a large, disheveled presence, paunchy, with strands of thinning brown hair flying off his head every which way. Devesh was scrawny and ridiculously ugly. He looked like a praying mantis, Winter thought. But he had a jolly way about him, full of humor and with a ready laugh. His wife was as shapely as he was narrow, pretty and dark and freckled and full of life.

Roger and Devesh were passing a device between them. They were goading this Frankenstein AI program of theirs to create shockingly realistic animated images of movie actors. They then instructed the program to invent dialogue for various movie genres, which the animated actors then proceeded to recite in voices indistinguishable from those of the real actors.

"Look at this. You literary types are finished," Roger told Winter and Adele. His tone was gruff and raucous. "Soon Taka2"—that was the name of the program—"Taka2 will be able to make an entire movie by itself, write it, direct it, star in it . . ."

"I thought movies were already written by computers," Adele said.

"Well, all right, I'll give you that. But artists in general are going to be totally obsolete, you'll see."

"He only says that because he doesn't know what artists are," Winter told Adele. "Because he doesn't know what human beings are."

"Ah, but that's the thing," said Devesh. "Taka2 isn't a human being. He's a god, just hatched."

Winter rolled his eyes. "Pure idolatry, you miserable sinner. A program that can calculate advantage but has no body to feel with isn't a god. It's a digital sociopath."

"Thank you!" said Laura Khan. "Dev can't wait for spring break when I go visit my mother. He'll be all alone with his machine. I expect to come home and find him murdered by the thing."

Devesh laughed. "One day when Taka2 gets tired of us, he'll hack our nukes and murder us all, blow us straight back to the Stone Age."

"The Stone Age?" said Adele, turning to Winter. "Why, you'd enjoy that, wouldn't you, Cam. You could club the cavegirls and drag them to your elfin grot."

Winter laughed—it felt odd on his face, as if he hadn't laughed in decades. He waved them all off skeptically as he excused himself to go to the bathroom.

As he reemerged, about to head back to the table, he spotted little Arthur down the hall in a playroom. The boy was submerged in the cushions of a sofa. He was fiddling with some sort of handheld gaming gizmo.

Winter went in and dropped down onto the sofa next to him. "What are you doing still awake, you perfidious rapscallion?"

"It's a weekend tomorrow," said the boy, pressing buttons expertly to move the pictures on the screen around.

"What is all this? How did you manage to fit all those people inside that little machine?"

Winter spent much of his mental life in the eighteenth century and was willfully ignorant of the modern culture he deplored.

"It's Mario!" said Arthur. His tone was thick with disdain for Winter's ignorance.

"Mario, eh? Italian fellow, is he? What's he up to there?"

"He's a plumber. He's going to rescue Princess Peach from Bowser, the evil turtle."

"Aha. An Italian plumber jumping on fanged mushrooms to rescue a princess from an evil turtle. One of us has been taking too many hallucinogens, my lad. I certainly hope it's you."

All this human interaction was like medicine to Winter. By the time the party broke up, he was feeling almost cheerful, almost relaxed. He had convinced himself that this fear in his gut—this fear that his past was about to catch up to him in some very unpleasant way—had not been brought on by the approach of an actual assassin. It was just memory—guilt—shame—fear of himself: all the same phenomena that kept him from calling Gwendolyn Lord.

Saying his goodbyes at the door, he kissed Adele on the cheek and thanked her with real feeling. She clasped his hand with one of hers and gave it a reassuring shake, as much as to say, *You'll be all right.* At that, he realized she had seen into him and spied the turmoil in his unhappy heart. Once again, he was moved and grateful to her.

"Did you walk?" said Roger gruffly. "I could use some air. I'll walk you home."

Adele smiled her approval as the two men went out together.

It was a sweet spring night. The air was cool and perfumed with fresh greenery. Winter and Roger moved leisurely along the sidewalk together, the big shambling hulk of Roger towering over Winter's smaller, more controlled figure. They passed under overhanging bur oaks. The scent of the trees was damp and woody. The fresh acorns crunched beneath their feet. There was almost no traffic here, though they could hear the rush of cars in the distance. There were no streetlights, only the lights from houses. They were both shrouded in shadow as they walked.

"That was a nice evening," said Winter.

"Yeah, it was fun."

"Much as I hate clichés, I can't help saying it: You're a lucky man."

Roger didn't answer. They walked on through the night, silent for long minutes. Then Roger said, "Actually, there's something I want to talk to you about."

Winter glanced at him. "All right."

"There just aren't many guys like you here," he went on. "Straightforward guy-guys I can talk to, I mean. Everyone here's got a—a pose of some kind. Some elaborate position. Either that, or they're like Devesh, you know. He's so far inside his own head real life can't touch him. There's no simplicity, that's what I'm saying. You're a down-to-earth guy. I appreciate that."

Winter hardly knew how to take all this. Roger was obviously winding up to something. But what? He hoped it wasn't anything too serious. The party had cheered him, and he knew his good mood was fragile. He went on walking, waiting.

"Look, if I tell you something in confidence, you'd respect that, right?" said Roger in that brusque manner of his. "So much gossip back and forth in a hothouse like this. Everybody talks about everything."

"That's true," said Winter. "But, yes, I'm a grave with secrets: they never come back from me."

"Good," said Roger. "Good. That's good. Good."

But then he was silent again, and Winter was left wondering, waiting.

There was a thoroughfare up ahead, the main street bordering the campus curving down to cross their path. Cars flashed back and forth at the intersection, Saturday night traffic. Moving as if with one mind, the two men turned the corner onto another residential street to keep the quiet around them. More house lights here, more shadows. More silent darkness. Winter's eyes drifted to a large lighted window showing an empty living room within. The lights from house windows always made him feel wistful, as if some warm and loving family life was going on inside while he passed by in the cold.

"I've met someone," Roger said—bluntly, suddenly.

Winter blinked back into the moment. "Someone. A woman, you mean."

"I'm in love with her, Cam. The whole way. I have to be with her. I mean it. I have to be. It's killing me."

Winter was startled by the stab of pain that went through his heart when he heard this, by the intensity of it. Roger's home had been a refuge to him that night. Adele's kindness to him. Their healthy, contented son. He hated to think all that might be destroyed. He could suddenly feel the blackness of his depression waiting for him back in his apartment, back in his oppressively lonely life.

"Well, that is messy," he said quietly.

"I know. Life, right?" said Roger. He had fished his phone out of his pocket. He fiddled with it, then pointed the screen at Winter. "Look at her though. That's her there. Barbara, her name is. Beautiful, isn't she?"

She was. The photo on the screen showed a girl of nineteen or twenty. Slender but full breasted in a short, flowery party dress. She was dancing, tossing her long black hair. She had small, pert features on a face white as paper. One bare arm was flung over her head. Her round hips were flung out. Winter could feel the draw of her even in the small picture.

"She's a student," Winter said.

"I know, I know. She was in Devesh's 101. His gen ed class, you know. She came to me for tutoring. One thing just led to another. It was like getting hit by a wave. By a truck. You had a thing with a student once, didn't you?"

Winter had. But he wasn't married. He didn't have a child. And the university rules had been changed since that time. Such affairs were grounds for dismissal now. They weren't back then. Even so, Lori Lesser had tried to get Winter fired for his fling. He could only imagine what she'd do to Roger.

He almost raised these objections, but he didn't. He knew they were beside the point. Roger was confessing a passion to him. He'd been hit by a wave or a truck or whatever. Mere morality and consequences weren't going to change that.

"Well," was all Winter said. "That was a different situation."

"I know, I know," Roger said again immediately. He had taken the phone back and was peering down at the photo himself. The glow of the screen cast a white light over his face as they walked beneath the trees. He was chewing on his lips. He was yearning with his eyes. Then the phone light went out. His face sank into silhouette. He shoved the phone back in his pocket. "I've thought about all that. I've thought about all the things. I don't care. That's the truth. I don't give a damn about any of it."

"No, of course not," Winter murmured. He was only now beginning to recover himself. His heart still hurt, but his brain had started working again. He was assessing the situation, trying to judge what his own best reaction would be. He saw it this way. He was not in charge of the world. He had very little power here. There wasn't much he could do besides listen and say whatever he thought might help Roger to see the full reality of his situation. He went on now, choosing his words carefully: "Rules and so on. Even losing your job. That's not the point. I see that."

"Good. Good. Yeah. I don't care."

"But I don't think it's too much to ask that you stop a moment and consider Adele. Adele—and Arthur especially."

Roger pushed the thought of his son aside with a backward wave of his hand. "Ah, Arthur'll be fine. Kids, you know. They're resilient. They adapt. He'll be fine."

It was strange. Winter had trafficked with real evil in his life. He had broken bread with villains. He had dealt death and witnessed murder. But these little wrongs that ordinary people did, the appalling way they treated one another, the lies they hid behind, the lies they told themselves to mask their guilt—these were the things that retained the capacity to shock him. *Arthur will be fine!* Arthur will be emotionally scarred for the rest of his life, he wanted to reply. And you'll have to lie to yourself every single day to keep from facing the fact that it was your fault. Irreparable damage to your own son's life—all your fault. By the time your fling with this girl comes to its inevitably stupid and ugly end, you'll be a lost soul, unable to assess yourself honestly in any way. And who knows what state the boy will be in. As for Adele . . . here, he remembered the touch of Adele's thumb on his palm as she squeezed his hand reassuringly. As for Adele, he hated to think what the bitterness of betrayal and divorce would do to her.

All this was just normal life, of course. Normal American life in the twenty-first century, anyway. It should not have been shocking to the erstwhile assassin. But it was. Somehow it was.

"How far has this thing gone?" he asked.

"Far," said Roger. "All the way."

Winter gave a soft grunt.

Roger turned on him fiercely. "What?" It was an angry challenge. "What's that supposed to mean? What are you, passing judgment on me now?"

Winter was, but he didn't see the use of saying so. It wouldn't change anything. It would just make Roger feel—well, the way he seemed to feel already: furious and defensive.

Winter made a small gesture with his head. "I do think it might be wise to wait a little."

"Oh—wait!" said Roger, disgusted.

"Just to see where it goes."

"I know where it's going. I'm forty years old, Cam. I know the real thing when I see it. Adele—she and I . . ."

They were nearing the center of town. The spotlit dome of the state capitol was visible at the end of the block to their left. The great lake, sparkling under a waning sliver of moon, was visible up ahead. Winter's apartment building, a tall, graceful brick tower, appeared now and then above the housetops.

The end of their walk was approaching. Time was growing short. Winter felt if he was going to say something worthwhile, he would have to do it soon. He wanted to do it, to say something worthwhile. He wanted to stop this wave/truck of Roger's from crashing into Adele's home, Arthur's home.

But he had no idea where to start. "What were you just going to tell me?" he asked Roger. "About Adele and you? You started to say something."

"Well . . ." The large, disheveled man made a large, disheveled gesture. "You see what it's like with us."

"Not really," Winter said. "Actually, I thought Adele was looking very content tonight."

"Yeah, well, she! She's got everything she wants, doesn't she? Little home. Little family."

"Those are not inconsequential things, Roger."

"No, they're fine. I know that. They're fine, they're fine. I didn't mean it that way. It's fine for Adele! But look—I'm not an old man. I still need some passion in my life. You understand what I'm talking about. A man can't just sit there while the days go past. He can't give up his life just to be nice about things. I mean, look, you know this: To be with someone like Barbara, just to look at her, touch her, it makes you feel so—alive! God, it was like I'd been dead and suddenly came back to life. It really was."

Winter had one of those moments sensitive people have—one of those moments of double vision when he could see the situation fully from his own perspective and from Roger's at the same time. To him, it was all such a shabby and stupid cliché. A man approaching middle age throwing away his family for a girl of twenty. When here was Winter—stuck in the past like a fly in amber—sick with a history of error and loss and death—whose fondest dreams were Roger's actual life: a woman, a home, a child, two children, three . . . what wouldn't he have given for all that?

Yet, he glanced at Roger and even in the dark he saw that for him this was—what?—a great romance, a last chance at happiness or fulfillment or authenticity or whatever he would end up calling it. A desperate grab at fleeting life. Somewhere deep down, even he must have realized the squalid comedy of it all. But that sort of clarity was buried under the bubbly valentines and orchestral music currently emanating from his gonads. Winter knew the feeling. He knew how complete and real it could seem.

The two men reached a corner. From here, it was a straight walk to Winter's building. Roger stopped. Winter stopped, hands in the pockets of his slacks. He looked up at the bigger man. He realized their conversation was over. They would part here.

"Look," Winter said. "Take some time to think it over. It's only common sense, Roger. It's a big decision. Give it some consideration."

"Yeah," said Roger. "Yeah. The thing is, though: I love her."

Oh, for Christ's sweet sake! Winter almost said, but he managed not to. "I know. I get it. Still. Take some time," he said.

"Yeah. Yeah," Roger said again, but he was shaking his head no, no. "I thought you'd see this. I thought you'd understand."

Winter couldn't help a small, mirthless laugh. "I think I understand well enough."

"Oh, sure, I know what you think. You think: 'Middle-aged man, he's thinking with his dick instead of his brain.' Right? And you know, I'm not saying that's not part of it. Sex. Sure it is. Good is good, you know? It puts some hair on your chest, no question about it." He made one last effort to get Winter to see the deeper reality. He held out his hands to him, an imploring gesture. "But in life, you have to go with your heart sometimes. Don't you? You know this. You only go around once. Sometimes you have to listen to your heart. You *know* this!"

What Winter knew was that if he heard one more trite phrase come out of his friend's mouth, he might lose control of himself and say something he would regret.

He said: "Roger. I'm not minimizing anything. I hear your passion. I do—and I do understand it. But that's exactly why you should listen to advice from a cooler head. Take some time. Think this through. It's what any friend would tell you. Adele is a good woman . . ."

Roger gave a derisive snort. "You haven't read her books."

Winter smiled. "I meant in real life, Roger. She's a good woman in real life. In fact, that's the point I'm making. This *is* real life—with real people in it, and consequences and death at the end. Irrevocable decisions should be looked at from every angle. That's all I'm trying to tell you."

Roger muttered something—something that sounded very much like, "Yeah, yeah, yeah." Aloud, he said: "Well, look. Thanks for listening. I appreciate it. I mean it. I do. I should be getting back."

Winter watched him walk away with a terrible sense of regret. He thought of Adele leaning toward him at the dinner table, that kindly, harmless flirtation. Arthur happily lost in the world of his game, confident that his real world was secure. Was there something else he could have said that might have stopped this? he wondered. Something that might have changed what was about to happen to them?

All the good feeling of the evening was gone. As he made his way home, depression closed around him like a suffocating cloud. He reached his building. He paused at the doorway. Looked over his shoulder. No one was there. And yet that feeling—that butterfly trapped in his belly—that sense he was being watched—it persisted. Someone was coming for him. Someone out of the past.

He pushed inside. He passed through the lobby with an absentminded nod to the doorman behind his desk. He rode up in the elevator, brooding. What was the point of anything? he wondered bitterly. Here he was, struggling to call Gwendolyn Lord, yearning to call her but paralyzed for reasons he didn't fully comprehend. And here was Roger, with everything Winter ached for—love, a family, a home, a place in life—and ready to toss it all away for sex with some dopey nineteen-year-old. What was the point?

The elevator door opened. He plodded down the carpeted hall. He reached the door to his apartment. Fumbled the key into the lock. He could feel the emptiness of the apartment waiting for him in there. It was unbearable. He did not know how long he could go on like this.

He started to open the door—but stopped. He stopped moving altogether, his hand still on the key. He drew a sharp breath in through his nose.

What was that? A scent. Not just a scent, but an entire world remembered. Christmastime and old songs and a beautiful creature, a little girl, sitting on his bed in the dark, holding his hand for comfort so he could go to sleep in a strange house. His first love. Charlotte Shaefer.

For a moment, he could not tell what had happened to him, what had brought those memories back to him with such force.

But then he understood.

It was perfume. Not imagined. Real. Wasn't it? Yes, there was a faint smell of perfume in the air around him. A woman had been here not long ago. Right here, in this hall. Outside his door.

What's more, he recognized her lingering scent. It was sweet, overly sweet, with a hint of strawberry in it. It was the sort of perfume a twelve-year-old girl might wear.

But then, that made sense, didn't it? Because Charlotte was so young when he had known her. And he was so young, just a boy.

It was all such a very long time ago.

3

He had thought he was going crazy before, but that was nothing. He smelled that perfume—Charlotte's perfume—and seemed to fall into an interior darkness. Was this the shadow of his past he had felt was haunting him? How could it be? Why would it be? What would it mean if it were? And why did he feel so afraid?

He passed a dreadful night, sleepless, nervous, weirdly paralyzed in his mind so that he could not think what he should do—and yes, afraid, though he could not have said why. In the hours after midnight, he barely recognized himself. He was not a religious man, but he imagined demons swarming the air above him, genuine entities, gibbering, laughing at him. Laughing at his nameless fear.

Three times during the endless darkness, he got out of bed, yanked a bathrobe shut over his underwear, and returned to the apartment door. He opened the door and stuck his head out into the hall. He breathed in to confirm to himself that the scent—the same perfume that Charlotte wore when they were children—was really there.

And yes, there it was. It was still there the first time he checked, anyway. He could smell it just as clearly as he had before, and all the memories came back with it too. The second time he poked his head out the door—three in the morning or thereabouts—the aroma was fainter. The third time, when it was nearly dawn, the scent had almost faded away. But not quite. He could still catch a trace of it. Enough of a whiff so that he couldn't doubt his own senses, as much as he wanted to.

The rest of the time, the rest of the night, he lay in his bed open eyed, sweating the pillow damp. He was too agitated even to turn on the light and read. He just lay there, staring, sweating. Remembering.

Winter had grown up with wealth. A metropolitan rich kid. But his parents had been distant and unloving. His father was always working at whatever financial business he had—Winter never really understood what it was. His mother wandered their town house in a daze, her face dancing with the rainbows that fell from the crystals on the chandeliers. Whenever she happened to bump into her son, she seemed surprised to see him, as if she'd forgotten that she'd once given birth. Whatever warmth Winter had gotten in his child life had come to him through his nanny and her family. The Shaefers.

They were a small clan of warm, noisy immigrants from Communist East Germany, two sisters and a brother. Charlotte was the daughter of the brother, a child so beautiful Winter could have dreamed her. A little porcelain housewife of a girl with perfect features and silky blond hair, she had mothered Winter in his loneliness, exactly what he needed. He had adored her, but was too young for her, just a boy.

But he never let that love go. They grew up. She had boyfriends. She went to college. Still, he yearned for her. Finally, as a young man, he managed to purloin one sweet kiss from her, just one. Then she had discovered the truth about her family. How her beloved father had worked as an informant for the Stasi. How her mother had killed herself when she learned her husband had betrayed his mistress to Communist torture in order to finance his family's escape to the West.

The revelations had driven Charlotte half-mad. The last time Winter saw her, she was partnered with an angry little troll of a protofascist. Eddie. A man deformed in body and mind, who went about accompanied by two Dobermans as vicious as he was.

After that, she had disappeared. She and Eddie both.

Maybe, in a different life, he would have gotten over her. Maybe he would have tracked her down and found her. But as things developed in their seemingly random way, he stumbled into joining the Division and became what he became. A killer. A cold stranger to his better self. His old life—his past—his childhood—all retreated from him. Everything—except for Charlotte. Charlotte—crazy as it was—Charlotte remained with him, the face of all his motherless longing. He could not stop loving her. He could not fully love anyone else.

The night went on and on in thoughts like these. In the morning, exhausted, Winter staggered to the door one final time. He put his head out. He sniffed the air. The smell of her perfume was gone. He must have imagined it, he thought.

But he did not believe he had imagined it.

He had a class that morning at 10:00 A.M. A seminar on the contemporary literary response to the French Revolution. Nine of his best students, far more engaged than the kids in his lecture class. He needed at least an hour to prepare.

But when he sat down with his books and computer at the dining room table, he knew he could not focus on his work. Almost immediately, he stood up again. He went out of the apartment. Down in the elevator to the lobby. He leaned on the doorman's desk until the doorman got off the phone. Bernie his name was, a young guy, round faced, pale faced, with a stubble of beard.

"Your security cameras record, don't they?" Winter asked him.

"Yeah, sure, Mr. Winter," Bernie said. "The video gets overwritten every two weeks or so."

"Somebody came to my door last night, somewhere between, I don't know, six thirty and midnight, say."

Bernie looked down at his record book, frowning. "There's no record of anyone coming in."

"Right. I think she must have snuck past Demetrius. I'd like to look at the tape though. I'd like to see if I can spot her."

Bernie was an intelligent fellow and knew not to ask any more questions. He invited Winter to join him behind the desk. They stood together looking down at the screens while he rewound one of the three video angles. This was the one that took in the center of the lobby. Even zipping through the recording on fast-forward, it was easy to see that the people going back and forth were all either residents, who waved as they passed, or guests, who stopped at the desk to check in with the doorman.

Then, at 10:36 P.M. according to the time stamp on the top left corner of the picture, a small figure went rushing by unnoticed.

"Ah, Demetrius," murmured Bernie reproachfully. "Where were you, my brother?"

He backed the video up and slowed its speed to give Winter a good look at the figure. A woman clearly. Her head was ducked down and a baseball cap pulled low on her forehead, the visor just above her eyes. She carried no purse. She was wearing a winter overcoat too heavy for the spring night. She was moving fast, her shoulders hunched, her chin sunk beneath the coat's raised collar. As she passed through the scene, Winter spotted a strand of hair escaping the back of her cap. Light hair. Probably blond. The color of the video was too washed out for Winter to be certain. Charlotte was blond, though her hair had been dyed black the last time he saw her. Charlotte was about the same height as this woman, with the same delicate build. But he couldn't be sure this was her. He couldn't get a clear look at her.

There was only one thing that stood out to him: She had a book tucked under her arm. She was pressing it close to her body. The image wasn't very clear but it seemed to be a thin paperback. Its cover was a black-and-white photo. He couldn't be sure what it was a photo of.

"Can you enlarge that section?" he asked Bernie.

The doorman enlarged the photo. It lost clarity but Winter could see the book a little better. The black-and-white cover photo showed a city skyline. Part of the title was visible, words on two lines. Small *r*, small *y* was all he could make out on the top line: "ry." "he Night"—probably "The Night"—was all he could make out on the bottom line. The woman's arm covered everything else.

Winter thanked Bernie and gave him a couple of bills. He went back up to his apartment. It was only when the door shut behind him that he realized his heart was hammering. He was breathless.

What the hell? he thought. What was he so excited about? What if it was Charlotte? So what? He wasn't in love with her anymore. He couldn't be. He didn't even know her.

But his heart wouldn't stop pounding. His thoughts wouldn't stop racing. How many nights had he sat alone in his apartment, staring at an old photo of Charlotte online, a portrait from her high school yearbook. And now . . .

He checked his watch. It was almost 9:00 A.M. He needed to shave and get ready for his seminar. Instead, he returned to the laptop on the dining room table. He called up amazon.com. He tried to find the book the woman in the video had been carrying under her arm. He typed in possible titles. *Memory in the Night. Fury in the Night.* Had she been bringing the book to give to him?

he wondered. Had she planned to leave it for him, then changed her mind? *Adversary in the Night.* Maybe it meant nothing. Maybe it just happened to be a book she was reading.

He came to himself and checked the time. Half an hour had slipped away. It was 9:30. He had to get ready to go.

He went into the bathroom and shaved. It wasn't pleasant. His face in the mirror was slack with sleeplessness. His eyes were frantic with—what? Agitation? Craziness? Fear? He scraped the razor along his cheek and suddenly an idea came to him. Eddie, Charlotte's boyfriend. He stared at himself as he shaved, stared into his own frantic eyes. Surely she had dumped that furious clown by now. He was not the stuff of a long-term relationship. He was just her angry reaction to her father's betrayal, a slap at the Socialist Stasi.

Unless he was something more.

He finished shaving. He wiped the remaining cream off his face in a hurry. He hurried back to his laptop. His heart was racing again, even faster than before, so fast it was painful. His head felt light.

He called up his search engine. He typed in: "Fascist book. 'In the Night.'" The answer came back at once: *Treachery in the Night.*

"The novel, self-published under the name Ivy Swansag, became an extremist cult favorite after it was deemed required reading by several fascist and white supremacist websites. The FBI has used it as a textbook on extremist psychology . . ." the first entry began.

Winter cursed quietly under his breath.

There was a picture of the book's cover. The black-and-white photo of a skyline. It was the book the woman in the lobby had been carrying under her arm.

He was barely breathing at all now. He was dizzy with surges of emotion he couldn't name. Amazon didn't sell the book. Other sites sold hard copies. It took him a few more searches before he found an e-book version on an obscure antisemitic site. The e-book was offered for free. He downloaded it onto his laptop.

It was almost ten o'clock now. He had to get to class. He had to go right now.

He didn't go. He called up his e-reader. He blinked back his dizziness as the now-familiar cover photo appeared on the screen. He turned the page. There was no dedication. No frontispiece. He was immediately at the book's beginning.

Holding his breath, he read the opening sentence.

Something terrible is about to happen.

4

The seminar was slow torture, an agony of waiting.

He sat at the head of a long table. His students sat along the table's sides. Five young women, four young men. Arty types, all eager, interested, engaged, looking his way.

This week they'd been reading William Blake's epic on the French Revolution.

"Sick, sick, the Prince on his couch! wreath'd in dim / And appalling mist . . ."

The students loved this stuff. They loved Blake's obscurity and his imaginative passions. This, they thought, was what poetry was supposed to be: feverish and hard to understand. None of that Wordsworthian plain speaking. They could make anything they wanted out of stuff like this. They could smother it under whatever insipid notions happened to be making the rounds. Winter had to work hard to rein them in and hold them accountable to the poet's actual words. And he had to do this while feeling pretty much wreathed in dim and appalling mist himself.

He did not know what was happening to him. He had had no time to explore and understand the emotions raging inside him. He had been so depressed for so long and was now so agitated, he really thought he might be losing his mind. And he did not know why. Somehow, it seemed to him the answers waited for him in the pages of *Treachery in the Night*. He wasn't sure why that should be so either, but he was desperate to return to reading it.

He pinned his attention to the class. He focused on those young faces to his right and left. He forced himself to wrestle meaning out of the Dense Fantastic that was Blake's vision. In the end, he managed to do a much better job of discussing the poem than he'd thought he would. But God, what a relief it was when the class was over.

The students gathered around him. They had questions, final comments, personal reactions. He tried not to be too curt with them. But as fast as he could, he was out on campus, striding through the wistful spring weather—practically running through it—to his favorite coffee shop, the Independent.

It was a quaint place, ivy-covered brick on the outside, stained wood tables inside. A swirly paisley mural on the walls and flowering trees at the long window. He usually came here later in the day, usually in the afternoon for a snack, a coffee and croissant. It was always crowded then. It was all but empty now. He was able to find a good seat: a singleton in a secluded corner. He set his black coffee down and snapped open his laptop. He brought the book to the screen again. He was embarrassed by his sense of urgency. His light head. His fluttering pulse. He did not understand himself. All he could think about was Charlotte.

He started to read.

Something terrible is about to happen.

When he finished the prologue, he sat back in his chair—dropped back into it, slack and stunned.

It was her. Charlotte. There was no doubt about it. The girl in the book—this supposedly fictional character named Miranda—she

36

was Charlotte. There was no question in his mind. Theo was obviously Eddie, malformed the way Eddie was, and with his two snarling dogs always beside him.

What did it mean? What could he make of it?

Was it truth or fiction? That was the main question. Had Eddie really been gunned down by this other man, this character called Evan Moran? Did Moran then become Charlotte's lover? With Eddie's body still warm out in the woods?

It made Winter sick to think it might be so. Charlotte an accessory to murder. His coffee burned in his stomach like acid.

He looked around the shop, the quiet shop, the familiar shop. Trying to settle himself. Trying to still this feeling that he was coming apart inside. The scenes from the prologue kept coming back to him. Miranda-Charlotte waiting in the Farmhouse. The rifle shots from the forest. Moran coming back alone. Lifting her onto the bed . . . the images raced through his inner vision again and again. He felt as if his mind was careening out of control.

It occurred to him that he ought to call Margaret. He was having some sort of emotional crisis. He ought to call her and request an emergency session so she could talk him down.

But the idea offended his masculine pride. He wasn't going to call his therapist like some child crying to his mother. *Help me! I'm lost!* It made him angry that he'd even considered it.

He went on reading.

Miranda only slowly realized she was afraid.

That was how the first chapter began. It was a flashback from the prologue. It told the story of how Miranda came to the place they called the Farmhouse.

A few months before the events in the prologue, Miranda had been living near her college with Theo and his dogs. The town wasn't named in the novel. Neither was the college. None of the places in the book were specified. But Winter recognized the description of Miranda's house: a modest clapboard in a row of aging clapboards. He had been in that house the last time he saw Charlotte. It had been a nightmare of an evening.

He had been so in love with her for so long by then. Ever since they were children together. So he was already tense when he arrived at her house. Plus he had a cold. He had taken some medicine and his brain was foggy. When he went inside, Charlotte poured him some wine. The combination of the alcohol and the medicine went to his head. It made the whole experience wavery and unreal, like something happening under water.

Charlotte was totally changed from the way he remembered her. The sweet, serious little lady of the house who treated him with deadpan maternal warmth—that girl was gone. This Charlotte was frenetic, bright eyed, miserable. Mocking their shared memories. Treating him as if he were still a child.

Then Eddie came home. His snarling dogs pinned Winter in a corner. There were strange art posters on the walls all around him: angels of death, a knight among monsters. Those pictures and the growling dogs and angry, misshapen Eddie and laughing Charlotte—the whole scene swam in a fog of wine and cold medicine. An awful, awful evening. And it took place in the very house the book described.

Winter wondered how long after that evening the novel began. It seemed to be some years at least. Charlotte—or Miranda, he should say—because, for all he knew, the whole thing was fictional—Miranda was out of college now. She was working as a barista in a coffee shop. Working full time but also keeping house for Theo. She had become his full-time helpmeet as he worked to get his master's degree in political science.

But Miranda's love for Theo was fading. It had been fading for some time. At first, she had come to hate the dogs. She was afraid of them. They were always glaring at her, baring their teeth. But she had also begun to distrust Theo's angry certainties. He thought he saw through everything, he saw the secret truth hidden behind everything that ordinary people cherished in life. Love, marriage, children, charity, Christmas, movies, business, government. He analyzed and dismissed them all. They were frauds. They were empty relics of what had once been real institutions, real traditions, real values. Now—what were they? Illusions! Meaningless remnants used to hypnotize the naive so they did not notice that their culture had been eaten hollow from within by stateless cosmopolitans with no loyalty to anything but their own wealth and power. If ever Miranda objected to these ideas, if ever she dared to protest meekly, *I don't think it's all that way, Eddie*, he shut her down, waved her off, as if she were an idiot or a child.

For a long time, she kept her resentment secret—secret even from herself. But after a while, she had to face it. She was unhappy. Almost without knowing it, she had begun thinking about leaving. She wanted to leave. But she was afraid.

She had seen the violence growing in him. Growing in his ideas but not just in his ideas. More and more, he was using phrases like: *It all has to be torn down and begun again. They all have to be gotten rid of. They won't give us the country back, we'll have to take it by force.*

And then there were all the people he hated. The Blacks. The Jews—especially the Jews. He regarded the Blacks as mere animals, but the Jews, *Oh, they know what they're up to, all right*, he told her. *They've got their claws into everything, don't they? We're going to have to start cutting some throats, I'm telling you.*

One night, as they were eating together, he had been going on and on like this, and she had finally said to him, *Oh, Theo, stop.*

That was all. It had just come out of her. She had spoken in the mildest possible tone. She had just been trying to bring him out of his furious fugue state for a few seconds. She said, *Oh, Theo, stop,* and she rolled her eyes.

He had leaped from his chair at the dinner table. The chair toppled back behind him. His glass tumbled forward in front of him, spilling red wine across the table like blood. Instantly, the Dobermans were on their feet, snarling—snarling at her, at her, who fed them and walked them and nuzzled them sometimes, nose to nose! She stumbled backward out of her own chair. She staggered away from the bared teeth of the animals.

Theo! she cried out.

But for a long moment—an endless moment—Theo just stood there. Glaring at her. As if he and the dogs were one mind, acting together. Any second, she thought, he might give some silent order and they would leap at her and sink their teeth into her flesh. Shake her to pieces between them like fighting over a rag doll. The spilled wine dripped off the edge of the table onto the wooden floor, tap, tap, tap. Only when Theo ripped his chair up off the floor and sank slowly back into it—only then did the Dobermans stop snarling. He barked their names. Reluctantly, they lay down at his feet, still glaring at Miranda. She felt her pulse pounding in her throat so hard she feared it would choke her.

Day after day, the situation between them grew worse. Theo became foul mouthed. His diatribes would devolve into a series of muttered four-letter words. The anger in his voice frightened her.

I don't like it when you talk that way, Theo, she told him. She could hear her own cringing tone, but she refused to believe what was happening to her. *I don't like it.*

His hand snapped out like a snake, and he grabbed her wrist, hard, a grip like iron. The dogs started barking loudly.

Then, almost at once, he let her go. The dogs fell silent. The moment was over. But his hand had left a bruise on her.

⊶

At this point, once again, Winter stopped reading. Again, he dropped back in his chair, nauseated, dizzy, unraveling. He felt as if he had been watching a horror movie—some violent grind house film full of monsters and butcher knives and screaming victims and gore. He had been sitting in the dark and watching and suddenly—suddenly he realized that one of the victims on the screen was someone he knew, someone he once loved. And she was looking at him—him out there in the theater audience. She was casting beseeching glances at him, begging him to come into the film and rescue her from the mayhem.

He shuddered. This was bad, he thought. Something bad was happening inside him. Right there in the Independent. He was falling to pieces. He really ought to call Margaret, he thought. *Like a child crying for his mommy*, sneered a voice in his head. So he didn't call her. He just sat there, gazing at the coffee shop around him. Gazing across the shop to the window and the flowers on the trees outside, a blur of white and green in his unfocused vision.

Was it true? he kept asking himself. Was the story in the novel true? Why had the woman in his lobby been carrying it under her arm when she came to see him? Was the woman Charlotte? Was Charlotte the novel's author? Was Ivy Swansag a pseudonym for Charlotte Shaefer?

But no, he didn't think Charlotte had written the book. The emotional tenor was wrong. Winter was a professional reader. A professional student of literature. He had a sharp sense of what an author was trying to communicate. The novel's description of Miranda was unsympathetic. She was passive, sniveling, unappealing. The author disdained her. The reader was meant to feel that Theo was discovering these great truths about evil Jews running the world and violent Blacks and so on and that Miranda was too conventional, too womanish, too nice to accept his revelation. The relationship between Miranda and Theo was meant to represent a decadent society. Stunted manhood, angry but impotent. Weak womanhood clinging to illusions. All in all, the way the book was written, Winter thought the most appealing characters were supposed to be the Dobermans. There was a reason the book had become a cult favorite among extremists.

Winter sat there motionless, staring into space. His heart was still in turmoil, but his brain was working with cool precision. This was his job. He was a literature professor. This was what he did, and for a few moments, the process of interpretation engrossed him.

Then he came back to himself. He glanced at his laptop monitor. He felt a strong urge to keep reading. But he knew he shouldn't. He was already too upset, too unstable. He was losing control of himself. He needed to get up, get out, get some air, try to calm down. He struggled with his competing urges.

Finally, he reached out quickly. But he didn't shut the laptop. He used the keyboard to close the e-reader. He took a deep breath and let it out in a long sigh. When he felt he was ready, he went into his search engine and began to search for Ivy Swansag.

There wasn't much information available. She had managed to remain largely anonymous. The novel had its following, but it wasn't well known to the general public. A few high-profile outlets had condemned the work, both from the left and the right. "A veritable handbook of hate," one writer called it. But most of the talk about it came from the more obscure corners of the web, and whether from the right or left, it was mostly just blather. It took Winter almost thirty minutes before he stumbled on a pilfered and reposted thread in which a neo-Nazi pseudointellectual waxed eloquent about an interview he'd heard with the author. The post included a brief quote from Ivy Swansag: "It is a deeply symbolic work, or at least that was my intention in writing it."

When Winter read that, the electric anxiety pulsing through him expanded into full-blown excitement. He copied the quote and fed it back into the search engine. Not many hits, but one of them led to a fragment of the interview itself, a very brief piece of video.

In the video, Ivy Swansag was sitting in her writing room, obviously speaking into her computer. The picture was small and the player was substandard. The image was unfocused and partially pixelated. Winter studied it carefully as he listened to the author's voice.

"There are ideas, and then there are the people who embody those ideas in time," Ivy Swansag said. "There is a perfect vision of something, you know, and then there are the imperfect people who will bring that vision to fruition or not. I'm not writing propaganda, you know. I'm telling a story. That said, it is a deeply symbolic work, or at least that was my intention in writing it."

Swansag was a smallish, plump woman, well over sixty whenever the interview was filmed. She had disheveled gray hair and a beaky, beady-eyed face that Winter found unpleasant. He placed her accent in the Pacific Northwest, Oregon probably.

The interviewer, a man, was off camera, not visible.

"Is the story true?" he asked the author.

Ivy Swansag gave a dismissive noise. She made a dismissive gesture with one hand, swiveling a little in her writing chair. "Awf, obviously it's *true*, or I wouldn't have written it. But do you mean did it really happen? Is it based on actual events, as they say? No, of course not. It's a novel. I made it up. That's what a novel is."

There the video abruptly ended, clearly cut off midstream. Winter watched the fragment several more times. He scanned the blurry scene for clues to the woman's identity or whereabouts. There weren't many. All he could see was a small part of her desktop. The wall behind her. The wall to her left with a window partially visible. He focused on the window for several minutes. Replaying the scene. Freezing it. He could make out mountains in the distance. He could make out what looked like a field of unmown grass closer up. He kept examining that area of the screen as the words played again and again.

"No, of course not. It's a novel. I made it up . . ."

It was not until the sixth or seventh time he watched it that he caught something he'd been missing all along.

He rewound the video further. Now he saw there was a wooden chair behind Swansag. Her body blocked it from sight. It came into view for only a second when she spoke the words, "Awf, obviously it's *true*." That was the moment when she gestured and swiveled slightly. When she swiveled in her chair, one corner of the chair behind her became visible. It was a small, ordinary wooden chair pushed against the wall. But there was a hat on it, an orange baseball cap lying on the seat.

It took Winter several tries before he could pause the video at the one brief moment when the cap appeared. When he did, he could make out a logo on the front of the cap. It was a face, a purple face wearing a purple cowl. The face was all but featureless with the shadow of a nose and all-white eyes. The moment he saw it, he thought the word: *Phantom*.

And he knew at once he could find her. He could find this so-called Ivy Swansag, the author of *Treachery in the Night*. And if he could find the author, maybe—maybe at last—he could find Charlotte herself.

Once again, he was taken aback by the force of his own reaction. The confusion, the runaway emotions. He had no idea what was happening to him. He only knew his mind was in chaos. He felt as if his personality were burning down inside him.

He really needed to get up and get out of here, he told himself again. Go somewhere. Anywhere. He just needed to be outside, away from this, before it drove him insane.

This time, he managed to will himself to snap the laptop shut. He stuffed it into its case. He stood and looped the strap of the case over his shoulder and headed out of the shop.

If ever the weather of a soft spring day was meant to sweep a fractured heart back into the past, it was the weather of that day. As Winter walked toward the campus, the mild noon air enveloped him in nostalgia. He fondly remembered his childhood visits to his nanny's house. The smell of her cookies baking. The sound of nattering voices, a loving family, unlike his own. He remembered the porcelain figurines from the old country arrayed on the shelves. And the glorious porcelain beauty of their little girl, the child Charlotte.

It was irrational—he knew it was—but he couldn't help but feel that that awful evening when he'd seen her last—that night with the dogs and the wine and the drugs—that night had been the crossroads of his life. That had been the moment when he had been diverted from his natural future into a weird and seemingly random descent into a world of cold-blooded killing. He couldn't help but wonder: Was there another man he would have been if he had not taken that turning, if he had not lost Charlotte?

And what would happen to him now, what would become of this fractured soul of his, this loveless life he lived—what would become of him, if he should track her down, if he should find her—find her and discover she had collaborated in a killing?

He stepped onto the campus. Students—young men and women alone, in pairs, in clusters—crowded the paths that wound through the grass, that traveled beneath the stone and brick buildings with their green and red roofs. Others were sitting on the lawns in the sunshine or in the shade under the greening oaks and elms.

Winter glanced at his watch as he wandered along. The hour had just struck. The kids were changing classes or heading to lunch. In his agitated mind, he felt isolated among them, a fritzing shadow amid solid flesh. In his state of confusion, it took a moment before he realized what he was looking at.

Up ahead of him, there was a couple walking together, a girl and a boy. As the flow of students thinned, as the crowd divided and headed off down different paths in different directions, he realized he had been watching them thoughtlessly for several moments. It was her laughter that awoke him from his reverie: a warm, high, feminine giggle of delight. He focused for a moment on the two of them.

The boy was a big, gangly athlete type. He wore a blue school T-shirt and jeans. His long, muscular arms were bare. He had his backpack slung over one shoulder. His stride was sloppy, easy, and self-confident. The girl was much shorter, half a foot at least, more probably. Seen from behind, she was slender and shapely in close-fitting jeans and a billowing flowered blouse. She had straight black hair tied in a ponytail that bounced and swayed as she walked.

Boy and girl turned together down a side path to Winter's right. Winter saw them both in profile and he understood why he had been looking at them.

The girl was Barbara. Roger Sexton's Barbara. He recognized her from the picture Roger had shown him as they had walked together through the night after the dinner party. This was the girl for whom Roger was planning to leave his wife and child. The girl who had awakened him from the gray blah of his midlife blah blah and awakened him to the high blah blah blah of his blissful blah-de-blah, or whatever testicular claptrap he had spewed out during their walk together.

What struck Winter about the girl at once was her casual attitude. Maybe it was foolish of him—he suspected it probably was foolish—but he was surprised by the . . . by the *everydayness* of her. Her expression, her smile, the way she was talking to the boy beside her. It just didn't seem to him to be the expression and smile and tone of a young woman in the midst of a romantic melodrama. He could only catch a word here and there of what she was saying, but it clearly wasn't anything remotely like, *I love him so, but he would have to leave his wife and child and I hardly know what to do!* It sounded more as if she were mocking the stupidity of some television show both she and the athlete boy had been watching earlier. Not thinking about Roger at all.

Winter wasn't exactly following the pair. Not exactly. After all, he was heading to his office in the building the students called the Gothic. And all right, he hadn't fully decided he was heading to his office until just about this moment, but now he had. Which made perfect sense. It was the easiest place for him to use the university's research tools, which he would probably need if he was going to identify and locate Ivy Swansag. And it just so happened that Barbara and her companion were heading along a path that would take him to the Gothic. Maybe it wasn't the exact path he would have taken normally, but it was a possible path. So he wasn't following the young couple, he was just, as you might say, trailing along in their wake.

The path became narrow. It descended. The crowd of students was suddenly gone. Barbara and her friend walked on alone with Winter a good many yards behind them. They were moving along the side of the Emery Building, a great stone block of a structure that housed the physical education department, including the gym and indoor track. There was a line of oaks to the right of them, their branches overshadowing the path. To their left, there were the white walls of the building.

Winter saw Barbara and the athlete lean toward each other as they talked. Their arms brushed together. He thought of Roger saying to him: *To be with someone like Barbara, just to look at her, touch her, it makes you feel so—alive! God, it was like I'd been dead and suddenly came back to life.* At the time, Winter had thought Roger sounded like a bad soap opera, a walking cliché, but then Winter knew he could be cynical at times, and who was he to denigrate the mystic joys of love's sweet song?

Just as he asked himself that question, Barbara and the athlete stopped beside a side entrance to the building, a heavy wooden door inside an alcove. The boy stepped into the shade of the alcove and Barbara followed him.

Without thinking—without meaning to—Winter stopped in his tracks and watched them from a little distance.

Barbara came into the boy's arms and he pulled her close and kissed her deeply. It was not the rarest sight one might see on a college campus but still, in that small, unpopulated piece of territory, it struck Winter as a moment of riveting intimacy. The girl's smaller body seemed to flow up into the man's greater frame and he clutched her bottom and lifted her with one hand while, with the other, he held her face to his as their mouths blended.

Winter became aware that he was staring at them. He stopped staring. He was about to start walking again, get past them. But just then, the kiss broke. Barbara had her hand on the back of the boy's neck, one of her legs curled around his leg. She was dangling from him like a pendant. And when his lips and hers came apart, she turned her head and looked directly at Winter as if she'd known he'd been watching them all this time.

She smiled a bright and gorgeous smile. She waggled her fingers at him in a mocking little wave. The boy glanced Winter's way and grinned.

Embarrassed, Winter bowed his head and charged forward, hurrying past them.

He continued around the corner of the building, and on toward the Gothic, his mind blank with confusion.

5

The Gothic was a looming stone ghost house of arches and gables and castellated towers. Winter's office was on the second floor. It was a tiny cubbyhole. The last phone booth on earth, he sometimes called it. His desk took up most of the floor space. He had to turn sideways and squeeze between the edge of it and the book-laden shelves in order to wedge himself into the chair that was itself wedged between desk and window. The space could make him feel claustrophobic at times, especially when he had to move around in it. He had once had to fight a Russian mobster here and had a visceral, somewhat traumatic, memory of trying to find the space to club the guy in the head with the complete poetical works of Lord Byron. That, however, had not been a normal day here at the university. Most days, he was more or less happily jammed into his chair, lost in his work, and glad for the fast internet and the privacy.

Now, ensconced behind his desk, he sat and stared blankly. There was not enough room for him to swivel his chair full around so he could face the window, but he swung it half the way and turned his head to gaze out into the branches of the spring trees.

He considered what he had just seen. Barbara and that boy. That kiss. It had been sensual enough to disturb any man's mind, but for him personally just then, it had been kind of medicinal too. Up until the moment Barbara had flowed up into the young man's arms, Winter's mind had been in a wild state. Reading those first pages of *Treachery in the Night* had unnerved him. The sudden nearness of Charlotte—the possibility of finding her again—the possibility that Eddie had been murdered with her passive consent—his thoughts had been scattered—his emotions had become electric and out of control. He felt as if some fissure in his damaged personality had quaked open and all sorts of toxic ghosts and gases were swarming up from the pit.

The kiss had shocked him out of his self-absorbed agitation. The simple comedy of the thing had centered him in the day-to-day world again. He thought of hulking forty-year-old Roger Sexton singing the aria of his middle-aged opera. *Oh, Barbara—she makes me feel so alive.* And here was Barbara herself, and she hadn't a clue that she was part of the show. Or if she did know, she didn't give a damn. Or something—he wasn't sure exactly what the situation was. But whatever was going on, it was comical, all right, in a grim and pathetic sort of way.

After all, the girl must have had some sense of the older man's passion for her. He was seriously thinking of throwing away his marriage so that they could be together. Yet here she was crawling so far down a boy's throat only her tennis shoes remained in the open air. Well, yes, it was sad but, let's face it, it was kind of hilarious too.

This, for Winter, was the medicinal part. Because wasn't he, Winter, just as ridiculous? Reading this weird little novel. Obsessed with finding the author so he could find Charlotte. Upset to the point of nervous breakdown over—what? A child he'd had a crush on when he himself was a child?

He had to shake his head at himself. What *was* this thing called love anyway? Who could solve its mystery? And so on—the rest of the song—which thankfully he'd forgotten, though the tune was now stuck in his head.

He turned back to his desk. He sighed. What next? He probably ought to call Roger and tell him what he'd just seen. If nothing else, it might wake the man from his romantic fantasies before he confessed to Adele or did some other stupid thing that couldn't be repaired.

Winter phoned his friend. Got his voicemail.

He said: "Call me, Roger. Soon as you can. It's important."

He powered up the computer on his desk. He sent Roger a text with the same message: *Call me ASAP.* Then he put this diversion out of his head and went to work to try to find Ivy Swansag.

He couldn't find her. But he came closer—as close, he thought, as he was going to get without leaving his desk and doing some footwork. He began by searching for a sports team called the Phantoms in Oregon. Happily, it turned out there was only one of them. Sure enough, they used the exact logo he was looking for: the cowled purple face on an orange background, the logo from the baseball cap on Ivy Swansag's chair. The Phantoms were a high school football team in the North James school district, centered in a small town named Cooksville about a hundred fifty miles south of Portland. He searched the town's directory for Swansag but the name wasn't there. It had to be a pseudonym, he thought. It sounded like a pseudonym. He figured he would have to go to Oregon if he wanted to track the author down.

He called up the video of the Swansag interview again. He captured a more or less clear picture of the woman's face and sent it to his phone. Cooksville had a population of about seventeen hundred. He did not think it would be hard to locate her there.

He sat back in his chair. He wondered if he should read more of the novel. He thought he probably shouldn't. He was too unstable. It had upset him too deeply. He should probably leave it alone.

He did not leave it alone. He opened *Treachery in the Night* on his office computer and continued reading.

"I want you to come with me," Theo said to Miranda. "There's something I want you to see."

As always, the Dobermans howled wildly when they realized they were being left at home alone. But soon, Miranda was in the passenger seat of Theo's old pickup, and he was driving them at a mad speed through the night.

"Where are we going?" she asked him.

He didn't answer. He stared straight ahead through the windshield. His intensity made Miranda nervous. It flashed through her mind that he might be taking her into the middle of nowhere so he could kill her. *What a crazy thought*, she told herself. This relationship was turning her into a complete neurotic.

They reached the center of town. They drove to a bookstore on a small street on the west side. Tomorrow Books, the shop was called. It was closed. The storefront window was dark. Theo parked the truck down the block and the two of them walked back to the entrance. As they approached, the glass front door swung open. A smallish, serious-looking young man in a black T-shirt and black jeans was waiting to receive them.

Miranda followed Theo inside. The serious-looking young man scanned the empty street up and down before he let the door swing shut. Then he bolted it.

The young man led them down a narrow flight of stairs into the cellar. It was a storage place for books, but the shelves had been arranged to make a space in the center of the floor. There were about twenty-five people gathered there. They were seated on metal folding chairs that had been set out in rows. They were mostly men but there were five or six women among them. The serious-looking young man in the black T-shirt took his place at the front of the room.

"OK, guys, let's get started," he said.

The young man's name was Frederick Bernard. He had jagged-cut black hair and heavy-lidded, sorrowful-looking eyes. He had a thin nasal voice that made him sound, Miranda thought, like some kind of nerd, a math nerd or a computer nerd, something like that. He had the soft, hesitant manner of an academic. He delivered his speech in a quiet voice with a slight stutter. Miranda found his air of serious intellectual intensity rather sweet.

The enemies of law and order were preparing for violence, Frederick Bernard told them. They were organizing in cells throughout the country. They were waiting for an incident—a questionable killing of a Black man by police somewhere or a school shooting or anything that would give them a chance to instigate protests. The media loved this sort of thing, he said. They would be sure to play along and glorify the anarchy.

Once the protests started, the enemy would employ their expert techniques for turning the marches into riots. It was easy to do. Someone would break a store window and that would get people looting. A couple of others would set a police car on fire and the adrenaline rush would drive the more excitable protestors wild. Once the chaos began, the enemy would take control of it and use it to bring the city to its knees. If the police tried to stop them, the media would accuse them of brutality. Politicians, afraid of media criticism, would maintain a cowardly silence. The whole nation would be intimidated into taking the rioters' demands seriously.

"It's up to us to make them pay a price for this," Frederick Bernard said in his soft, hesitant way. "If we're ready for them, if we establish good communications between our own cells, we can mobilize quickly and have people on the scene ready to fight back and bloody some noses."

Frederick Bernard went on speaking for a long time. It seemed like a long time to Miranda anyway. She found the young man's speech soporific. The truth was, while she pretended to care about politics when Theo was ranting at her, she'd grown tired of the whole business. She wanted to be done with it. She wanted to leave Theo. She wanted to find some nicer man and settle down with him and live an ordinary life. She had to pinch her arms to keep herself awake.

Her gaze wandered, the novel said. *Her eyes passed over the titles of the books on the shelves, over the shadowy corridors between one shelf and another.*

Then her gaze stopped wandering. It had fallen on a man.

He was a big man. He was tall and lean and muscular. He had a round face that seemed at once vulnerable and cruel, boyish and dangerous. He was not sitting on one of the metal chairs, but leaning his shoulder against one of the shelves, his arms crossed on his chest. Like Miranda, he was not listening to Frederick Bernard. No. He was looking back at her. He was looking up and down her with hot eyes. She felt the heat of those eyes deep down in the core of herself. Something almost forgotten stirred inside her.

That was the first time she ever saw Moran.

Winter had reached this part of the text before he realized with dismay that he had agitated himself all over again. His thoughts were going every which way, like a mob in a panic. His blood was on fire.

He could picture the scene in the bookstore clearly. It was not Miranda he saw, of course. It was Charlotte. And it was not Charlotte as he'd seen her last, with her hair dyed black and her eyes frenetic. It was the old Charlotte, the Charlotte he had loved, delicate and blond with skin of rose and ivory, pretty as the little figurines that bedecked the shelves in her family's home. He imagined her with those eyes locked on the eyes of the big man leaning there. Moran. Moran was the hero of the novel, Winter knew. He was the Nietzschean superman that decadent society was waiting for. Blah blah blah.

Winter swiveled away from the page on the monitor. He stared out the window again, frantic minded and forlorn. Was the scene real? Was the girl Charlotte? Was the story true?

Suddenly, with a quick movement, he brought his hands up and smacked his brow with the heels of his palms. He clutched his head as if to hold his inner world together. What was wrong with him? What was happening to him? He felt as if he were going mad.

Just then, there was a knock on the office door, soft, diffident. The door cracked open. A young man stuck his head in. Winter knew him. His name was Jim Yarrow. He was gawky, tall, eager. He was a student going for his PhD in literature. Winter was advising him on his thesis.

Winter forced a smile. "Jim . . ." he said. "Come in. Come on in."

The boy entered. At the same moment, Winter's phone buzzed. He glanced down at the screen. It was Roger Sexton calling him back.

Winter gestured Yarrow to the chair in front of his desk as he picked up the phone.

"Hey, Roger," he said. "I'm with a student, but we need to talk."

Roger's voice sounded friendly enough, but Winter heard an edge of suspicion in it. "Sure. What about?"

"That matter we talked about last night. I have something I need to tell you."

Jim Yarrow was working to fit his long legs into the small space between the office chair and the desk.

"Oh, listen," Roger was saying over the phone. "Don't worry about it. Really. It's all right. I mean, I got your message. And believe me, I'm thinking about it. I'm proceeding with care, trust me."

"No, this is different. Something new. Some information you'll want to hear."

"Like what?"

"Well, like I said, I'm with a student right now," said Winter. "Let's find a time to get together. I have a department meeting at seven, but maybe before that."

"No, I've got a club thing. Look, Cam. Really. It's nice of you to worry about me. I appreciate it, and I appreciate your advice. I'm serious. I really do."

"Yeah, but it's not about that . . ."

"OK, well, look," said Roger. "We'll get together soon, all right?"

"Roger—"

"Look, I gotta go. I'll call you. I promise."

He hung up before Winter could say another word.

Winter spent the night as he had spent the night before, wide eyed, mind racing, sleepless into the early morning hours. He knew enough not to read more of the novel. He felt it would tear him to pieces. As it was, the scenes he'd already read would not stop replaying themselves on the movie screen behind his eyes.

Eventually, sheer exhaustion carried him off into fitful dreams. Then, in the morning, foggy headed, he had to start preparing for his lecture that afternoon.

He did not read any more of *Treachery in the Night* until the next day when he was on the plane to Portland. Even then, he hated to return to it. He had stopped himself from opening the book several times over the previous twenty-four hours. He didn't think he'd be able to stand any more of it. What was wrong with him? What on earth was wrong with him? Reading the book made him feel like there were spiders scrambling around in his brain.

But now, here, in the plane, in a window seat, nothing but kingdoms of clouds to look at in the sky outside, he could not help himself. He opened his laptop. He returned to the story.

When the meeting broke up, the men cleared the chairs away and two of the women set up a table with wine and snacks on it. The people stood around chatting, eating crackers, and drinking wine from plastic cups.

Theo was at the front of the room. He had fallen into a heated half-whispered conversation with Frederick Bernard. The calm, thoughtful Bernard was working hard to remain patient with Theo's urgency and passion, Miranda thought.

Miranda, meanwhile, was left awkwardly alone in a roomful of strangers. She sipped her chardonnay. She moved among the shelves and read the book bindings.

"I haven't seen you at one of these talks before."

She looked up at the voice. Moran was standing over her, looking down at her from his greater height. The heat Miranda had felt from his eyes seemed to be coming from his entire body now, a great wave of heat. It somehow seemed to wash over her and fill her at the same time. It made her feel weak inside, as if it had melted her.

"No," she managed to say. "This is my first."

He nodded. Took a long, slow look around at the others. All of them chatting, sipping wine, munching on crackers. "Talk is what it is. A lot of talk." He had a deep voice, solid and rich. He sounded very sure of himself. "A lot of philosophy. People up in their own heads. You know what I mean?"

Miranda rolled her eyes. "Oh yeah, believe me, I know."

Moran took a long look at Theo where he stood making excited gestures at Frederick Bernard. Then he looked back at Miranda with a quirk of a smile. "I figured you might," he said.

Just like that, Miranda felt there was a secret bond between them. As if he knew all about Theo and his rants and his theories and his impotent anger. As if he understood her whole situation and how trapped she felt in her relationship.

"Evan," he said to her. "Evan Moran."

"Miranda," she said. She held out a hand and his much larger hand engulfed it, but gently. She lifted her face to his, her eyes to his, connecting with him gaze to gaze. He held her hand a second longer than he should have.

A moment or two later, Theo came humping back to her with his odd, rolling gait. He ignored Moran, who towered above him. "We should go," he said to her tersely.

"This is Evan," Miranda said with a gesture. "Evan . . ." She glanced at him.

"Moran," Moran said.

Theo glanced up at the bigger man. He nodded at him curtly. "We should go," he said again to Miranda.

As they were heading to the stairs, Theo holding her by the wrist, drawing her along by the arm like a wayward child, Miranda could not help but glance back over her shoulder at where Moran was standing. His eyes were still on her. He was watching her go. The knowing smile was still on his lips.

Miranda felt her cheeks flush. She was embarrassed to have Theo dragging her away like this. She was embarrassed to have this misshapen and humorless man pulling her along while Moran watched. Watched and smiled knowingly. With his hot eyes.

6

Winter rented a car in Portland, a black Ford Expedition. He drove away from the airport and was quickly on country roads. He'd crossed two time zones and it was still early afternoon here. A vast blue sky stretched above him. An armada of cumulus clouds sailed across his windshield. Low brown mountains ringed him round and forests of conifers, pale green. Before him, the road wound out of sight into an obscure and misty distance.

But all he could see were scenes from *Treachery in the Night*. They kept going off in his mind like fireworks, flaring, fading, sprinkling down into the dark center of him.

By the time his plane landed, he had reached the part of the story where Miranda and Theo had moved into the place they called the Farmhouse. It stood in a field beyond the suburbs of an unnamed city. Miranda had deep misgivings about the move. She wanted to end her relationship with Theo. She wanted to break free of his increasingly furious philosophy and lead a normal life.

But somehow, she had been swept along into this move as if against her will, like a swimmer who sets out northward and is carried east on an undertow. Was it her fear of Theo? Fear of his rage and simmering violence? Or was it something else? The prospect of seeing Moran again?

She had already met with Moran a second time. There'd been another gathering at the bookshop, another talk by Frederick Bernard. After the speech, as the guests mingled, Moran had drawn her in among the shelves where they could stand together hidden from Theo and the others.

"Miranda," he had said to her in a soft, deep voice. When he touched her bare forearm, she had pulled back so sharply some of her chardonnay sloshed over the rim of her plastic cup onto her hand.

"Don't," she whispered, quickly wiping her hand on her jeans. "I mean it." She tilted her head toward the main section of the room. "I'm with Theo."

Moran snorted. That was what he thought of Theo.

When Theo told her they were moving to the Farmhouse, she did not even protest.

Of all the many agitated thoughts that were pinballing around in Winter's brain, one of the most agitating was this: He did not like the character of Miranda. She was weak and whiny, a bobbing toy on the current of her emotions and desires. He told himself this was the author's work. She was meant to represent a womanish and self-indulgent society waiting to be reclaimed by the glorious manhood of Moran. But no matter how often he lectured himself about this, he couldn't bring himself to separate Miranda from Charlotte in his mind. Was this really what she was like now? Were these really the people she mingled with? Was this really what she had become since he'd last seen her?

Looking ahead to where the road vanished in the mist, he felt as if he were on another, darker road inside himself, on a midnight highway, chasing the ghost of this girl into an unknown and unknowable past.

The Ford growled its way up a long incline. As Winter reached the peak of the hill, he saw the village of Cooksville spread out in the valley below him. Blackish mountain clouds gathered over it, but the light of early afternoon made the clouds glow at the edges. Where sunbeams fell through, they seemed like bright pillars holding up the heavens. Beneath this dramatic skyscape, Cooksville seemed to him like a fine, magical town from the old Western days. He could make out cow-town brick and clapboard shops on the main road, a church in the distance, houses among the trees. It looked as if no time had passed since the place had been settled who knew back when.

As the Ford began the winding ride downhill, Winter's phone rang. It was Roger Sexton again.

Winter pressed a light on the dashboard. When Roger's gruff voice came out of the audio array, Winter could picture his big, shambling presence.

"Hey. You still wanna talk?"

"I do, yes," Winter said.

"Well, why don't we get together? I'm about done here. I could get away for a drink at the Nomad in half an hour."

Winter sighed, watching Cooksville rise up toward him. "I can't. I'm out of town. I have some business to take care of."

There was a long pause. Winter was about to speak, when Roger said, "So what did you want to tell me?"

Winter tried to gather his thoughts. He had wanted to do this face-to-face. That seemed right somehow. This seemed wrong. He considered putting the conversation off until he got back home. But time was of the essence. He was afraid if he waited too long, things would get Shakespearean, with messengers passing each other on the road and the truth arriving too late so that everyone ended up committing suicide. Metaphorically speaking.

So out it came. "I was walking to my office a couple of days ago, and I saw your young friend," Winter said.

"Wait. Barbara? You saw Barbara?"

"I did. It was lunchtime and all the students were out and there she was."

There was another pause, a briefer one this time. "OK . . ." said Roger warily.

Winter made a face. This was giving him a bad taste in his mouth, but he didn't see any other way forward. The first houses of Cooksville were now appearing in the forest around him. Simple ranches on small patches of cleared land.

"She was with another student, a boy," Winter said. "Big kid. Looked like an athlete type. I don't know how to put this exactly but . . . well, look, it got pretty romantic between the two of them, Roger. It got very romantic."

"What do you mean?"

"I mean it got romantic," Winter repeated helplessly. "They were kissing each other. Passionately."

"What do you mean?" Roger said again. And when Winter couldn't think of an answer, he said: "What were you, spying on them?"

"No, I wasn't spying on them." Winter shook his head to himself as if the idea were ridiculous. "I was just walking behind them to get to my office. I guess the boy was going into the gym at Emery. They said goodbye and it . . . it got very passionate."

There was one more longish pause. Then Roger said, "Up yours, you son of a bitch."

"What?" said Winter. "Hello?"

But Roger had cut the connection.

Winter made a whiffling noise, a noise of frustration. What the hell? he thought. How was this his fault? But strangely enough, he did feel it was his fault somehow. Just as he felt he had, in fact, been spying on the girl. Well, he told himself, in any case, he had done his unpleasant duty. He had acted the part of a friend. Still, he did feel a bit like a son of a bitch.

He drove past a few more ranch houses, a lumberyard at the base of the mountain, a Victorian-style mansion that seemed out of place in that setting, then some more or less stately clapboards on tended lawns. Then he was on the village main street which, even close-up, looked to him like the main street in an old Western movie.

His GPS guided him to the church at the end of the road, then past the church down a winding wooded lane, and finally off to the right down a dirt side road. There, he found what he was looking for.

It was an isolated two-story clapboard house. Painted white, chipped with age and weather. There was a worn-out wooden sign in front, lopsided and broken but still legible: *Yesterday's Books*.

That pretty much described the place indoors. Old books were everywhere. Lined up on shelves, three deep. Stacked against the wall in towers. Even arrayed on windowsills one row balanced on top of another. Beyond the first room, there were other rooms and Winter could see through the doors to the books crowded into those rooms as well. There was also a flight of stairs with books on the steps and books on the built-in wall shelves beside the steps. Winter could feel the rooms of books upstairs too. He could feel the sorrowful weight of neglected words pressing down on the ceiling.

Winter loved used bookstores. Another day, another trip, he would have shopped through this place for hours. He would have searched through the abandoned volumes in a blissful daze, gathering up a few lost works in the hope he might rescue them and give them a good home. But today, his business was with the man sitting at the table against the left wall. He was the only other person in the shop. He was swimming in piles of books there, books on the tabletop, books at his feet. He was writing in a ledger with a gnawed pencil.

The guy looked so eccentric he could have been imaginary. A wizard from a fantasy novel maybe, or maybe a forty-niner from Gold Rush days—yes, probably that. He looked about two hundred years old. Small and so dwindled his arms looked like skeleton arms and his shirt and pants billowed around him. Wisps of silver hair covered his liver-spotted skull and a dirty white beard flowed down to the center of his chest.

He didn't even glance up when Winter came in. He probably hadn't seen another human being since the gasman checked the meter last month. Nonetheless, he didn't even say hello. He just went on doing what he was doing: picking up a book, looking at the inside page, writing some information in the ledger, then scribbling something on the book's inside cover—a price, Winter guessed. Then he set the one book aside, picked up another, and did the same again.

"I guess you haven't heard the good news about the invention of the computer," Winter said.

"Never use 'em," said the old man. He didn't stop writing.

Winter nodded. He waited for the old man to look up. The old man didn't look up.

"So," said Winter. "How's it going for you otherwise?"

"About how it seems, I guess," said the man. He set one book aside and picked up another. "What's your pleasure?"

"I'm looking for an author named Ivy Swansag."

The bookseller nodded, still writing. "Back room, back shelf, we should have some copies left."

"Thanks, but I'm not looking for her books. I'm looking for her. The author."

"The author?" The bookseller ruminated. "Why would I know the author?"

Winter raised one hand to indicate the store. "Oh, I'm pretty sure you know her. Where else would a writer hang out around here? Plus in her novel *Treachery in the Night*, she has a bookstore called Tomorrow Books. Your shop is called Yesterday's Books. Stands to reason there's a connection."

"Stands to reason, eh?" This seemed to amuse the old man. Something shivered deep in that beard of his anyway, and Winter figured it was probably his mouth fighting a smile. In any case, he had the bookseller's attention. The old man had actually paused in his work. He laid his book aside. Looked up. Leaned forward in his chair, his elbows on his knees, his hands dangling down unseen under the table. He raised his rheumy eyes to Winter. "As long as we're talking about reasons, what's the reason I would want to talk to you about her?" he asked.

Winter shrugged. "There's no reason not to. I'm an English pro-fessor." He took out his wallet and showed the man his university ID. The old man didn't even lower his eyes to look at it. "I'm writing a paper on *Treachery in the Night*."

"Are you now?"

"I am."

"How do I know you're not lying?"

"Why would I be lying?"

"Well, you could be a federal agent," said the bookseller.

"Do I look like a federal agent?"

"A little, yeah."

Winter rolled his eyes. He wondered if being a federal agent ever washed off or if he'd look like this forever. "How about this: Could you just give her a call and tell her I'd like to speak with her?"

"I could," said the old man thoughtfully. "If she had a phone."

"She doesn't have a phone?"

"Nope."

"Well, could you just tell me where she lives so I could speak to her myself?"

"Nope."

"Could I bribe you or beat it out of you or something?"

"Well. You look fit enough, but I'm pretty ornery."

Winter laughed. "I'll bet you are."

The bookseller was quiet for a moment and Winter thought they had reached an impasse. But apparently not. Because now the old man said: "You have a gun on you?"

"Sorry, what?"

"Are you carrying a firearm?"

"No, of course not. I told you. I'm an English professor."

The old man examined him a few more moments. Then he brought his right hand out from under the table. He was holding a revolver. It was huge, a real cannon. Ancient too, by the look of it. Winter thought it might have been the very gun with which the old man had killed Jesse James or someone like that back in the day. All the same, it seemed to be in good working order, and its sudden appearance made his heart skip.

"Well, you have a gun on you now, son. And I'll tell you what," the old bookseller said. "You gimme a second to use the john and you can drive me out there. I'll personally ask Susannah—Ivy Swansag—if she'd like to talk to you. If she says yes, then there you are. If she says no, off you go home. And if it turns out you are a federal agent, I'll blow your head off."

7

They drove together in silence. The old man sat in the Ford's passenger seat, the gun in his hand, his hand resting easy in his lap. Winter eyed the enormous weapon from time to time, mildly worried it might discharge and blow off his kneecap if they so much as hit a pothole. Other than that, though, his mind felt settled, calmer than before. He was in action now. On the hunt. It focused him. Steadied him. For the moment anyway.

It didn't take long before the town sank out of sight behind them. They followed an empty two-lane out of the valley, into a pass. The mountains loomed over them. The dark glowing sky loomed above them. The rays of light fell to earth here and there like a hint of heaven.

The bookseller gazed out the windshield. Winter stole a glance at his gaunt, wizened face. He seemed comfortably nestled in his silence. It would be up to him, Winter thought, to get him talking, to see if he could pry any useful information out of him.

"Do you come out to see her often?" he asked. "Susannah, I mean. Is that what you said her name is?"

The bookseller's long silver beard waved a little as he nodded. "Susannah Woods. Not often, no."

"But I take it you've known her for some time."

Even under the sound of the engine, Winter could hear the old man draw breath. He said: "Some time, yes. And since we're making conversation here, you have a mind to tell me why you want to see her?"

"I told you," said Winter. "I'm an English professor."

"I know what you told me. I meant the real reason. If you're not a federal agent—and I'm guessing you're not since if you were I'd have killed you by now—what are you? One of her political friends?"

Winter snorted. "No. Are you?"

"Not me. I'm saved by the blood of the lamb, brother. The burden of hatred has been lifted from my shoulders."

"That must be a relief."

" 'Tis. Now I love everybody. Even the Jews."

"Big of you."

"They shouldn't have killed Christ though."

"Well," Winter said. "Maybe it was a case of mistaken identity."

To his surprise, the bookseller let out a wheezy laugh. "Mistaken identity. That's a good one."

The Ford emerged from between the mountains into another valley. Farmland stretched to a river on their left and to the horizon on their right, a little vastness of green fields dotted by brown cows. The black mountain clouds dissolved. The sky turned blue, pale blue under a layer of mist.

"The truth is," said Winter, "I did work for the government once. A long time ago," he added quickly, before the bookseller could pull the big gun's trigger. "Believe me, if that doesn't take the politics out of you, nothing will."

"Yessir. If there's a boot on your neck, it doesn't much matter whether it's the left boot or the right boot," the bookseller said.

Winter gave half a smile. "I'm looking for a girl, that's all."

"Handsome young fellow like you, that shouldn't be too much of a problem."

"I meant a specific girl."

"Ah." The old man's withered head rose and fell. "Miranda from the novel."

Winter glanced over at him. "Yes, that's right."

"In-ter-resting. I mean no offense to you, son, but it'd go a long way to convincing me to trust you, if you could prove you know her—let's say, by telling me her real name."

"Charlotte."

"Uh-huh. Charlotte Shaefer. That's the one."

"So you knew her?"

"I met her a few times. When she was staying with Susannah. It's years ago now. Haven't seen her since."

"You don't know where she went?"

"I do not," said the bookseller. "Don't want to neither. I know a woman on the run when I see one. When whatever is after her catches up, I don't want to be the one they come around to asking questions."

Winter drove on at a steady pace. He kept his expression calm, but he was excited now. This man had seen Charlotte. Met her, spoken with her. Knew her name. It was the first contact Winter had had with her since that last time he'd seen her so long ago.

"So she was on the run and she hid out with Susannah?" Winter asked. "Is that it?"

"That was it as far as I could tell," said the bookseller. He chewed the inside of his cheek. "Some of it I'm just guessing, I admit. A sort of deduction, you might say. One day, Susannah came by the bookshop to ask me for a favor. Asked me if I'd do some shopping for her, bring some things out to her, food and so forth. Normally, she'd have done it herself, but this time, she asked me. So of course

I did it, being a Christian man. And when I got to her house, there this girl was. This Charlotte."

Winter was quiet for a moment as he recited this narrative back to himself to make sure he had the sense of it. Charlotte had shown up at Susannah's house on the run. Susannah had not wanted to be seen in town shopping for two instead of one. So she asked her friend the bookseller to bring her deliveries for as long as the girl was there.

"How long did that arrangement go on?" he asked.

" 'Bout a month, I'd say. Five, six weeks maybe. Like I told you, it was years ago."

"And you don't know who was after Charlotte, who she was hiding out from."

"I do not," said the bookseller. "Could've been the feds. Could've been some of the political people. Left or right. They're all the same. None of them's worth a pig's fart, you ask me."

"Why'd she come here? To Susannah?"

"Oh, Susannah, she was always playing mother to that bunch. Knowing her, she saw the girl among them, took pity on her, and slipped her her address in case she ever was in trouble and needed it. That's just a guess, of course, but I'd bet a dollar on it, if I had a dollar."

Ahead through the windshield and out through the windows on either side, the valley had opened into a broad blue-green plain with smoky blue-gray mountains ringing the horizon. Winter was barely aware of the scenery though. He was too busy reconstructing the old man's story in his mind. He could imagine Charlotte sitting with Susannah at a kitchen table, drinking coffee, telling the older woman the story that inspired *Treachery in the Night*.

"So basically, something happened," he said aloud. "Something happened to the political group Charlotte was with, and Charlotte had to run for it, so she ran here."

Winter felt the bookseller's gaze on him. He took a look over and saw, yes, the old man was giving him a suspicious eye. His thumb was caressing the hammer of his pistol.

"Didn't you tell me you read the book?" the old man said. "The book tells the story. Leastways, I always figured that was the story more or less."

"I haven't finished it yet," said Winter.

"Pretty easy read, I'd think."

"Not for me."

"Oh. I get you. This girl—she means something to you."

"She did once."

"One of those women who leaves a mark, huh."

"That's it."

There was silence in the Ford for a moment or two. Then the bookseller said, "Well, I'm going to choose to believe your story, since blowing your head off hardly seems the Christlike thing to do. Just so you know, though, Susannah'll kill you faster than I will, she catches the stink of G-man on you. And if she misses, I won't. Turn there. Cluster of mailboxes on your left."

Winter spotted the cluster and made the turn onto another dirt road. This one was hardly a road at all, just a track really, worn into the grass by pickup tires. The Ford bounced hard and wobbled side to side.

"I don't suppose I could get you to take your finger off that trigger till the road smooths out," Winter said.

"Nope," said the bookseller.

On they drove.

They passed two side roads, even narrower and rougher than the one they were on. Winter saw farmhouses in the distance. Cows. A big old monster of a green combine sitting idle by a brown furrowed field. Finally, up ahead a last house came into view.

The sight of the place startled Winter. It was, he knew at once, the Farmhouse from the novel. Which meant Susannah Woods must have transposed the action of the novel to her own home. Which meant, assuming the book was based on true events, those events must have looked very different in real life. It was just as she'd said in that fragment of interview: *It's a novel. I made it up. That's what a novel is.* Reading the book, Winter had felt that he was learning something about Charlotte's life, but maybe not. How could he know where the truth lay?

They pulled up in front of the house. It was just as it was described in the novel: a slump-roofed, ramshackle two-story clapboard, scraped raw by the weather. An ancient green pickup truck was parked beside an ancient cedarwood garden shed to their left.

When Winter killed the Ford's engine, a deep silence settled over them. It was a country silence, loud with the chitter of bugs, the twitter and flutter of birds, and the whisper of wind moving through the unmown grass. The house itself stood silent with a deeper silence, the windows dark, no movement visible within.

Winter rolled out on one side of the Ford and the old man worked his skeletal frame free on the other. The two men tromped up the house's porch steps side by side. The bookseller waited, gun held down by his thigh, as Winter knocked. There was no answer. Winter knocked again and then again. The bookseller lifted his chin to tell Winter to try the door. Winter tried it and it swung open.

"Susannah!" the bookseller shouted through the doorway. "Susannah! It's Old Bill. You here? You got a visitor." Still no answer. The bookseller looked around at Winter. "Must be she's working. Her workroom's upstairs. She doesn't always hear me knocking when she's up there."

He went inside and Winter followed him. There were no lights on and the house was cool and shadowy. As in the novel, the building had a chaotic feeling to it, hallways running off in various directions like kids dispersing for a round of hide and seek. Winter caught a glimpse of the kitchen through a doorway and peeked in. It was a shabby country kitchen, the counters grimy, the terra-cotta floor tiles worn to a thin film. There was nothing in the copper sink but a coffee mug. The dregs in the mug were moldy as if it had been there a long time.

"Suzy Q, it's Old Bill," Winter heard the bookseller shouting.

He left the kitchen and caught up to the old man as his skeletal figure climbed the stairs with weary tread.

They reached a landing, first the bookseller, then Winter. The wooden floors were as tilted as the deck of a ship at sea. Small windows looked out on a backyard of unmown fields bordered by a distant tree line. Winter thought of the prologue of *Treachery in the Night* when Moran and Theo walked off together into the forest, rifles in their hands, Dobermans loping along beside them. Was that story true? Had Charlotte known that only one of them would come back?

Hunched and brittle, the bookseller creaked along the creaking hallway. Winter followed him. There was a closed door at the end of the hall.

"Susannah!" the bookseller called. "This is where she works," he said to Winter.

The old man knocked on the closed door then opened it and looked in. Winter heard him make a clicking noise with his tongue.

"Damn me," the old man muttered.

He went into the room and Winter went into the room and both stood just inside the threshold, staring at the desolation.

The place had been ransacked. The floor was littered with books and papers. Two corkboards and a whiteboard had been knocked off the walls. A file cabinet had been turned on its side and emptied. The computer—a Bronze Age desktop—was over-turned, the monitor smashed. All the drawers were pulled out of the antique wooden desk and emptied onto the desktop or onto the floor around the overturned chair.

Winter crouched down and lifted one corkboard, then another. There were index cards tacked to them, handwritten sentences on each. Some sort of story outline, it looked like. He couldn't make much sense of it. He noticed a streak of what looked like dried blood on the cork.

He spied a photograph near the overturned cabinet. He shifted over to it, still crouching. The photo was buried under other papers. There was blood smeared on some of the papers too. No finger-prints. Whoever had done this was wearing gloves.

Winter pulled the photo free. It was a picture printed on paper: a man in his thirties, thin faced, pale, aesthetic, with serious eyes and shaggy black hair. When Winter plucked it out, he spied another photo underneath it. His heart sped up. He recognized the face immediately. It was Eddie, Charlotte's boyfriend. He remembered the dull and furious face and the strangely shaped shoulders. He looked at the first photo again. He figured that must be the man who was called Frederick Ber-nard in the novel, the intellectual guy who'd made the speeches in Tomorrow Books.

Winter began to page through the scattered papers more urgently. He noted more blood on some of the pages. He found another picture. Was this Moran? he wondered. He thought it was. He recognized the round face, its boyish vulnerability, the cold and savage cruelty in his eyes. The photo showed him from his belt buckle up, and Winter could see he was a big man, powerful, broad shouldered, with muscles bulging through his work shirt.

Now Winter's heart was beating hard. He was breathless and paging through the papers faster and faster.

"Hey, professor, have a look at this," said the bookseller.

For a moment, Winter didn't listen, paging and paging through the papers, searching for another photo. Charlotte's photo. Proof of life.

"Have a look here at this," said the bookseller again.

Winter turned to him. The old man was crouched down, too, pawing at the papers, studying the floor beneath. With his spindly body and his billowing clothes and that long white beard, he looked like some sort of shaman—a haruspex was the Latin word that came to Winter's mind—a haruspex reading the entrails of a lamb.

Taking deep breaths to quiet his heart, Winter straightened up and went to stand over him. He looked down over his shoulder. The old man had pushed some papers aside and uncovered a stain on the floor.

"Blood, you think?"

"Yeah," said Winter. "That's blood. There's some smeared on the papers too."

The old man sighed. "Damn me."

The two men were thinking together now. They didn't have to speak. They left the workspace. They went down the stairs, Winter first, then the old man, moving more cautiously, behind him. They didn't search the rest of the house. They both knew there was no need. Winter went out the front door and waited at the bottom of the porch stairs for the old man to catch up with him. Then they walked side by side toward the green pickup truck, and around the truck to the cedarwood garden shed.

They smelled the old woman before they found what was left of her. Winter wrestled the shed door open and made a noise of anger and disgust. Then he turned sideways to breathe the fresher air outside, and the bookseller moved past him to take a look.

Animals had had at the body, but there was enough remaining so they could see the woman had been torn up pretty thoroughly even before that, before she died most likely. She was tied to a chair and slumped over, her gray hair spilling down over what once had been her face. She was wearing a woolen housedress, its flower pattern faded and covered with crusty blood. The plump figure Winter remembered from the interview video looked small and pitiable now, as if it had caved in on itself.

"Damn me," said the old bookseller once again. His face was stern with righteous indignation.

Winter moved farther into the shed. He had spotted something lying beside the dead woman's chair. There was a page of paper on the floor there, crumpled up as if a man had bunched it into his fist, then cast it down.

Winter crouched and picked the paper up and opened it. His heartbeat was so loud, the sound of it filled his head. Another picture was on the page. It was the picture he couldn't find up in the workroom. Charlotte. Older than when he'd last seen her. Her blond hair had grown back. The frantic madness was gone from her eyes. The solemn stillness of her childhood had returned to her face. She was gazing into the distance as if her thoughts were far away. Winter looked at the photo and his pounding heart ached with longing and fear.

Behind him, he heard the old man give a heavy sigh. He looked up over his shoulder at him.

"Well, professor," the bookseller said. His voice was thin but still steady. "Looks to me like whoever your girl was running from is coming after her." The old man's sad old eyes passed slowly over the shed's interior. "Looks to me like he's catching up too."

PART TWO

THE PHANTOM OF THE ZONES

I made my way to Istanbul to look for Jerry Collins. What I remember most about that trip was my sudden sense of solitude. Of abandonment even. A very intense feeling that the usual organizational support for my mission was gone.

It's a funny thing about that. That support, those structures you count on to back you up: They're there in your mind even when you don't realize it, even when in fact you're most alone. You're on assignment in a foreign place, a hostile place. But there's still a sense that, even if everything goes sideways, in the last extremity, you have a layer of protection, an authority to which you can appeal. It's not a sense of safety exactly. I always knew I could be captured. I knew I could be killed, even in a city of allies. But I also knew the Division was there somewhere. Back home. The Recruiter was sitting deadpan at his desk in DC. His hands clasped on the desktop as usual. The world at his command. I knew if I fell off the radar for sixty minutes straight, the most powerful nation on earth—plus our kick-ass savior Jesus Christ and all his angels and the Air Force besides—would use all their resources to try, at least, to find me. Maybe that was an illusion, but it was a reassuring one.

And now, that mental security blanket—it was just gone. That walk we'd taken, the Recruiter and I, that walk to Mount Vernon in the *autumn evening—it had been such a sinister affair, all sorts of unspoken things going on in it. I just didn't know what to think anymore. Was the Recruiter acting alone now? Was he at odds with the last best hope of earth? Was he suddenly acting behind its back? And who was I working for then, him or the nation? I didn't know. And if I should fall off the radar into eternal darkness, I didn't know if there would be anyone to appeal to this time, anyone who might come to my aid.*

And where the hell was Jerry Collins anyway? What did it mean that the most clean-cut straight-arrow Christian patriot in the long history of clean-cut Christian straight-arrow patriots had disappeared without a trace?

And then there was Istanbul. Do you know it at all? It's a mysterious city. Everything about it underscored my sense that I was plunging into an alien solitude. You get there—the airport is new and beautiful. Full of sparkling shops and vaulted ceilings. Pillars of white and pillars of gold. When you fly in from DC, it feels as if you've just gone around the corner. But only at first. Then you step outside. You get a cab. All the cars are small, dented, dated. The highways are dilapidated, packed with all these small, dented, dated cars. And all of the cars are tearing along the highway at unbelievable speeds. Dodging and weaving like carnival bumper cars but without the rubber bumpers. The drivers are insane in Istanbul. Stoned on khat and crazy as loons. You tell yourself they must know what they're doing—driving so recklessly, so fast—you have to tell yourself that or you'd faint from fear—but it's totally untrue. They have no idea what they're doing. I'm not even sure they know where they are. There are wrecks everywhere, all along the highway. Cars overturned by the side of the road. Cars in flames. You reach for your seat belt, but there is no seat belt. The car was built before seat belts were invented. So you're flying through traffic, past wrecks, toward death, and does anyone even know you're there? If you were crushed to pudding in a twelve-car pileup, would anyone ever find you?

The cab dropped me off in the old quarter just in time for afternoon prayer. The muezzin was singing from the minaret of the great Blue Mosque. The mosque—it looks like a fairy kingdom unto itself, the huge ballooning dome, and all the elegant towers—an image from the cover of a sword and sorcery novel. And that weirdly mesmerizing nasal chanting filling the air. Muhammad is the prophet of Allah. Come to prayer. *It all added to my nagging sense that I was far from home, in another world altogether, and completely on my own.*

My hotel had been Jerry's hotel so I showed Jerry's picture to the clerk at the reception desk. First I gave him some money, then I showed him the picture. He pretended to study the picture—that's what I got for my money—then he shook his head: Don't know him. But I could see in his eyes that I'd gotten what I wanted. I felt pretty sure that, as soon as I was out of sight in my room, all the relevant people in Turkey would know I was here. Sooner or later someone would show up to give me some information or possibly slip a knife into my kidney, one or the other. Either way, I'd have a clearer sense of the situation.

So it turned out. I dropped my bag off in my room. Washed up. Cat-napped. I must have been there an hour. It wasn't any more than that. Then I headed out to the police station and instantly—ten seconds after I stepped out through the hotel door—I realized I was being followed. That's how fast it all went down.

My shadow was a willowy brown-skinned man in a white shirt and gray trousers. He wasn't much good at keeping out of sight, or maybe he didn't care whether I saw him or not.

It was a fine mild day with the scent of the ocean in it. The streets were crowded with natives and tourists, but it wasn't hard to keep track of the man. He was strolling along with his hands in his pockets, relaxed and steady. He didn't fall back. He didn't draw near. He was just always there, always visible.

As for me, I didn't want to lose him, but I didn't want to confront him alone either. If he was going to talk to me, he could do it in a crowd. If he was going to try to kill me, I wanted witnesses.

I remembered my way to the Grand Bazaar, so I led him there. Past the outer awnings, under the stone arch. It's one of the largest indoor malls in the world, maybe the largest, I don't know. It's been there practically since the Turks conquered the city in the fifteenth century. I've always found it a sort of dazzling place. Dazzling crowds, dazzling colors. People shouting at you as you pass. Meat markets, gold markets, displays of brightly colored bowls and colored baskets and rugs, shop after shop, all of them under arched ceilings tiled with elaborate designs. Packed with tourists and locals all moving at a summer pace, studying the merchandise, haggling with the sellers.

I drew my shadow as deep into the corridors as I could. I paused to pretend to peruse some knitwear. The shadow didn't notice and kept coming for a step or two. A step or two too close. I straightened and turned on him.

He didn't hesitate. He flowed toward me with the flow of the crowd. His shoulder touched my shoulder as he brushed past me. And when he was gone, I was holding a ferry ticket in my hand.

OK, I thought. I guess I'm taking a ride on the ferry.

The next morning, early, I was out on the Marmara Sea. It was a fine day. The sky bright blue. The air just cool enough for my windbreaker and my cap. The minarets and domes and colored buildings of the city fell away from me, all very beautiful against a backdrop of small white clouds. The glaring water surrounded me.

I hadn't brought a gun. I wished I had, but I knew it would have been useless. Whoever I was going to meet, they would strip it off me first thing. So away I went on the ferry, unarmed. And all I could think about was that this was where Jerry Collins had vanished, out on the water. And I wondered, if I vanished too, what then? What would the

Recruiter do? Who would the Division send to find me? Anyone? Did they even know I was here? And if not—if the Recruiter was acting on his own—was there anyone else he could trust the way he trusted me?

We chugged past the islands and on until we reached Bandirma in the later morning. It was a jaunty little workman's town, very shabby in those days. I haven't seen it since. I got out in a small crowd of other passengers and saw my man right away. He was a thug for sure. Short but stocky, dome-bellied but clearly made of muscle. Wearing a blue tracksuit. What it is with thugs and their tracksuits, I don't know, but they love them. He wore a windbreaker over the top with a gun underneath, out of sight but visible to the practiced eye.

He was leaning against a black Caddy, his thick arms crossed on his chest. The car was new and polished bright, which made it unique in those parts, easy to spot.

He gave me a slow nod of his head and I walked over to him. He patted me down—pretty expertly, I have to say. I was right not to bring a gun. It would have been a waste of good artillery.

"Phone," he said.

He held out his hand. I gave him my phone. He pulled the card out and threw it a long way into a distant patch of scrub. He gave the shell of the thing back to me.

"Thanks," I said dryly.

"Get in," he said.

He pulled the back door open for me just like a real chauffeur. I got in and he got in up front behind the wheel. We took off like a rocket and shot out of town at mind-boggling speed. Half an hour later, we were in the middle of a brown wilderness covered with scraggly brush and litter. And with old tires, and with old home appliances that had been thrown away. Not another car in sight. Not a living thing anywhere.

The thug pulled the Caddy over to the side of the road, the two right tires in the dirt. He killed the engine.

"Get out now," he said.

I got out. Really, there was nothing there. No birds singing. Not even the noise of wind. I don't know what to compare it to. It felt as if the movie had frozen around us and we were the only characters still moving. It's hard to give a sense of the isolation. If the driver had gotten out and shot me and left me in the middle of the pavement, the buzzards would have eaten me before anyone found my corpse.

Instead, the guy gets out of the car and he takes a little leather pouch out of the pocket of his windbreaker. He unzips the pouch and removes a hypodermic needle.

"I don't think so, friend," I said.

"It will make you sleep," he said. "So you don't see the way. You have no choice. Take your jacket off."

He squeezed a few drops out of the needle and waited for me. When I hesitated, he urged me on with a gesture of his chin. He waited, holding the hypodermic upright, the point toward the sky. I sighed and stripped my jacket off.

He stepped toward me. I threw the jacket over his head and it hung there, covering his face. With the same motion, I grabbed his wrist with one hand. With the other hand, I hit him in the crook of the elbow so his arm bent up. Then I jammed the hypodermic needle into the side of his neck. I pressed his thumb down on the plunger.

My jacket fell off him and fell to the ground. The guy stood there staring at me in open-mouthed terror. The hypodermic was still stuck in his neck. Then his hand dropped. The hypodermic just waggled there until I pulled it out and tossed it into the brush.

"I hope that stuff wasn't meant to kill me," I said. "But I guess we're about to find out."

He started to answer, but he never got around to it. His eyes rolled up in his head and his knees gave way. His sturdy little body wafted to the ground like a dropped towel. I knelt down and felt his throat. He was still alive—for now anyway.

I took his gun—a nice Glock nine—and his belt clip. I hooked the weapon onto my belt.

His phone was in the cupholder next to the driver's seat. I fetched it, but it was dark. I held it to his sleeping face. That worked. The phone unlocked and came to life. I checked the GPS. Sure enough, there were the directions to wherever the hell we were going.

I thought of leaving the thug where he was, but that seemed unkind somehow. He was just a thug doing his thug job. Anyway, I didn't want to leave a trail. So instead, I hauled him around back and hoisted him into the trunk. Then I retrieved my windbreaker, got in the car, and set off to wherever, bumping along a narrow road through absolute nothing.

An hour went by. More than an hour. Trees closed around me, tall Turkish pines with bare trunks and spreading crowns. The road began to wind and climb. I was going up a mountain through a haunted forest of tangled evergreens.

After a while, I got a glimpse through the trees of a house above me. I didn't see it clearly until I broke out of the forest near the mountaintop. It was vast, a vast villa, a white palace of columns and arches and enormous arched windows. Blue pools and fountains all around it, curling jets of water arching into the air. Beyond the building, suddenly, there was the sea. It hadn't appeared on the GPS map, and I didn't know it was there until I saw it.

I stopped the car, killed the engine, and got out. It was different here than in the wilderness. There was life. Wind whispering off the water. The sound of waves, and the fountains plashing. Seagulls sailing overhead, crying out. And the smell of the sea.

I heard the thug banging feebly on the trunk. I could hear him moaning too. I figured he hadn't been planning to murder me with that injection. Lucky for him. I ignored him and walked toward the mansion.

The entryway was a long, arched gallery decorated with nude statues, ancient statues for all I knew. I walked past them and came into a court-yard, a marble-floored space surrounded by the wings of the building but open in back to the sight of the blue sea. The distant water sparkled in the sun. There were fountains in the alcoves in the walls on both sides of me: carved stone faces drooling water into basins. More statues. It was very elaborate.

There, in the middle of it all, sat a man. He was a young man, tall and fit. He was sitting on a white metal chair at a round white metal table. The marble floor was white and the walls were white and he was wearing a white tracksuit, very clean and bright. He was grinning as if he were glad to see me and his teeth were white. Other than that, he was scruffy, unshaven, his light brown hair long and unkempt.

There was a bottle of champagne in a bucket on a stand beside him. He held a flute of champagne in one hand, and there was another flute waiting on the table beside a carved wooden tray of Turkish savories.

But what struck me—what struck me first as I continued walking toward him—were the women. Girls, I should say. Three of them, just standing at his shoulders like servants, and four more standing by the walls like living statues. All of them were wearing white skirts and nothing else. Judging by the looks of them, they were various nationali-ties, Middle Eastern, Asian, Slavic. They had fine young bodies, but too young, young enough to make me uncomfortable and I was young then too. I was no monk, but there was definitely something unwholesome about the scene, like I'd come into a harem or a den of slavery. There was something decadent here—or maybe wicked *is the word I want.*

Anyway, that's what struck me first. But what struck me next really struck me, struck me hard, like a blow to the belly.

Because after a few more steps I was close enough to see the man clearly—the man sitting on the white chair at the white table with his flute of champagne and his half-naked underage girls.

And—call me a feather and blow me away—I'll be damned if it wasn't Jerry Collins.

8

"All right, all right, all right," said Margaret Whitaker impatiently. "That's enough of that, Cam. That is absolutely enough."

"Really? The story's just getting good," he said.

"Never mind," she answered. "What on earth is wrong with you?"

"What do you mean?"

She glared at him, tight lipped. As if she really were his mother instead of just a therapeutic stand-in. And in fact, she was cross with him as a mother might get cross when she's worried about her child. And the way he was gazing at her—with that expression of bland innocence as if he didn't know what she was making such a fuss about—well, it really did make her want to smack him a good one. Instead, she gestured at him.

"You look like death warmed over," she said.

"Well, thanks."

"You're welcome. Your eyes are the size of saucers. Your skin is the consistency of paste. You look like a truck just ran over your best friend right in front of you. And you come in here and start talking about this . . . just start telling me this—irrelevant story as if I weren't going to notice."

"I thought you'd want to hear the rest of . . ."

"Enough, Cameron. I mean it. I'm your therapist. Tell me what's wrong. What on earth happened to you since I saw you last?"

She watched as he reluctantly surrendered to her. He seemed somehow to sink deeper in the brown client armchair. His shoulders slumped. His bland expression was replaced by a look of open misery. He stared down at the brown carpet—which seemed almost colorless in that brown and tan room—as if it were the Pit of Darkness. Margaret waited, very still in her brown leather swivel chair, her face serious but no longer stern.

"I think I've found Charlotte," he said finally.

"What? Oh, my Lord!"

She hadn't meant to blurt that out. His announcement had caught her completely by surprise. But as it turned out, her reaction seemed to comfort him. He was, she thought, glad—relieved—that she had grasped the importance of the situation.

"All right," she said. "Tell me all."

Staring and staring into the unseen black depths of the brown carpet, he told her.

"I came home one night and smelled her perfume outside my apartment door. The same perfume you and I had talked about. I had the doorman show me the security videos. There was a figure on one of them that looked like her. It was her, I'm sure of it. She was carrying a book. A novel. I downloaded it and started reading it. The main character was obviously based on Charlotte. So I went to see the author out in Oregon. A woman. About your age. When I got there, I found her—the author—dead."

Margaret caught herself this time. Only a soft, startled grunt escaped her lips before she clamped them together tightly.

"She'd been murdered. Tortured first, then murdered."

Margaret remained still, but she could feel her blood was racing through her. "You called the police."

"Yes, of course."

Of course, my eye! she almost said, but she managed not to. He looked so desolate, she didn't have the heart to scold him.

"What did they say?"

He let out a sigh that made his whole body deflate. "Not much. I got the feeling this woman was some sort of local favorite. They were being protective of her. But I have a pretty good idea what happened."

Now she could wait. She knew he would tell her the rest. Still, her blood was running so fast she was afraid she would grow faint.

"You remember that creepy guy she was with the last time I saw her?"

"Yes," Margaret said. "I remember. Eddie-my-boyfriend."

"Eddie-my-boyfriend. The protofascist. Right. Well, if the novel is true—and I really don't know yet how much of it actually is true—he went all the way down the rabbit hole of his political ideology."

Margaret couldn't help but wrinkle her nose with distaste. "Well, that sounds about right. That was more or less in the cards, if anything was."

"He joined some group somewhere during the riots, not the last riots, the ones before that. And he took Charlotte with him."

"Oh no. Cam, I'm so sorry."

"Yeah, it's the usual fall-of-the-republic stuff, you know. The violent leftist thugs were going to burn down some cities to gain political leverage so the violent rightist thugs were going to take to the streets and fight back. Gang war, red versus brown. American Weimar, and so on. Anyway, this woman, this author who was murdered, she was a friend of the browns and she must've given

Charlotte her address to use as a hideout if something went wrong. Well, apparently something did go wrong and Charlotte went to hide out with her. I guess she told the author her story and the author then turned it into this novel about a mighty superman rising up to fight the evil Blacks and Jews."

Shaking her head, Margaret clucked her tongue. "So—what then? You think someone tortured this woman—this writer—trying to get Charlotte's location out of her?"

"That's my guess."

"Do you think he succeeded?"

"No. He ransacked her papers, looking for information. There was blood on the pages so I think he did it after he killed her. I think that means he hadn't gotten what he wanted out of her."

"Why not, I wonder. How hard is it to torture information out of an old lady? If it were me, they'd only have to make a scary face, and I'd tell them everything."

"It's possible she didn't know where Charlotte had gone. In fact, I think that's the most likely scenario."

Margaret took a silent moment to consider all this. It was too much information to process on the spot. She would have to proceed from here with care, feeling her way through the fog.

Winter was obviously very upset; deeply troubled. She only had to look at him to see it: He was a mental mess. And how else could he feel? His life in the Division had stripped him of all respect for political ideology. He had nothing but disdain for true believers of any stripe. To think of his Charlotte—this childhood idol with her mysterious power over him—to think of her sinking into this underworld of rage was enough in itself to make a torment of his nights. But then—then to find that she was on the run, that some torturer from that raging underworld was hunting her . . .

"You think she came to your apartment to ask you for help, is that it?" Margaret finally said.

He nodded, still staring into the carpet, into that pit she couldn't see.

"That would make sense," Margaret murmured, as much to herself as to him. "She would have looked you up on the internet from time to time, the way we all do nowadays. She would have known about some of your adventures. You'd be a natural person for her to turn to."

"If she couldn't turn to anyone else. Yes."

"But why didn't she leave a note or try to contact you again?"

Winter shook his head miserably. "I don't know, Margaret. Maybe something spooked her. Or maybe she didn't want to leave a message without being sure I'd get it. I don't know. Maybe . . ." He lifted his face to her. It was, she thought, as if he had been peering into black hell and the vision had branded itself onto his eyes. "Maybe the killer found her. Maybe the chase is already over."

"Cameron. Don't get ahead of yourself. There's no sense thinking that."

"I guess not."

Eager to help him, to soothe him somehow, Margaret tried to play detective, thinking out loud. "She must have brought that book to show it to you, yes? Which means the story the book tells must be more or less true. In principle, at least. She must have thought it was the best way to explain her situation to you."

He didn't answer. She watched him closely. The seconds stretched out, dragged on.

Then something terrible happened. It was terrible to Margaret anyway. Later, she thought she should have been expecting it, or something like it. But she had been so taken up in their conversation that, when the moment came, it took her by surprise.

Winter lifted his right hand to his lips and she could see that it was trembling—trembling violently.

This was awful to her. The worst event in their therapy so far. They had been through all sorts of moments together. She had listened to his tales of horrific deeds. She had seen him depressed and in an anguish of guilt. She had watched him, him sitting right in that same chair, weeping pitifully over the death of a friend. But through all this, she was always aware of the solid core of him, the emotional steel that made him unlike anyone else she had ever treated or ever known.

Now, though—the anguish in his eyes—the pallor of his cheeks—the slackness of his body—that trembling hand: The man was simply crumbling to bits in front of her.

His voice trembled too. "Something's wrong with me, Margaret."

"No, no," she said soothingly.

"For God's sake, look at me."

"I see you. It's all right."

"It's not. Something terrible is happening to me. To my mind . . . it's not all right."

"Well, it will be. It will be all right. I've got you, Cam. We'll go through it together."

"I don't even understand it. I don't understand why I feel this way." He looked at her with that hollow, hell-branded gaze. His voice was as plaintive as a child's.

"Well," she said. "Charlotte means a great deal to you."

"Yes, but I was like this before. I tried to hide it from you but I was coming apart before she showed up."

"Yes," Margaret answered quietly. She hesitated before she went on, unwilling to explain too much. There were some concepts a client had to discover for himself or they would be worthless to him. They wouldn't sink in. She could guide him toward the tangles of his inner world, but he had to untie the knots on his own.

She continued slowly, choosing each word with care, trying to tell him what he needed to know without telling him too much. "You were troubled before because you were beginning to realize how emotionally paralyzed you are. It was being made manifest to you in your inability to call Gwendolyn Lord, a woman to whom you're powerfully attracted."

"What's that got to do with Charlotte?"

"Well," Margaret went on carefully. "The thing is, Cam, it's not really about Charlotte. OK? I mean, Charlotte—the image of Charlotte—has become a sort of vessel inside you for all kinds of meanings."

"So you mean . . ." Winter began. She watched him as he tried, through his pain, to make his way toward understanding. "You mean Charlotte showing up just now is like a ghost story—one of those ghost stories where the ghost represents some emotional truth in the narrator's life."

"That's it. Yes. The old Charlotte, the little girl Charlotte—she no longer exists. Just like the little boy Cameron no longer exists. If you were ever to see the real Charlotte again, she wouldn't be anything like the girl you remembered."

"Oh, I know that," he said irritably.

"Well," Margaret pushed on patiently. "There's knowing it, there's understanding—and then there's grasping it, really feeling and accepting it. Those are different things." She took a deep breath. She felt she needed to come to the end of this. "If you were to find Charlotte now, if you were to look at her, really look at her as she is, it would be very, very painful. Not just because of what she might have become. But because it may also entail facing certain things about yourself, the sort of things that brought you to me in the first place."

Vague as that was, it did seem to reach him. He put his arms on the arms of the chair, gripped them as if to keep himself from floating away. He sat back and tilted his face up at the ceiling. He nodded to show he understood.

She let him have that moment. She waited till his body relaxed, till he lowered his head so he could face her again.

Then she said quietly: "That's why you must not try to find her."

He blinked. He shook his head as if he hadn't heard her. "Sorry? What?"

"Listen to me, Cam. Look in a mirror. You said it yourself: Something's wrong with you. You've had a shock. You're rattled. You're decompensating. That's what we call it. Which is fine. We can deal with that. We will deal with it, I told you, together. But whoever this person is who is hunting for Charlotte—well, think about it: He tortured and killed an old woman. He. They. There may be more than one of them, you don't even know. But even if it's only one, he's violent. He's brutal." She held up one hand before he could object. "I know. I know. You can be violent and brutal too. But you're too upset to operate at his level. In the emotional state you're in, your perceptions will be uncertain, your skills will deteriorate, even the habits of your training might desert you at times. You'll be operating at a disadvantage against an utterly ruthless killer."

Winter sat still and silent. He went on looking at her with those hollowed eyes. His hands still clutched the arms of the chair. Then one hand, his right hand, lifted a little and turned palm up, a gesture of helplessness. The hand, she saw, was still trembling. She thought the sight of it would break her old heart.

Then Winter said, "I have to do this, Margaret."

And miserably, Margaret answered him: "I know."

9

Winter left the therapist's office and walked toward campus. It was a spring day of fragile beauty. The sky was pale blue. The air was very still and neither warm nor cold. The city felt balanced between one season and another.

He pushed up the main street, past the shops and taverns. For the first time, he noticed that there were Easter decorations in the storefront windows. Cardboard bunny rabbits and painted eggs. He wondered how long they had been there. It was almost time for the university to close for spring break, he thought.

The white dome of the state capitol rose up before him. He gazed at it as he walked without really seeing it. He was thinking about Charlotte. What Margaret had said about her. Her image had become a vessel of meaning inside him. To truly look at her would mean facing the truth about himself.

Maybe she was right. Maybe that was why he felt so shaken, so crazy. Every time he read more of *Treachery in the Night*, he felt another patch of his mind begin to unravel. He hated returning to the book, but he knew he had to. The murder of Susannah Woods—Ivy Swansag—had given his work a new urgency. Someone was after Charlotte. Someone brutal and violent, as Margaret said. Winter had to find her before the killer did. The novel was the only clue he had to follow.

He had made his way deep into the story by now. Miranda—Charlotte—was living in the Farmhouse. From the kitchen window she could see the nearby city burning. Every day, the leftists staged another riot. Every day, a pillar of black smoke rose from the unseen streets. At night, the red glow of the flames played over the face of the velvet sky.

The other denizens of the Farmhouse sat in the living room, huddled over their laptops and their devices. They watched the news online. They scanned the websites for videos. They saw the rioters rampaging, not just here but in cities around the country. The rioters were dressed in black bloc—black clothes and bala-clavas, sunglasses and body armor. They threw Molotov cocktails at the police. They threw stones and firecrackers at them. They set cars aflame. They broke shop windows. They swarmed passersby and beat them and bullied them and forced them to shout red slo-gans. Then they chased them out of the area, punching and kicking them and whipping them with batons as they went.

At one point, the rioters laid siege to police headquarters. The police were forced to evacuate under a shower of firecrackers and bottles. The rioters then laid claim to several city blocks around the abandoned HQ. The chief of police, a youngish Black woman named Letty Neeson, told reporters she was helpless to stop them because the mayor and the city council would not allow it. There was no point even in making arrests because the prosecutor was also in the same political camp as the rioters and would only set them free.

The people in the Farmhouse watched all this on their devices, and it inflamed their rage. At night, they gathered around the living room fireplace and discussed the situation and tried to make battle plans.

There were seven people living in the house full time. There were Miranda and Theo. There was the soft-spoken intellectual leader Frederick Bernard. There was Billy Mayhew, who had been a stand-up comedian and TV comedy writer until he went off his medications and became, by his own description, "a high-functioning psychotic." There was Pete Dolan, once a left-wing writer, then a right-wing writer, now a full-time street brawler. Both Mayhew and Dolan were witty and energetic and full of ideas. Miranda thought they were also dangerously insane.

Mayhew's wife was there too—her name was Andrea—and Dolan's girlfriend, who was named Fiona Maclean. Miranda liked these women. They were warm, intelligent, and devoted to their men. Like Miranda, they tried at first to contribute to the nightly political and philosophical conversations in the house. But the passion and intensity of the men overwhelmed them. The men interrupted them and talked over them and filibustered until, after a while, the women fell silent. Like Miranda, they spent most of their time keeping the house, cooking for the group, shopping for supplies, and taking walks in the woods. They were glad of one another's company as they waited for the violence to come.

That was the Farmhouse Seven. Then there was Moran.

He wasn't in the house all the time. Like the wind, he came when he would, and no one knew from where he came or where he went when he left or how long he'd be gone. But Miranda did know this: she could not stop thinking about him.

Whenever he was there, he filled the house with the power of his presence. When he slept on the sofa in the living room, Miranda, lying beside Theo in her bedroom upstairs, could feel him down below. She could feel him breathing. She could feel his blood pulsing. She could feel him staring up at the ceiling, staring through the ceiling at her where she lay. During the day, his eyes were always on her. And everyone's eyes were always on him. He was always the center of attention. He dominated the nightly conversations, sometimes without even saying a word. When the others spoke, they looked to him to gauge his reactions. When he spoke, everyone else fell silent. Even Theo's Dobermans stayed close to the floor, their heads lowered to their paws, when Moran was in the room.

One night, he arrived suddenly during one of their sessions. He stepped in out of a lightning storm that rocked the Farmhouse with thunder and hammered on its roof with rain. The rain had put out the fires in the city so the sky was pitch black at the windows. It felt as if the house were floating amid tumultuous nothingness.

The Farmhouse Seven were sitting in the living room. They had dined on spaghetti marinara and were now drinking red wine from water glasses. They had arranged the sofa and chairs in a semicircle around the fireplace. The rain and thunder were at the windows and a merry blaze was burning in the grate. It was a cozy atmosphere. Miranda liked the feeling of it. It reminded her of nights with her family back home.

"Right now, I'm in touch with five other cells around the city, and there are more on the way," Frederick Bernard told them. "But it's slow work. We need more soldiers before we can go in. We'd be crazy to go as we are."

"Crazy's not a bug for me, it's a feature," said Mayhew the comedian. He tapped his foot rapidly on the floor. "I'm crazy as a squirrel on acid, man. I feed on blood. I piss on death. I piss blood on death and then feed on the whole thing together. I'm ready to go in now, now, now."

He downed the rest of his wine by way of punctuation and poured himself another glass by way of having more wine. As always, it was impossible to tell whether he was joking or serious. The women in the circle laughed uncertainly.

But Pete Dolan said, "I agree with him. I'd rather do what damage we can instead of just sitting here night after night, watching our jaws go up and down—blah blah blah—while the city burns to ashes."

At that moment—on the word *ashes*—the lightning flashed at the windows, the thunder rolled, the latch of the front door turned unheard, and in the doorway, all at once, there stood Moran.

He was dressed in work boots, blue denim, a black jacket, and a yellow watch cap, all soaked with rain. The moment he entered, he seemed to fill the whole house. The men in the living room fell silent at the sight of him. Theo's Dobermans lifted their heads, then laid them down on their paws again.

Moran's eyes went over them all and, as always, lingered on Miranda. She felt his gaze on her flesh like hands, like strong hands touching her softly.

Moran thumped among them, thumped between their chairs, and stood before the fire. Water dripped from him and darkened the braid rug.

"Talking," he muttered. It wasn't a question. It was an insult. He stripped off his watch cap. He stuffed the cap in his jacket pocket. He held his hands out toward the flames to warm his palms.

"We were just discussing tactics," said Frederick Bernard in his serious way.

Moran gave him a quick, dismissive glance over the shoulder. He turned back to the fire. "They've extended their zone. They've chased out the cops. Red restaurants and shops are sending them free food and bottled water. The media is calling them peaceful while the city burns. And you're discussing tactics." Frederick Bernard started to respond but Moran went on speaking into the crackling flames as if the other man weren't there. "They're afraid though. The rioters. They are now anyway. They're afraid to walk alone, even on their own turf. Bad things happen to them when they walk alone." Moran turned. His rough, round, cruel, and boyish face was twisted in a smirk. "Very bad things," he said again.

Moran unzipped his black jacket. As he did, Miranda saw the raw red bruises on the knuckles of his right hand. Then his jacket was open and she saw the muscles of his torso etched into the black T-shirt underneath.

Theo watched him too, but his dogs kept their heads down.

"I need a shower," Moran said.

He started to thump out of the room.

"Moran . . ." said Frederick Bernard.

He got to his feet but Moran went past him without a pause and headed up the stairs. Frederick Bernard followed him.

"Moran," he called again.

That left Theo, Mayhew, Pete Dolan, and the women around the fire. For a moment, they were silent there.

"What do you think he did?" Andrea asked softly then.

Miranda shook her head: she didn't know.

"The last thing we need are loose cannons," said Theo solemnly. The dogs at his feet glanced around at him.

Miranda stole a look at the others and thought, *Theo sounds like a weakling to them too.*

They all fell silent again. They listened. There was a soft roll of thunder outside. The rain came down hard on the roof.

Winter reached the campus. He walked up the broad central path in the sweet spring sunshine. The path took him past stately university buildings, brick castles, and stone temples. There were students here and there but not many. Most were in class or in their dorms at their books, studying for their exams.

Winter himself had to give a lecture in a couple hours, one last talk before the break: the influence of the German philosophers on the English poets. He could do that off the cuff if he had to, he thought. He knew he ought to prepare, but it was more important to him to locate Charlotte.

He headed toward his office in the Gothic.

Inside that haunted stone monstrosity, the halls were busy. Faculty and administrators passed from office to office or conferred in doorways. Office doors swung open and students went in or came out. There was always a lot of business to take care of before the break.

Winter climbed the stairs, smiling absently at the descending faces he recognized. He was still thinking about *Treachery in the Night*. About Miranda and Moran. He was so far gone in these thoughts, he was barely present in the moment. He crested the stairs and turned the corner to his office.

Then, startled out of his meditations, he came to a full stop, staring.

There was a woman waiting for him at his office door. A student. Her back was to him.

Even before she swung around to face him, he knew it was Barbara.

10

Barbara smiled. Winter, already rattled, was struck by the power of the girl's attractions. She was pretty, but not beautiful, yet something came off her that reached him, some kind of heat.

"Hi, Professor Winter!" she said in a sprightly Hi-Professor-Winter sort of voice.

He moved toward her. Close enough to catch her scent. Close enough to see the color of her eyes, an arresting hazel. Her figure troubled his heart. He was tempted to say something charming. He fought the temptation. "Your name is Barbara, I think, isn't it?" he said.

She opened her mouth in an *o* of surprise. "How did you know that? How did you know my name?"

Winter found her skin very smooth, very white. And how glossy her hair was. "Professor Sexton—he told me."

"O-o-o-h," she answered. "Roger."

"Would you care to come into my office and sit down?"

"Sure!" she said.

She was wearing a light spring dress with a pink gingham pattern, not too short at the skirt, not too low in front. It gave her an appearance of youth and innocence. Which Winter found mesmerizing. As he moved past her to his office door, she turned eagerly to follow him, bouncing on her toes. Winter realized he was going to have to make a serious effort to come out of this encounter with any self-respect at all.

Inside the tiny office, he went through the vaguely embarrassing ritual of squeezing between the desk and bookshelf to get to his chair. Barbara, meanwhile, settled into the chair in front of the desk. She was arranging her skirt around her knees as Winter sat across from her.

"Should I close the door?" she asked.

"No, leave it open," he said, a bit too quickly.

"Why?" she laughed. "Are you afraid to be alone with me?"

"Mm. Let's just leave it open."

"Well, I mean, wow. What all did Roger tell you about me? What am I, like a femme fatale or something? How deadly did he make me sound?"

By force of will, Winter had begun to recover his equilibrium, such as it was. He still couldn't quite account for the effect she had on him. It was just some quality she had. He hadn't felt it when he saw her before, outside, with the athlete boy, at a distance. He felt it now though.

"How can I help you?" he asked.

"I notice you didn't answer my question. Are you not going to tell me what Roger said about me?"

Winter studied her for a moment, longer than he meant to. "No," he said slowly then. "No, I'm not. Why don't you tell me why you're here?"

"Well . . ." She played with her long black hair a moment, twirling it speculatively around a finger. It was the first thing she'd done that was even vaguely flirtatious. "I saw you before. Outside on the path. I just thought, you know, if you're going to ogle me from afar, we might as well get up close and get acquainted. You know?"

"Yes. Yes, I did stare at you," Winter said. "I'm sorry about that. I was startled when you began kissing that boy."

"Jody? Why? Kissing's about all you *can* do with him. He's cute as hell, but dumb as a rock."

Winter made a noncommittal noise. He was trying to think of how to answer that, and he couldn't quite come up with anything.

While he was trying to work it out, Barbara went on. "It's not that I minded you watching us or anything. I didn't mind at all. I kind of liked it even. I've always noticed you around campus. All the girls do, you know. You get voted Most Handsome Professor a lot." She paused to let him respond. He forced himself not to respond. She went on: "Some girls say you're a sexist or whatever, but I kind of think that adds to the attraction, right? I mean, most men are such toys. I like it when a guy stands up for himself."

Winter laid a finger along his lips. He had managed not to react openly to any of this. He hadn't even laughed at her remark about Jody being dumb as a rock, though he wanted to. He felt fenced in. He couldn't think of what to say to her. He felt she made it impossible to say anything safely.

But he had to say something, didn't he? And there was no sense being subtle. It was the unspoken things that got you in trouble in the end. So why not just come out with the truth?

"The reason I was startled to see you kissing Jody," he said, "is because I thought there was something between you and Roger Sexton."

She opened her mouth wide in mock shock. She was still playing with her hair. "Really? Did Roger say that?"

"That was the impression I got."

"Ah," she said, teasingly. "The impression. Well. I guess there was something between us. I mean, there was *something*. What did he think it was?"

"I can't speak for him. But clearly it wasn't much of anything to you."

She side-eyed the open door. "Are you sure I can't close that? I don't really want to talk about my personal life with anyone who passes by in the hall listening in."

"No, leave it open," said Winter. He was working hard to keep his eyes on her face, off her breasts, off her legs, off her hand in her hair. "It wasn't, was it? Serious. This—thing with Roger."

She shrugged. "Not really. I mean, we did it, if that's what you want to know. We did it a few times actually. Roger knew I was doing it with Devesh and I guess that turned him on so . . ." She shrugged again. "Roger's nice in his big dopey-bear way. I like him and all, it's just . . . you know, it was what it was." She gave another bright smile. "Why are you looking at me like that?"

"How am I looking at you?"

"I don't know. Like you disapprove of me. Do you? Why? Because I broke school rules by doing some professors?"

Winter could only gesture. He wanted to say that he didn't disapprove of her, but he didn't quite know how he felt.

"Well?" she said. "Are you going to report me to the authorities? Roger would be fired if you did."

Yes, that was true. If Lori Lesser ever found out about all this, the first thing she'd do when she got back from her rest cure would be to have Roger fired. Devesh too.

"Personally, I think it's stupid, all these rules," Barbara went on. "I mean, we're all adults. What happened wasn't any more Roger's fault than it was mine. It's not anyone's fault really. There's nothing to be at fault about. We wanted to do it so we did. What's the big?

It's like nobody knows how to feel about anything anymore. It can kind of make you crazy if you think about it too much."

It could, Winter thought. It could make you crazy. He almost said so, but he caught himself.

"I just like to do it. Most people do, right? It's not that complicated. I mean, don't you like to?"

Winter ignored this. He answered carefully: "So this was a casual thing for you, in other words. Your relationship with Roger, I mean. It was a casual sort of . . . fling."

Barbara tilted her head and gaped at him with quirky condescension—like a teenage daughter gaping at her hopelessly outdated dad.

"A *fling?* Well, we're not exclusive or anything, if that's what you mean," she said—said as if she were talking to an idiot. She leaned forward in her chair. "*Is* that what you mean? That we're exclusive somehow? Because we're not. If that's what's holding you back."

Winter was reduced to awkward silence, his lips moving, nothing coming out. Finally, he managed to say: "Holding me back?"

"Yeah!" said Barbara enthusiastically. "Like I said, I liked it when you were watching me kiss Jody. It was a turn-on. So, you know, I thought maybe you wanted to, like, do it." When he continued to hesitate, she added: "You don't have to worry. It's not like I'm going to rat you out or anything."

Winter drew a slow breath in through his nose. That last sentence—*it's not like I'm going to rat you out*—that struck him as an implied threat. Like she could rat him out if she wanted to. It didn't worry him. No one was going to fire him. He knew enough of the dean's dirty secrets to end the man's career entirely. Still, the fact of the threat chilled him. It broke the spell he was under—and he really had been under some kind of spell. He had been so discombobulated even before Barbara arrived—shaken by his therapy session, by *Treachery in the Night*, by the idea of finding Charlotte—that the sight of Barbara waiting for him at his office door, the attractions of her, all that chatter about *doing it*—for a moment, it had all enveloped him in a kind of haze of possibilities. Poor Roger, he thought.

He lowered his hand from his lips. He clasped his two hands together at his belt buckle. Professor-like. "Well, thank you, Barbara, for coming by. I'm sorry if I stared at you. As I say, it wasn't anything personal. I just thought you were involved with Roger, that's all."

Barbara stared at him, expectant. As if he hadn't spoken at all. As if she were still waiting for him to take up her offer.

"I think you should leave now," Winter said.

"Ooh," said Barbara, drawing back from him. "That's grumpy. You're a lot more grumpy than I thought you were going to be. Look, hey, I just thought we could have fun, that's all. I didn't mean anything by it."

He smiled thinly and kept an iron silence.

Barbara rose from her chair. Winter's eyes automatically went up and down her. He still couldn't quite define her appeal, but it certainly was appealing.

"I don't like you at all as much as I thought I was going to," she told him.

This time, it was Winter who shrugged.

11

On the evening after the storm—after Moran arrived at the Farmhouse—Miranda and Theo were on bad terms. Theo had been in a mood all day, growling at her like one of his dogs. Miranda knew it was because of Moran. It was because Moran had been hanging around her, openly looking at her and making remarks. He liked her dress. He liked the way she wore her hair. He acted as if Theo couldn't hear what he was saying when Theo was right there, right there with them in the same room.

It got to Theo. It made him angry. He took it out on her. He started to talk to her harshly. He ordered her around. He criticized every little thing she did or said. Even his dogs glared at her. By afternoon, Miranda was getting sick of it. It pissed her off. It wasn't her fault that Moran was dogging her. If Moran annoyed Theo, he should've taken it up with Moran. Only he wouldn't do that, would he, because he was afraid of Moran. So he was bullying her instead.

Later, Andrea and Fiona went to the store for supplies. Miranda had volunteered to stay behind and hang the laundry on the back-yard lines since they hadn't been able to do it during the storm. She was hoping the women would come back in time to take a walk in the woods with her. The rain had cleared the air, and the autumn day was fresh and cool. There was not even a sign of smoke from the city. A walk in the forest would be nice.

But the afternoon grew late and the other women didn't return. Soon it would be too dark to go into the woods, she thought. So she decided to take a walk alone. She went up to the bedroom to change into hiking clothes. There was Theo, sitting at the small desk in the corner, typing on his laptop, the dogs at his feet. The Dobermans looked up as she came in. Theo went on working.

Miranda stripped her dress off, tossed it on the bed. She stood at the dresser in her bra and panties, rummaging through the drawers for some good walking jeans and a fresh T-shirt.

"Where are you off to?" Theo said with a dark glance.

"For a walk. Want to come?" She hoped he wouldn't. She only asked out of a sense of obligation.

Fortunately, he said, "I've got to finish this article. What about you? Don't you have anything to contribute?"

The Dobermans tensed when she looked at him. They could feel her anger. *What the hell is that supposed to mean?* she wanted to say. But she didn't say it. She just pulled her clothes on roughly and stormed out.

Usually she enjoyed the forest. It was always peaceful there and right now, it was beautiful. The sinking sun was streaming through the changing leaves. The paths were hazy and golden and mysterious. But Theo had made her so angry, her walk was ruined. She tromped over the mud and the soggy duff, hugging herself and scowling.

She stopped dead and let out a high-pitched cry.

Suddenly, there was Moran. He was leaning against a nearby tree, watching her. Smiling.

"Oh my God!" she said. Her hand flew to her chest as she tried to catch her breath. "You scared the crap out of me."

Moran laughed. "Sorry. Sorry." He pushed off the tree and swaggered toward her. "I didn't want to say anything because I didn't want to startle you."

"Well, *that* didn't work out, did it?" she said.

"I guess not. Sorry."

"It's all right. I just—I didn't notice you standing there, that's all. What are you doing out here?"

"I was just about to head into the city. Wanna come?"

He was close to her now, hovering over her. He smiled. She looked away. "I thought Frederick said we weren't supposed to go there yet."

"Do you always do what you're supposed to do?"

She gave a short laugh. "Too much probably, yeah."

"You're a good girl, huh."

"I know, I know. It's my upbringing."

"That's too bad."

"Is it?"

"Yes," said Moran. "To me, it is."

Miranda knew what he wanted her to say, and she knew she shouldn't say it, but she said it anyway.

"Why?"

"Because I want you to do something you're not supposed to do," he said.

"Oh yeah?"

"You know I do, Miranda."

He stepped even closer. He slipped his big hand through her golden hair until his palm lay warm against her cheek. He leaned down and kissed her.

She didn't stop him. Not at first. She rose into it and kissed him back. It felt good to finally do it. It felt as if a ball of solid heat at the center of her had melted and flowed down the length of her.

She knew the tide of sensation was about to carry her away. She pulled back and turned her face away, but he pressed in against her cheek. She tried to break free of him, but he held her.

"Don't, Evan. Stop," she said.

He didn't stop. He slid his hand to her bottom and pressed her body into his.

She struggled harder. "Don't. I mean it!"

He tried to turn her head toward him.

She bent her head back from his. She met his eyes with a fierce stare. "Stop. I won't forgive you if you don't. I'm serious. I won't."

At first, he smirked as if he didn't care whether she forgave him or not. But he did care. He liked her. She was something different, golden like the forest light.

He loosened his grip on her. She slipped out of his hands and turned her back on him, breathing hard.

"I'm sorry," he said. "I thought you wanted to."

"That's not the point."

He was silent, as if he didn't know what to say. Then he said, "Look. Come into the city with me." She didn't answer. "I won't do anything. I just want to show you what it's like."

Miranda didn't know what to do. She didn't even know what she wanted to do. She didn't want to go back to the Farmhouse, back to cranky, angry Theo and those stupid dogs.

She turned back to Moran where he stood hulking and sheepish. Sort of pitiful and lovable, she thought, like a big dog who'd had his nose rapped. "OK," she said. "OK. Yes."

Moran had a great black beast of a pickup, a four-door Ford with a blunted crew cab. Miranda felt safe in the front passenger seat with the monster-big console set between them. He drove them through the twilight swiftly, past empty fields. He didn't say anything, and she worried he might be angry at her. Maybe he felt she'd led him on. Maybe she had led him on a little.

"Look, I'm really sorry if I sent some mixed signals back there," she said. "I have some things I need to work out. I just want to do what's right, that's all."

"Yeah, sure, I get it. Do your thing," he said.

"You're not mad at me?"

He glanced her way and smiled. "Hell, no. We all have things. I get it."

That was a relief to her. She didn't want to cheat on Theo, but she didn't want Moran to give up on her either.

"What do you do?" she asked him. "When you're not, you know, doing this?"

"Ranch work mostly."

"Really? You mean like a cowboy, with horses?"

"Sure. Horses sometimes. Tractors and chain saws a lot of the time."

"Cool," she said.

She pictured him sitting on horseback at the top of a ridge, a thrilling silhouette against the sunset sky. So different from Theo.

"Sometimes when I'm out on the range—when I'm alone out there, just me and the sky, you know, and the cattle—I can almost feel what it was like when the first white men came, what it must have been like for them to see this country, all wide and empty and free. Before it all went rotten."

"Yeah," said Miranda. For a few moments, she could see it too.

It was dark by the time they reached the city. They parked the truck on a peaceful residential block. There was no traffic here. The houses were small but trim, and they could see families and couples at dinner through the lighted windows. Moran walked a little ahead of Miranda and she followed him. The buildings grew bigger around them. Soon she could see damage from the riots. Boarded shop windows. Litter cluttering the gutter. Cars scarred and blackened by fire. Then they came to tents, one after another. Homeless men with baleful stares shuffled here and there, muttering, clutching their groins. Some gathered around a fire that burned in a trash can.

"We have to go this way to get into the Zone," Moran said. He had dropped his voice almost to a whisper. "It's the only way we can avoid the checkpoints."

They reached a row of burned-out shops. Moran stepped into an alley beside a tattoo parlor. He climbed a ladder up to the roof and was waiting there when Miranda came up after him. He took her hand and drew her up beside him. They crossed from shop roof to shop roof, with little leaps over the low brick walls that separated one roof from the next. Below her, Miranda saw the beginning of the Zone—the streets the rioters had taken over.

It looked like a market in the midst of a ruin, a new, more primitive city growing up in the ashes of the city the rioters had destroyed. Rows of makeshift shops offered vegetables and bottled water under awnings made of dyed sheets. Heavy plastic barriers were set up in the middle of the road to cut off car traffic. The windows of the stores were boarded with plywood. The walls were charred, smeared with graffiti, and hung with banners. There were slogans and curse words. *Anarchy!* was scrawled in red letters so large, the single word stretched a full city block.

Under the awnings, women with strangely colored hair handed out water and food. At least Miranda thought they were women. She couldn't be sure. Men—at least she thought they were men—gathered around fires that burned in trashcans. Here and there was a figure in black bloc, the face covered by a balaclava. Some of these masked people wore guns on their hips. Some carried batons.

There were no cars anywhere, Miranda noticed. It was as if the car hadn't been invented yet, she thought. Really, it was as if the riots had driven the city back to an earlier age.

Moran descended by another ladder. She went down after him and they were in another alley.

"Just act naturally, like you belong," he murmured to her. "Avoid conversations. Keep moving."

She did as he told her. The guards in black eyed them, but no one stopped them. They passed clusters of people chatting with one another. Everyone was weirdly dressed. To Miranda, it seemed as if they were all in costumes of one sort or another. Many of the men were styled and decked out like women. Many of the women seemed gaunt and sexless. She couldn't tell who was what.

On one corner, a young man was standing on a crate and addressing a small crowd of men and women in black bloc. The young man made dramatic gestures with his hands and spoke in ringing tones as if he were orating for ages yet unborn. Most of the audience were masked. Most of them wore belts with batons attached, and pepper spray. One of them had a holstered gun.

To Miranda, the scene seemed sinister. She had watched the riot videos. She had seen people beaten bloody and carried off to the hospital in ambulances. Word on the socials was that two men had died when the mob forced their car off the road and it hit a wall. There were stories that women were being raped every night.

After a while, Miranda had a creepy feeling. She looked around. Sure enough, a man dressed all in black was following them. He was ambling casually along at a little distance, looking this way and that, pretending not to watch them. He was carrying a baton in his hand. He tapped it against his leg like a cop on the beat.

"I think that guy is following us," Miranda murmured.

"He is. He has been for a while. Just keep walking," said Moran.

They came into a small plaza. There was graffiti all around. Litter filled the gutters and blew over the sidewalks. At the center of the plaza, there stood a large tower of white stone. It looked like some sort of official building or the office building of a corporation, but any identifying signs had been torn down or covered with banners.

Miranda and Moran entered a narrow parking lot on one side of the building. The lot was empty—there were no cars—and it was very dark. There were streetlamps but the lights had all been shattered.

"Don't look back," Moran told her.

Miranda walked a few more steps into the lot, into the dark. Then Moran was suddenly gone from beside her. Miranda started to look for him, then realized: This was why he'd told her to keep looking ahead. He wanted her to keep walking into the darkness even after he vanished. But where had he gone? She didn't know. She was scared. Her breath grew short. Her heart sped up. She could hear the footsteps of the man in black behind her. She could hear his baton tapping against his leg.

Up ahead, where the parking lot ended, there seemed to be a park or something. Some sort of open space. It was too dark to see what it was. Without meaning to, Miranda started to walk faster. She was hoping the man in black would just leave her alone. Where was Moran?

"Hey. Hey, you," the man in black called to her.

Miranda heard a woman whimper someplace near. It was a moment before she realized she had made the sound herself. She kept on walking, but whatever courage she had was rapidly draining out of her. Her legs were weak and shaky.

"Hey! You," said the man in black. "You better stop, OK?"

Miranda did stop. She was almost at the end of the parking lot. She saw a fringe of grass beyond that, but that was all she could make out. If she tried to run it would be easy for the man in black to catch her there, there in the dark where no one would see.

She turned. The man in black came toward her. He was small and willow thin, a dangerous weasel. He went on tapping his baton against his leg. He looked this way and that as if to satisfy himself there was no one else with her. Miranda could see his eyes through the mask. They were not good eyes. They were bloodshot. Glazed with drugs and with hunger for her. She could see his mouth through the mask's breathing slit. His lips turned up at one corner, a sneer of power. He was in control.

She started to tremble. The man was about ten yards away from her, closing on her quickly.

"What happened to your friend?" he said. Teasing. His voice seemed to drip disdain. "What happened to the man you were . . . ?"

Out of some shadowy nowhere, sudden as death, Moran flew into him and struck him to the ground.

Miranda stood absolutely frozen, gaping. Moran rose up, straddling the man. He punched him in his masked face, once, twice, three times, four times, hard. He tore the baton from his hand. His arm flashed back and forth, back and forth, as he whipped the stick across the man's head. The man threw up a hand to try to protect himself. Moran knocked the hand aside and knelt on his arm. He hammered the baton down on the man's head again and again.

The man's arms fell to the ground, twitching. Moran stood up, stood over him, enormous. The man in black groaned and rolled onto his side. Miranda could hear him gasping for breath. She thought she saw blood on the ground near his head, but it was so dark she wasn't sure.

"Evan!" she hissed. She didn't want to shout and draw attention to them.

With a backhand motion, Moran sent the baton spinning into the darkness. Miranda heard it fall and clatter on the macadam. Then Moran drew back his boot and kicked the man in black. He kicked him from behind between the legs. The man let out a curt, awful cry of despair and pain. He curled up, clutching his groin.

"Evan!" said Miranda. Her voice was half a whisper, half a piping cry.

Moran kicked the man in the spine and in the head. The man grunted weakly trying to protect himself with his arms and hands. Moran walked around him and kicked him in the guts, then kicked him in the face.

"Evan! Evan!" Miranda managed not to shout but she ran forward and grabbed clumsily at Moran's arms. Moran kicked the man in black again. "You'll kill him!" Miranda cried.

Even with Miranda trying to interfere, Moran managed to kick the man several more times.

"Please, please, you'll kill him," Miranda said. She was crying. She finally managed to wrap her arms around Moran's massive torso, trying to hold him back even a little. She clung to him and sobbed.

"They ruin everything," said Moran. He was panting. His voice rasped.

Still clutching Moran, Miranda looked down at the man on the ground. She could see him more clearly now. Blood was spilling out of his balaclava. The blood was making a small puddle near the man's head. His arms were still in front of his face but they were spasming helplessly.

"We should call for help," she said.

But when she looked up at Moran, he was staring into the distance, alert. She listened. She heard what he heard. Voices murmuring urgently. Coming their way.

"Let's go," he said.

He took her hand and before she knew it, they were running out of the lot and into the grass beyond. Darkness closed around them. Miranda couldn't see anything. She had to run as fast as she could to keep up with Moran. The black night raced by her. All she could think about was the man on the ground and Moran kicking him and the terrible sounds he made. Her heart was filled with horror—horror, and a mindless animal rush of excitement that blew through her mind like a roaring wind.

12

As soon as Barbara left his office, as soon as he worked himself out of his chair, as soon as he had fought his way between the desk and shelf and closed the office door behind her and then fought his way back to his chair, Winter went to work tracking down a man named Gerald Dinh.

This was what he needed. In his half-crazed state, he needed to be on the hunt. His mission—to find Charlotte before the killer or killers who were after her—this was the only thing that was holding him together. He tried to put Barbara—and Roger and Adele and Arthur—out of his mind and concentrate only on this.

The idea to go after Dinh had come to him the night before, when he was reading the scene in *Treachery* where Moran ambushed the weaselly black bloc rioter in the parking lot. The scene had upset him, more than he acknowledged even to himself. The way it was written, Moran was meant to be seen as the hero. He was not a stunted, weak-willed complainer like Theo, but a romantic man of action willing to do brutal violence in the name of his philosophy. Winter already knew from the prologue that Moran would go on to murder Theo and that he would then become Miranda's lover. Though he did not yet know for certain how much of the story was true, he could not help believing that Miranda was Charlotte, little Charlotte whom he'd loved. The idea that his childhood flame had become the lover of a man like Moran sickened him.

So the scene in the book—that violent scene—would not stop nagging at him. He wanted—needed—to find out if the ambush story had any basis in fact. He began hunting the internet for stories about the riots, videos that might resemble the ambush in the parking lot. He could not find anything like that.

What he did find was Gerald Dinh. Dinh was a young freelance journalist who had covered the riots. He had been repeatedly beaten, chased, and pepper sprayed by rioters while trying to film their activities. But he would not be stopped. He had videoed the red thugs mobbing and assaulting innocent passersby, throwing heavy fireworks at police officers, terrorizing women, and setting cars and buildings on fire. At one point, he had even disguised himself in black bloc and joined the rioters' clandestine meetings. He had secretly filmed them planning their violence—until they discovered him and he had to run for his life.

Dinh's work had been banned and demonetized on social media sites, and wholly ignored by the major news outlets. But as far as Winter could judge, Dinh's stories were straightforward and accurate. Winter figured if anyone would know the truth behind the fiction of *Treachery in the Night*, Dinh would be the man.

Now, in his office, with Barbara gone, he set about tracking the reporter. It was not long before he found a phone number with a New York City area code.

Winter called the number. He checked his watch as the phone rang. He had to get to work preparing his lecture on the German philosophers. But he didn't care. He needed to find Charlotte. He did not feel sane enough to deal with German philosophy.

The reporter answered the phone on its third ring. He had a soft, youthful voice, American but with some sort of Asian inflection. Winter began to tell him who he was and what he wanted, but the moment he mentioned *Treachery in the Night*, the kid stopped him.

"No. Don't go on," he said. "Not over the phone."

"All right," said Winter. "I'll meet you anywhere you want, any time."

There was a pause. Winter waited. He thought he could feel the young man's fear.

"I'll check you out and get back to you," Dinh said—and he cut the connection.

Winter tried to work on his lecture as he waited for Dinh to call back. It was useless. His mind was on fire with a million little flames. He was thinking of Miranda—of Charlotte. Of what Margaret had said about her: *She's a vessel of meaning.* He was thinking about the novel's description of her after the ambush, how she lay in bed next to Theo, how she lay awake in the Farmhouse dark and thought of Moran kicking the man on the ground.

She felt the horror again, and the excitement too, the wild, windy thrill that had gone roaring through her as she escaped with Moran into the night. She had felt almost as if she were a part of him then, as if they had blended into one person, and as if together they had become one with the darkness too.

Oh, oh, oh, *she thought*, it is a frightening thing to be a woman!

Yeah, yeah, yeah, thought Winter bitterly. He tried to keep his focus trained on the writings of the German philosophers, their tortuous reasoning, their *Is* and *not-Is*, *das Ich und das Nicht-Ich.* But it was no good. He kept thinking about the novel instead. Miranda—Charlotte—lying in the dark . . .

With his mind divided between the novel and his academic research into the Germans, a revelation suddenly came to him.

He suddenly understood the code baked into Susannah Woods's pseudonym, Ivy Swansag. Ivy was IV—Roman numeral four—and Swansag was a near homophone for twenty in German, *zwanzig.* Four twenty, April 20, a favorite shibboleth among the extremists: Adolf Hitler's birthday.

"*Ich,*" murmured Winter.

He managed to stumble through his lecture that afternoon. It started out well anyway. Halfway through, he felt his phone vibrate in his pocket, and he supposed that it was Dinh calling him back. It distracted him. It was all he could think about as he rattled on about the eighteenth-century Jena set. And yes, when he finally did get outside to check, the message was from Dinh. The reporter had texted him an address in Brooklyn, and a time—tomorrow, 6:00 P.M.

So, a few minutes before six the next evening, Winter emerged from a yellow cab in the middle of a street of dilapidated brownstones. A light rain was falling on the city, dripping from the drooping leaves of the weakish trees that stood at intervals along the sidewalk. A mist rose from the pavement. It made the oncoming headlights look jagged and blurred.

Winter was glad to be on the hunt again. The tension of focus and expectation steadied him. He went up one brownstone's stoop and continued through the front door into the foyer. He pressed the button for 3B. He recognized Dinh's soft, tremulous voice on the intercom.

"Come on up."

As Winter crested the stairs onto the third-floor landing, Dinh's door opened just a crack. A pair of brown eyes looked out over a taut chain. Winter waited through an elaborate examination, the eyes traveling up and down the length of him. Then the door closed. Winter heard the chain slide off. Slowly, the door opened.

Warily, Dinh peeked out. He checked the hall a long moment before stepping back to let Winter enter.

Gerald Dinh was a small man, still in his twenties by the look of him. He was short and thin and flabby faced. He had a faint, scraggly mustache and beard, like an adolescent not quite ready to shave. He was wearing a billowing oversized T-shirt, dark gray. It made him look even smaller than he was, as if he'd dwindled suddenly, leaving the shirt half-vacant. And he was afraid. His eyes were bright with fear and there was fear scored into the flesh of his brow and jaw.

His apartment was cramped. The furniture was worn. The rug was faded. Two dusty windows looked out on the rain and the darkening end of the day. The room itself was neat enough, but grimy. Winter suspected Dinh had hurriedly tossed his dirty laundry into a closet just moments before, right after he'd buzzed Winter into the building.

Soft music was coming from the kitchen, tuneless jazz, nearly drowned out by what sounded like a range hood exhaust fan. A blond-haired cement block of a weight lifter leaned out to have a gander at the visitor. The weight lifter was holding a spatula and wearing a flowery apron.

"This is my husband, Ray," said Dinh.

"You want anything? Coffee? Wine?" Ray called, raising his voice above the fan noise.

"Thanks, no," said Winter, and Ray withdrew into the kitchen, just out of sight.

Dinh gestured vaguely toward the sofa. As Winter sat, Dinh wandered in the direction of a weary wing chair. The young man ran his hands through his black hair as if he couldn't quite remember where he was going. But he managed to reach the chair. He plunked down into it.

"I won't stay long," Winter told him. "I've got to catch my plane home."

"I'm sorry to make you come all this way, but I've gotten . . . what's the word?"

"Paranoid," Ray sang from the kitchen.

"Well, it's not paranoid, Ray," complained Gerald Dinh. "I get death threats every single day. The reds showed up at my parents' house one night and threw a brick through the front window. They put out my last address on social media. And anytime one of them spots me on the street, he sends out a message, so they all know where I am and anyone who wants to can come and get me. And they do want to. They want me dead. They already put me in the hospital twice. I'm deaf in one ear from the last beating. So it's not really paranoia, is it?"

Winter gestured sympathetically.

"So who—who are you again?" said Dinh, distracted.

"I'm an English professor," said Winter.

"And this is about that crazy novel?"

"*Treachery in the Night*, yes. I'm writing a paper about it."

Dinh nodded slowly for a long moment, as if working to take this in. "Well, that sounds like bullshit," he said then. "I mean, the author was just murdered, wasn't she? I saw it online. Is that what this is really about?"

"Paranoid!" sang Ray on a higher note.

Winter smiled and leaned forward, his elbows on his knees. "Actually, you're not paranoid. You're right. In a sense, this is about the author's murder—although it's actually more personal than that. Have you read the book?"

Dinh's narrow shoulders lifted and fell. "Not really. I glanced at it once. Seemed pretty trashy. I'm not a fascist, you know. Despite what the media says about me. I just love this country, that's all.

My parents came here on a raft from Vietnam. The socialists have sworn to destroy everything. So they can build paradise. My parents escaped from paradise—"

Winter held up a hand. "I'm not here about any of that."

Gerald Dinh blinked. "What do you mean?"

"The browns, the reds, the right/left, they're all nothing to me. I'm just looking for a girl. That's all."

"What do you mean?" said Gerald Dinh again, as if he were stuck on the question.

"The main character in *Treachery in the Night*—Miranda—I think she's based on someone I know. Or used to know. And I think she's in trouble. I think whoever killed Susannah Woods is looking for her. I want to find her before the killer does."

Dinh stared at him, shaking his head. "That's crazy."

The weight lifter leaned out of the kitchen with his spatula. "It doesn't sound crazy to me."

Dinh barely glanced at him, but he seemed to hear him nonetheless. "OK," he said. But what's it got to do with me?"

"It doesn't have anything to do with you," Winter told him. "You're just the only journalist who did any actual reporting out of the Zones. I thought you might know something that could help me."

"Like what?"

"In the novel—in *Treachery in the Night*—there's a character named Moran."

"I didn't read very much of it," said Dinh with a vague movement of one hand.

"Well, what Moran does is he goes into the Zone and he lures the rioters into secluded spots, one by one. He's this big, tough guy and when he gets one of the reds alone, he beats them senseless."

Dinh grunted. "So he's supposed to be the Phantom."

"The Phantom?"

"The Phantom of the Zones."

Winter sat back in the sofa. "It's a true story then."

"Well . . . is it a true story?" said Gerald Dinh. "It was more like a legend, really. Maybe true, maybe not. I was in a lot of the cities during the riots, a lot of the different Zones around the country, and I kept hearing about him—the Phantom. The only place I ever saw any evidence that he was real was in one Zone in Indiana."

Winter did not move. His heart felt sour, but his mind was suddenly still. Indiana. That was where Charlotte had gone to college. That was where she'd lived with Eddie. This was what he had come to find.

"A few of the rioters there did get beaten up," Dinh went on. "They were lured away from the crowd, like you said. They got caught on their own and someone jumped them. Really wrecked them too. They had to be hospitalized. They all said it was a single attacker—and they said he was big, a big guy like this guy in the book . . . what's his name?"

"Moran. That's his name in the book anyway."

"Moran, right. There was this one guy—what was his name now?—Moscow. Larry Moscow. He was totally destroyed. He's in a wheelchair, or he was at least last time I heard. Probably still is. He got the worst of it."

"Moscow?" said Winter. "Was that, like, a code name or a nickname or something?"

Dinh managed to give a small, mirthless laugh. "No, I know, but that was actually his real name. That's why I remember it. Moscow. The story was on some local news site. Here, wait, I may even have it in my files. Let me look."

He climbed out of his chair like an old man, piece by piece. He shuffled off into what Winter imagined was a bedroom. Winter could hear him rummaging around in there, kicking his way through obstacles. He could hear the clack of keyboard keys.

Ray, the weight lifter, leaned out of the kitchen with the spatula again. "I have to tell you," he called over the fan noise. "I am so sick of this. He's right about one thing. He's not being paranoid. These creeps are going to kill him one of these days. He knows that. But he just keeps aggravating them. And for what? Because his parents came here on a raft? It's not like there are any good guys anymore. I keep telling him. What's the point? There's nothing left to fight for."

Winter didn't answer right away. Ray went on leaning out of the kitchen, waiting for more of a response. Finally, Winter said. "I'm just looking for a girl."

The phone in Winter's pocket buzzed. He dug the device out and glanced at it. Dinh had texted him an article about the attack on Larry Moscow. As Dinh returned to the living room, Winter got to his feet.

"Thanks," he said. "That's exactly what I need." He shook Dinh's small, childlike hand. He waved to the spatula guy. He moved to the door.

"They make Moscow sound like a martyr," Dinh said bitterly. "In the article, I mean. They make him sound like an innocent victim. And all right, he was a victim. But not innocent. He was known for going after women, even in his own camp. He'd look for any excuse to whip them with his baton. Some kind of creepy sadist . . ."

"Right," said Winter. "Thanks." He opened the door.

"These people are monsters," said Dinh.

"Well . . . I'm just looking for a girl," Winter said.

He was glad to get out of there. Too much fear, too much emotion, too much relationship stuff crammed into such a small space. With his own psyche fragile as it was, it was more than he could handle. He needed to focus on this one thing. Charlotte—Indiana—Moscow. This hunt he was on.

He stepped out of the brownstone into the evening and the misty rain. He worked his ivy cap out of his windbreaker pocket and tugged it down over his brow. The cars whizzed by along the wet pavement in front of him, their white headlights glaring as they came, their red taillights fading after they passed.

He was about to start down the stairs of the stoop—but he hesitated on instinct. Or not on instinct—not just on instinct. He had seen something.

He scanned the gloaming. Yes. There it was. A figure on the sidewalk across the street. Other figures went walking by, but not this one. This one was motionless. Facing him. Watching him. A large man in denim—bareheaded, tall, broad-shouldered with a powerful physique.

Winter caught his breath. He peered through the mist at the big man as the big man peered back at him. It took a moment before his mind could register the uncanny truth.

He knew this man. He recognized him: a fictional character who had stepped out of the pages of a novel into perilous, threatening life.

It was Moran.

13

The moment their eyes met through the mist and darkness, Moran turned and started to walk away.

Good, Winter thought. He understood exactly what Moran was doing. The Phantom of the Zones—he was trying to lure him into a secluded spot where he could ambush him and beat him down.

Let him, Winter thought, with a flash of anger.

He followed after him.

Moran's stride was relaxed, but his long legs carried him quickly. Winter tried to cross the street, but the traffic was steady. He had to wait for a pause in the flow, find a gap, then bull his way through in the glare of headlights, a horn carping at him as the traffic started up again. By the time he reached the far sidewalk, Moran was at the end of the block, turning a corner. Winter quickened his pace as the big man moved out of sight.

Winter's thoughts raced as he raced after him. He was glad of this—glad a fight was coming. He needed a fight. He needed something, some kind of action. An old ferocity was coursing through him. It knitted his fractured self together. He'd been too agitated too long, too mired in his own turbulence. Now there was no turbulence. There was only this, and it felt good.

All the same, as he moved through the rain, Margaret's words nagged at him. Her warnings about him being upset over Charlotte. What was the word she used to describe him? Decompensating. That was it. He was decompensating, she said, so his focus would be off, his skills would have eroded. He came around the corner. His eyes searched the mist until they found Moran again. He did not feel like he was decompensating. He felt fierce and fine.

Up ahead of him, Moran made his move. Winter blinked and he was gone. That fast. Winter could see the mouth of a narrow alley midway along the block of brownstones. Moran must have ducked down there to draw him in.

Swiping the damp from his face, Winter put on speed. At the same time, to appease his inner Margaret, he lectured himself: If this real Moran was anything like the Moran in the novel, he was hard and fast and brutal. Much bigger, much heavier than Winter was, with a much greater reach. All the training in the world wouldn't help him if he got sucker punched by a man that large, that strong. And he couldn't lose his footing either. Most fights go to the ground in a hurry. He couldn't let that happen. The guy was too big to grapple with.

Winter told himself all that. He told himself to slow down. He told himself to be careful. But he wasn't careful. He didn't slow down at all.

He reached the alley mouth and stopped. He looked into the gloom between the walls, inky patches beyond the glow of the car lights and the streetlights. The alley was empty. Or it seemed empty. Trash cans stood against the walls. Litter lay soaked on the pavement. A lone rat nuzzled the debris beneath a fire escape—that was the only thing moving, the rat in the rain.

Winter remembered the ambush scene in the novel. How Moran had come flying out of nowhere like sudden death. How even

Miranda hadn't known he was there until he suddenly was. But hard as he looked, he couldn't see anyone in the alley.

He noticed the fire escape ladder was pulled down. A man as big as Moran could have jumped and grabbed it, pulled it down out of its ready position, then headed up the ladder toward the fire stairs. Or he could have pulled it down to make it look like he'd headed up, so when Winter made to follow him and started to climb the ladder, Moran could fly out of nowhere and hammer him into the dust.

Winter started to move into the alley. Margaret's voice kept nattering at him, warning him about his deteriorating skills. *Yeah, yeah*, he thought back at her. He reached the metal ladder. The bottom rung was just above his head. He stood another moment, trying to scope out every inch of the alley darkness, trying to make absolutely certain that Moran was not there.

Nothing moved but the rat, edging away from Winter down the alley, trundling casually as if to say *Screw you, human man, this is my city.*

Winter took his cap off, stuffed it back in his windbreaker pocket. The rain misted his glasses. He grabbed the rung of the ladder and pulled himself up. No Moran, no sudden strike out of the dark. Not yet.

Winter climbed. He reached the fire escape stairs. He had to pass four windows on his way up to the roof. Each window was a possible ambush. Moran might break through, shattering the glass. A bullet might break through and take him down. He bent low, moved quickly. He tried to stay sharp. He couldn't let his frazzled brain make him sloppy.

He reached the first window. It was dark, no one home. He assured himself there'd be no bullet. Why would Moran kill him? He must want to question him. He must have followed him because he thought he knew where Charlotte was. He must have seen Winter at Susannah Woods's farmhouse. Or maybe one of the Cooksville locals had tipped him off. A cop maybe. Then Moran must have followed him here. And now—the idea struck Winter with the solid ring of truth—now he was leading him someplace where he could take him down and torture Charlotte's location out of him, just as he'd tried to do with Susannah Woods.

The second window was lit. There was a young couple inside, sitting on the sofa, eating Chinese food out of white cartons. They looked relaxed. Winter kept climbing. The third window was lit too, but he couldn't see anyone in the apartment.

The fire escape ended at the fourth window. There was no way up from there to the roof. The window was dark, but it was open at the bottom, raised from the sill about an inch. Moran wanted him to see that, wanted him to see he'd slipped inside here, wanted Winter to follow the Phantom of the Zones into the dark apartment so he could ambush him there.

Winter told himself he wasn't going to do what Moran wanted, but he knew he was going to do exactly that. He couldn't stop himself. He crouched down. He grabbed the open window. Forced it up. Vaguely, he wondered if this was the sort of stupid decision Margaret had been warning him about. He paused to take a look in.

The apartment was dark. Nothing but shapes and shadows. Winter cursed, crouching there, trying to see more. He got out his phone, turned on its flashlight. Passed the beam over the scene inside. Concert posters on the wall. Cheap wooden chairs, a cheap wooden table. Threats lurking in the pools of night beyond the reach of illumination.

Winter turned the flashlight off and slipped the phone back into his pocket. His breathing was quick. He still felt focused, ready, but the doubts were still there too. Margaret's voice still fretted at him. He monkeyed himself through the window feet first. Barely felt his shoes touch the floor because he was so tense, so ready for Moran to fire himself like a missile out of the inner nowhere.

But nothing was moving inside. The apartment was empty. Winter could feel the emptiness, he could sense the absence of breathing life. He waited a second to let his eyes adjust. Then he edged forward slowly, cautiously, eyes moving.

Without warning, a sudden black flame rose at the corner of his eye: Moran's silhouette flashing in the shadows. With a vicious whipping movement, the big man swung a nightstick at Winter's head.

Winter dropped fast, dropped low. The club sailed over him with a wicked whistle. Crouched and off-balance, Winter pistoned a right jab into the attacker's groin.

Moran grunted with pain and surprise. He hadn't expected that from the midsized professor. In the first shock of the blow, he dropped his club. Winter seized the moment and sprang at him. But even damaged, Moran was quick. He swiveled into profile, shot his elbow into Winter's chest. It was a stunningly powerful strike. It knocked Winter sideways. Winter was quick-witted enough to keep dropping till he hit the floor, and a backhand swing of Moran's massive fist missed him completely.

Winter leaped to his feet, arms up for defense. But where was Moran now? In a moment of panic, he realized he'd lost sight of him. Then unexpected light made him squint. The apartment door was open on the lighted hall. Moran's enormous shape blotted the glow as he dashed out of the apartment, slamming the door behind him.

Winter rushed after him—and cracked his knee against a chair in the dark. He shouted in pain and went down to the floor again, gripping his leg. He reached up blindly in the darkness until he caught hold of a table edge. Grimacing with the pain, he pulled himself up to standing.

He limped to where he'd seen the door, his hands out in front of him as he felt his way. He reached the door and pulled it open just in time to see Moran climbing through the roof ladder at the end of the hall. Moran disappeared through a trapdoor in the ceiling.

Should he go after him? The Margaret-of-the-mind told him not to, but he did anyway. The pain in his knee was quickly subsiding. He figured the punch to Moran's crotch had to have hurt him. That's why he'd run, to get his strength back, to regroup, maybe for another attack up on the roof. There'd be light up there though. Not as easy to flash out of the dark like he'd done. Winter liked his chances, but was vaguely worried that Margaret was right, that he only felt confident because he was nuts—decompensating—out of his idiot mind.

Whatever. There was no chance he would stand down. He would not allow this fictional character to escape back into his novel.

He ran down the hall, his limp smoothing out as his leg grew limber. He reached the flimsy scissor ladder that led to the trapdoor. He thought: *No, no, no.* It would be too easy for Moran to wait in the dark up there and kick him in the head as soon as he poked through.

But even as he thought *no*, he began climbing. Some part of his brain understood that this was exactly what Margaret had been talking about. His decision systems were warped. His emotions were making him stupid. But no matter how well he understood this, he could not stop doing what he was doing. He wanted this guy too badly. He wanted the fight too badly. He needed the fight.

He climbed the ladder.

The trapdoor didn't lead directly to the roof. There was a little enclosure up there, a foyer. As Winter got closer, he could see it by the light from the hall below. It was a narrow space. No room for Moran to hide there, no room for an ambush. So maybe his judgment wasn't as bad as Margaret thought it was. Or maybe it was bad, and he'd just gotten lucky.

He pulled himself up into the little anteroom. There was nothing here but a heavy metal door with a crash bar. He hit the crash bar. There was a loud clank. He pushed the door open. The roof lay before him. Mist. Rain. The lights of the city beyond, dim in the fog. No one in sight. Everything still.

Winter stepped out onto the roof. The door swung shut behind him with a reverberating metal crash. The rain dampened his hair, streaked his glasses. He took the glasses off, slipped them into the windbreaker's inner pocket.

He stood in front of the closed door and panned his squinting gaze over the roof, left to right. Nothing rose from the small expanse of aluminum-painted asphalt but a couple of air vent pipes and the door enclosure at his back, like a little outhouse. A low brick parapet ringed the roof's rectangular space. Beyond the parapet, ahead and to left and right, the roof dropped off into nowhere.

His raised his arms into a fighting pose. Crouched, taut, and ready, he moved slowly forward.

Moran was on the roof of the door enclosure. He jumped down and tackled him.

The two went tumbling to the asphalt. Winter hit the roof hard, and Moran fell hard on top of him, knocking his breath out. In an instant, Moran's huge, powerful arms were snaked around him, working toward a choke hold. Winter knew he had no time at all before he was grabbed, blacked out, beaten. He tucked in his chin, fighting Moran's tightening grip. He rolled halfway out of the choke and squirmed half-free. He tried to jam his thumb into

Moran's eye but missed. Moran quickly maneuvered back on top of him, grappling into position to strangle him. Winter reached for Moran's groin. Moran twisted to avoid him. That gave Winter some room to move. He broke Moran's hold and jabbed at his eye again. This time, his finger sank into soft matter. Moran let out a short, ragged scream. Winter pulled free and scrambled away like a skittering insect. He stumbled to his feet.

Moran was on his feet too, dropped into a fighting stance, his wounded eye narrowed, swimming. The two faced off in the mist, both panting, both wet with rain. Winter's instinct was to act fast before the bigger man got close, so he shot a kick at him. It was a stupid mistake—he knew it even as he launched the kick. Moran was quick and agile for a big man—and he had that long reach. He grabbed Winter's leg, and turned to twist it, to drop him. But Winter was fast too. Faster. He hopped close and smashed the heel of his palm into Moran's nose. Cartilage crunched, and blood spurted from the big man's nostrils, spattering Winter's face before the rain washed it off him.

Moran fell back, losing his grip on Winter's leg. Winter staggered, off-balance. By the time he got his feet planted, Moran was facing him again. His round face was bloodied. His broken nose ruined his boyish good looks.

They dodged around each other, but neither attacked. Moran knew now: Winter was a fighter, dangerous. He was cautious. And Winter, still breathless from that first blow that drove him to the asphalt, felt too unsteady to strike again. They circled, breathing hard, eyes glaring.

"Where is she?" Moran rasped.

"I don't know," said Winter.

"I'll find her."

"Why?"

Moran's right hand shaped itself into a claw, as if to strangle the missing woman right then and there. "She's mine."

"For God's sake . . ."

Moran feinted a punch. Winter pulled back. Moran cut to the side and ran.

The move caught Winter off guard. Moran was at the parapet in less than a second. As Winter stood staring, frozen with surprise, Moran leaped off the edge of the roof.

Winter rushed through the rain to the parapet. He looked down.

The building next door was one floor shorter. It was a long drop to that roof—an ankle-breaker. But Moran had made a good landing. He was already on his feet, already running. He leaped over the next parapet onto the next roof. Then he leaped off the front of that roof—leaped into nothingness.

Winter's breath caught when he saw it. It looked like suicide. But a second later, he heard the echoing metallic jangle and he knew Moran had hit the platform of the fire escape. Then there was the pound of Moran's footsteps as he continued down the metal stairs.

Winter went on standing there, went on watching. He was unwilling to try the jump himself, unwilling to risk twisting his ankle or breaking his leg. His bones ached from being driven to the ground, and his throat hurt from the choke hold. He didn't have enough fight left in him to give chase to the bigger man or tangle with him again. And anyway, he didn't trust himself to make the decision. He was—what was the word again? Decompensating. Right. He was batshit decompensating. Margaret had been right. As always.

Winter shook his head and cursed. His arms fell to his sides. He raised his face to the rain. He let the cool water wash down over him.

14

During the plane ride home, Winter grew angrier and angrier. The fury was like a glowing coal in his belly at first, but it soon became a raging fire all through him. As the plane cut through the misty midnight, his fight with Moran replayed in his mind repeatedly like a video on a loop. How could he have let that Nazi thug get the jump on him? He'd come within an inch of being throttled into unconsciousness. And then he'd let the bastard get away. What the hell?

After Moran had run off, Winter found that the access door back into the building had automatically locked when it swung shut behind him. He'd had to jump down to the fire escape to get to the street. The jarring landing on the escape's rattling metal platform brought the pain back to his knee and now it was throbbing. His whole body was sore and grubby, and he felt like a failure. He sat in his window seat, watching the darkness, nursing a whiskey, wishing there were someone near at hand whom he could repeatedly punch in the face.

But who? Who was he angry with? Moran? For being the brute he was? Margaret? For making him doubt himself? Himself—for not having the brains to listen to Margaret's doubts? Or maybe

Charlotte—for living in his head all these years as the image of loving-kindness while in real life she was descending into a world of violence and rage and degradation.

Or was she? Or was that just the fetid imagination of "Ivy Swansag" in *Treachery in the Night*? Wasn't it at least possible Charlotte was still that porcelain woman-child he'd so desperately loved?

He despised himself for even wondering. What an emotional cripple he was, stuck in lost time. Coming to pieces the moment he was confronted with present reality. If it was reality . . .

He grew angrier and angrier. He was furious with everyone, each in turn. He bared his teeth at his own reflection on the night-black window. He needed to stop all this crazy nonsense. The minute he got home, he told himself, he was going to call Gwendolyn Lord. He was going to call her and ask her out to dinner and propose to her over dessert and after a brief wedding ceremony during their digestif, he would impregnate her, and then continue to infuse her with children, one a year, until he died of blissful exhaustion without ever thinking of Charlotte or the Recruiter or all the people he'd killed or other people's mysteries or anything but the taste of his dear wife's lipstick ever again.

By the time he returned to his apartment, grimy and disheveled and limping, he was so angry he really thought he meant it. He actually took out his phone and glared at it, as if daring it to deny he was going to call Gwendolyn Lord right that very moment. Which, all right, happened to be eleven thirty on a weeknight, local time. But never mind. This was important. A good woman, that's what he needed. A good, warm, loving, maybe even intelligent woman would solve all his problems. Why had he wasted so many years falling slow-motion into madness when all the while the answer was only a phone call away?

Whether he would actually have phoned Gwendolyn right then and there, he would never know. Because just at the moment of decision, his apartment buzzer buzzed. Who the hell bothers a person at this time of night? he wondered furiously. The thought made him see the phone he was holding as if for the first time. He slipped it sheepishly back into his pocket. He'd call Gwendolyn later, he told himself. First he had to deal with whatever nonsense this was.

He went to the intercom.

"What?" he said.

"A Roger Sexton is here," said the doorman.

Winter wanted to shout curses at him. "Send him up," he said with a sigh.

The big shambling Roger-Sexton-bear came stomping into the apartment, shaking his head at the floor. It wasn't raining here as it had been in New York. Roger was dressed in slacks and a button-down shirt, and the shirt was coming untucked at his sloppy waist.

"It's late, it's late, I know, I know, I'm sorry," he muttered. "I didn't know where else to go."

"You want a drink?" said Winter, because he wanted one.

Roger waved a hand distractedly. Which was as good as a yes as far as Winter was concerned. Winter went to the liquor cabinet and poured them each a generous dose of single malt.

"I don't know what to do," said Roger, pacing the floor as Winter was still pouring. "I don't know what to do."

"Go home to your wife and son," said Winter. He was in possibly the least suitable mood to play the understanding, nonjudgmental friend. Whatever that mood was, he was in the opposite mood. He brought the glasses to where Roger was pacing and handed him one as he shambled by.

Roger seemed not to have heard his advice. Which was a shame, Winter thought, because that was pretty much the best advice he had to give.

Drink in hand, Roger stopped pacing and collapsed heavily onto the sofa. *Flumpf.* He leaned back. He took a gulp of scotch. He didn't look at Winter. He hadn't looked at him once since he'd come in. Winter settled into his armchair.

"I went to her. After you told me about her kissing that guy, I went to talk to her. To Barbara, I mean."

"I know who you mean," said Winter irritably. He was having flashbacks to that fight on the roof. He could feel Moran's muscular arm trying to snake its way across his throat. The fascist monster had come within a second of destroying him.

"I told her how I feel," Roger continued. He seemed to be explaining this to the empty space between them.

"What?" said Winter, startled. "You told her?"

"Yes."

"That you loved her?"

"Yes!"

"Oh, my God, Roger! What a stupid thing to do."

"I had to."

"No, you didn't."

"She laughed at me."

"Of course she laughed at you. You were being ridiculous."

Roger clunked the whiskey glass down onto the coffee table. He leaned forward, clutching his head as if to keep it from exploding.

"I do love her, Cam."

"No, you don't. That's absurd. You love your wife and son."

"I don't."

"Yes! You do. You have to. They're your wife and son. That's what that means. That's what they're there for."

Roger fluttered his hands violently in front of his face in an eruption of anguish. "She laughed at me!" he cried again in his disbelief.

Winter sighed. He took a shot of scotch. He wished he'd poured himself more than he had. Soon he'd have to get up and go to the bar again, and he was too tired to even think about it. Plus his knee hurt.

Roger sagged, his arms on his thighs, his head hanging down. "You don't understand."

"Oh, the hell I don't," said Winter. "You're a middle-aged man. You can smell death and you don't like the smell so you dipped your stick in a young girl and it felt like life to you, so you're acting like an idiot. You think that's never happened before? It's probably happened two or three times within a mile of here since you came in."

"I know it looks like that, but this is different."

Winter laughed.

"She made love to me!" Roger cried.

"She does that with everyone. She likes it."

"If you call her a slut, I'll punch you in the face."

If you punch me in the face, I'll rip your leg off and make you eat it, Winter didn't say, but he sure as hell wanted to. He took another drink instead. "Go home to your wife," he said again. He thought it was such good advice, it was worth repeating.

Roger brought his hands to his chest. He clutched the front of his wrinkled shirt. He was experiencing another eruption of anguish apparently. "I can't go home to her. That's all over now. Barbara showed me that. I know she's young, but she's very wise in her way."

Winter made a rude noise.

"She is!" Roger insisted. "She showed me who I am. This is my authentic self."

"Oh, well, get another one then," said Winter. "Get a better one. Put your back into it, boy. It's not that hard."

For what seemed long minutes on end, Roger gaped at him. It was as if he hadn't heard a word Winter had said until just now. "What the hell are you talking about?" he asked.

Winter rubbed his eyes. He was trying to erase the image of Moran from his mind—Moran or whatever his real name was when he sprang out of the pages of his novel and started putting real people in choke holds.

"All right, Roger," he said wearily. "I'm your friend. So I'm going to be your friend. I'm going to solve your problem for you, OK? Free of charge."

Roger just continued staring at him blankly, so Winter continued saying what he had to say.

"Your problem is this. You did something wrong when you slept with this girl."

Roger blinked at him. "What do you mean? Wrong. I never did anything more right in my life. Wrong. What's that supposed to mean?"

"It means wrong," said Winter. "Immoral. Against the laws of God and man."

"What the hell are you talking about? You're babbling."

"You cheated on your wife, Roger. That's immoral. That's what the word *wife* means. Someone it's immoral to cheat on. Because you promised you wouldn't. And now you're thinking about leaving her and you promised you wouldn't do that either. It's immoral to break your promises. That's what the word *promise* means, something that's immoral to break. If we're going to change the meaning of every word that doesn't suit us, we might as well just grunt at each other and act like demons."

"This is the stupidest conversation I've ever had. I shouldn't have come here. I'm leaving," Roger said.

But he didn't leave. He just sat there. So Winter just went on. "And the worst, the most immoral thing you're doing? Is breaking up the marriage of your son's parents. That's a disaster for him. Your marriage is the planet he lives on, and you're going to blow that planet up."

"Oh!" Roger waved this away as if it were flies. "Kids are resilient. He'll get over it."

"Stop lying to yourself, you fat stupid shit!" Winter answered him, annoyed. "He'll never get over it. It'll traumatize him for life. That's what happens to children when their parents get divorced. You're going to ruin his life, Roger, and you're his father. That word has a meaning too. And it'll ruin your life also, by the way, though you probably won't realize it. You'll never get over it either, same as him. You'll just pretend to. You'll just tell yourself you have and after that, it'll be all lies all the time all the way down. That's no way to live, if you're a man. There's another word for you. The word *man* has a meaning too, Roger. So knock this garbage off and try to act like one."

Roger was staring blankly into a corner of the room. Winter could tell he'd stopped listening, so he gave up the effort. Instead, he got up and returned to the bar. It was too bad, he thought, as he refreshed his whiskey. It was too bad Roger had stopped listening, because Winter had more he wanted to say. He wanted to go on berating Roger—not to help him, but just because he was angry and Roger happened to be there and it felt good to take it out on him. Specifically, he wanted to tell Roger a story—a true story about his own life. He wanted to tell him what it felt like to see a girl you loved lying dead in a ditch, tortured and murdered because of something you'd done, a mistake you'd made. He wanted to tell him how you didn't change the meaning of words after you saw something like that, because it didn't matter a damn if you did. It didn't matter what words you used, it didn't matter what theories you concocted, it didn't matter what you believed, because there she was, tortured and dead, and it was your fault and there was no getting out of it. A girl you loved lying dead in a ditch marked the outer limit of philosophy.

But he didn't say any of that. What was the point? He carried his whiskey back to his chair, already drinking it as he went. Roger was still staring into the corner. Winter had no idea what he was thinking about. He didn't care either. He doubted it was anything interesting. Probably something about Barbara and the magical place between her legs that made all things new like Jesus. Something like that.

Roger came out of his reverie with a quick shake of his head, a dog shaking off water. "No," he said, as if to himself. In fact, Winter realized, Roger had been talking to himself ever since he arrived. "No, no, I . . . I gotta get out of here. This is . . . this is not what I need. This was a mistake, coming here."

He rose clumsily from the sofa. He walked past Winter as if Winter was a ghost he couldn't see. Winter sighed again. He set his drink down on a side table. He followed Roger to the door.

Roger opened the door, then looked back at Winter as an afterthought—remembering his manners maybe. "Thanks for the drink," he said from someplace far away inside himself.

"Go home to your wife and son, Roger," Winter said wearily.

Roger stared at him a moment longer. "You keep saying the same thing over and over," he said.

"Yes," said Winter. "Strange, isn't it?"

Roger left and all at once Winter was plunged back into the darkest darkness of his depression. He wandered as if aimlessly into the center of the living room and stood there as if wondering where to go next. Oppressed by a crushing sense of solitude, he fished his phone out of his pocket and looked down at it, at the clock on the face of it.

It was probably too late to call Gwendolyn now, he thought.

PART THREE

A BEAST IN FLAMES

Humor me, Margaret. I know what you think. You think I'm avoiding the subject, right? You think I'm trying to distract you so I don't have to talk about Charlotte and what she means to me. Or whatever it is you think I don't want to talk about. But that's the point: It's all connected. In my mind, at least. In my mind, it's all one story. And sure, whenever I'm talking about one part, there's always some other part I'm not talking about. I can't talk about everything all at once. So I have to tell you this and maybe I'm avoiding Charlotte, but maybe if I were talking about Charlotte, I'd be avoiding this. You see? It's all connected because it's all in my mind, all together in my one mind. Anyway. Anyway, just . . . humor me.

Jerry Collins. Remember? In the villa in Turkey. Straitlaced, uptight, evangelical Jerry Collins. Sitting at the white table in the white court-yard dressed in his white tracksuit and surrounded by bare-breasted statues and bare-breasted girls beneath the age of consent.

He lifted his champagne flute to me as I approached him. "Cameron Winter, as I live and breathe," he said. "Champagne?"

I gestured that that would be fine and sat down across from him.

"You didn't kill poor Hamza, did you?" Jerry asked as he poured. "I'd take it badly if you did. I'm very fond of poor Hamza."

148

"He's in the trunk of the car. He was alive last time I looked. It all depends what you put in that drug he was going to give me."

Jerry laughed with what sounded like delight. I'm not sure it really was delight though, because his eyes were all over the place, blue eyes, dancing around, like he was either drugged or crazy, or both.

"Well, then, he'll live," said Jerry, setting a champagne flute before me and sitting back in his chair with his own. "I mean, I wasn't going to kill an old pal, was I? I told my people just to knock you out."

"Funny," I said. "I thought I was your people, Jerry."

He shrugged. It was an odd gesture, louche, cynical, so unlike him. But looking at him, all unshaven, long haired, I wasn't sure who he was anymore, or what he was like.

"Whatever," he said. "Anyway, it's Hamza's own fault really. I gave him fair warning about you, what you'd do to him if he let his guard down. You were always the best of us, Poetry Boy. You were the chief's favorite, that's for sure."

The champagne was so good I can still remember the taste of it, even now. I said, "And you were always . . ." I looked for the right words.

"A pious stick-in-the-mud?" Jerry suggested. "An evangelical pain in the ass?"

"Something along those lines, yeah. I remember Roy and I would go into town hunting for girls, and you would frown sternly and read your Bible. You ruined many a hangover by lecturing us about the things of the flesh and eternal hellfire and I've forgotten what else."

"You embarrass me, Winter."

"Oh, I don't know. For all that, I always sort of liked you, in a vaguely ironic way."

Jerry laughed again. I still couldn't tell what he meant by it. "By the way, if you're still into the whole girl-hunting business"—he gestured with his free hand at the bare-breasted girls standing by his shoulder—"*you've come to the right place. Not a lot of sport to it, I admit. Like shooting fish in a barrel, as they say. But help yourself. I'm happy to wait.*"

I rubbed my chin as if considering the offer, but I was considering him, really, this new Jerry, all unkempt and crazy eyed. What the hell had happened to him? It had happened so fast too, in just a matter of weeks. He'd only been missing a month or two.

"*You know, I would, Jerry. I would help myself. I wouldn't mind at all except . . .*"

"*Except?*"

"*Except I can't help noticing that some of them look to be about twelve years old.*"

"*Ah,*" *he said sadly.*

"*And a couple of them, at least, seem Syrian.*"

"*You have some issue with Syrian girls? All cats are gray in the dark, Winter.*"

"*It isn't that. It just makes me suspect that our fat friend Kemal Balkin culled these children out of the refugee camps, you know. Little Syrian girls on the run with nothing to their names, no one to protect them. Rounded up and sold as sex slaves.*"

"*Only the presentable ones. The others are forced into laboring as telemarketers. I mean, talk about abusive.*" *He laughed again.*

"*Mm,*" *I said.* "*Either way, it's all a bit of a turnoff for me.*"

He stopped laughing. He scowled.

"*Now who's the moralist?*" *he said grumpily.*

"*Am I? I mean, I'm not as well versed in the Bible as you are, but I have to imagine this sort of thing violates a commandment or ten, no?*"

"*Oh, my goodness, yes,*" *said Jerry mildly, gazing out toward the sparkling sea.* "*After all, this Kemal Balkin the chief sent me here to exterminate—he's a very bad man, you know. Very, very bad. A monster, really, once you get to know him.*"

"Could be that's why the chief sent you," I said. "Just a guess, but it would be in keeping with his character. The chief's character, I mean. And yours too, I would have thought."

"Mm, well, thereby hangs a tale, as someone used to say."

"Shakespeare."

"Was it Shakespeare? Sorry, Poetry Boy, I know you're a stickler for that sort of thing. Shakespeare then. Thereby hangs a tale, as jolly old Shakespeare used to say. And yes, character is at the heart of the story, as you suggest. The chief's character. And mine. And our country's character also. You remember our country, don't you, Winter? The place we're killing people in service of."

"I remember our country, yes," I said.

There was a breeze coming in off the water. It felt very pleasant in the heat of the sun. And the plash of the water in the fountains sounded pleasant. And the view of the sea with the light sparkling on it was very pleasant to look upon. It wouldn't have surprised me to discover that the girls attending to us were pleasant to look upon too, but I couldn't look upon them because it made my gorge rise.

Jerry went on in this new man-of-the-world casual way he seemed to have acquired.

"Do you know what my mission was?"

I shook my head. "Not exactly. The chief didn't go into detail."

"No, of course. He wouldn't, would he?" Jerry said. And now, beneath the frantic movement of his eyes, I saw a bottomless depth of sadness. And more than sadness: horror, I think. "I imagine you've heard the name Abu Ali Dakkak?"

I had. Dakkak was a Syrian warlord, backed by the Russians because of his harsh stance against the West. Anyway, he was a bad guy.

"Dakkak had a daughter. Hana," Jerry continued. He was gazing out at the water again, but I don't think he saw the water. I don't know what he saw. "There was some sort of family mess, as I understand it. It's *not easy being a warlord's daughter, I guess. Anyway, Hana ran off with some man and got herself abandoned in the middle of nowhere. A sad story, but an old one. Somehow—a series of unfortunate events—Hana ended up in the clutches of none other than Kemal Balkin, who set her to work turning tricks for Chinese gangsters in the Golden Triangle, doncha know."*

I was in the middle of raising my champagne flute to my lips, but my hand froze midway. I could already see where this story was going. At least, I thought I could.

"So you get the picture," said Jerry. "Our beloved chief, working as always for the last best hope on earth under the aegis of our all-American kick-ass Lord and Savior Jesus Christ, managed to come into some fairly lurid evidence of Hana's doings and whereabouts, along with some highly convincing documentation as to who was to blame. Namely our fat friend Kemal. So you can imagine what he sent me to do, can't you, Winter."

I could. This was a more or less typical Division operation. The Recruiter would have sent Jerry to Ankara, say, under cover as an attaché to the ambassador. There, Jerry would have gotten drunk on raki with just the right corrupt policeman or some other Syrian spy. During their revels, Jerry would have dropped just the right amount of information about the fate of Dakkak's daughter Hana. Then we all would have sat back with innocent looks on our faces and waited for that information to reach Dakkak and for Dakkak to react with typical Syrian restraint by spiriting Balkin off to some private Mediterranean retreat somewhere where he would slowly disembowel him without ever knowing that he was doing the Recruiter's will, and thus the will of the last best hope on earth under the aegis of our all-American kick-ass Lord and Savior Jesus Christ. Kemal would get his just deserts and it would all seem less like a US-engineered assassination and more like an act of God—though I'm not sure the Recruiter ever bothered to make that distinction.

I lowered my champagne flute to the table. "So it actually was the Recruiter who sent you?" I asked. "The Recruiter personally."

"Yes. Of course. The chief. Who else?" said Jerry.

I thought about this. I thought about the Recruiter and I walking by the Potomac as night fell. I remembered wondering why we were meeting as if in secret, away from the Division offices, away from everyone. Who were we hiding from? And why?

While I was thinking about that, Jerry went on: "He couldn't send me to Syria directly. Too much chaos. Not to mention the fact that I'd've stuck out like a sore thumb. I'd've had my sore thumb cut off, more than likely, and various other bits and pieces of me as well. The chief figured I could make contact with Dakkak through his people here in Turkey much more plausibly, though that was dangerous too, knowing how Kemal has his eyes and ears in Istanbul's every corner. Still, I thought I set the thing up perfectly. Managed to link up with a Syrian spy who couldn't know I knew he was a Syrian spy. Didn't even leak the intel to him. Just let him know I had it, so he would break into my hotel room, hack my device. Which he did. The whole operation went off without a hitch. A Division classic, if I say so myself. I returned to my hotel room that night with the warm feeling of a job well done. Trundled off to my trundle bed and so on. And woke up with a pistol stuck in my face."

"I hate when that happens."

"Yes. Yes," said Jerry. And I thought I saw that sadness in his frantic eyes again, that sadness and that horror. "I was driven . . ." He gestured—at the statues, the fountains, the water, the half-naked girls. "I was driven here. Just as you were to be driven here. In fact, I sat just where you're sitting now, Winter. Kemal Balkin sat where I'm sitting. I drank champagne with him, just like you're drinking champagne with me. He offered me a girl, you know, as I offered you one. And I refused as you did, and for the same reason. They really are

just children, after all. Poor children with nowhere to go, enslaved for the enrichment and pleasure of this devil-spawn Balkin. And I said all that to Kemal. I did. Just as you said it to me. And you know what Kemal said? He laughed. Ho ho ho. Like a whoremongering Turkish Santa Claus. The fat bastard. And he said, 'Ho ho ho. So the Recruiter wants me dead, does he? The infidel dog. I've been expecting him.' "

"He'd heard of the Recruiter?" I asked, surprised.

Jerry Collins nodded slowly.

"But how could he?"

"Yes," said Collins. "How could he? And how could he have known I had leaked his information to a Syrian spy?"

"Well, the spy was a double agent," I said. "Balkin had bought him."

"That was my first guess too. But no," said Jerry. "Because then Balkin said to me, 'I'm sorry to tell you my assassination is not going to happen. Do you want to know why?' I said I did. And he said, 'Come with me, Mr. Collins.' " Jerry set his champagne down and stood up from the table. "Come with me, Mr. Winter," he said. "And I'll show you what this is all about."

I got to my feet. I followed him along a column-lined arcade. Into the mansion. Along a hallway covered in Turkish rugs and lined with Greek statues. We reached a door with a keypad lock. Jerry pressed the keys. The lock clicked. He pushed the door open.

"The holy of holies," he said.

We went in together. The room was nothing special. At first glance, you would have said it was the library of any prosperous man. A spacious wooden desk. Studded leather chairs. A wall of books. And pictures. Lots and lots of framed photographs. Everywhere. Side by side on all the walls. On the small tables. On a fireplace mantel. Everywhere.

" 'Ho ho ho,' said Kemal Balkin," Jerry Collins said.

He gestured to the walls, to the pictures on the walls. I went to them. I studied them. One and then another and then another until, in a single sickening moment of vertigo, I began to understand what had happened to Jerry Collins. Jerry, the true believer in his Bible and his flag.

The pictures on the wall were photographs. Of men. Men I recognized, most of them. Men anyone would have recognized, if he read the news. I moved from one picture to another, one familiar face to another, one high official to an even higher official, and another even higher than that. Congressmen, men from State, men from Intelligence, journalists, publishers, media moguls, billionaire entrepreneurs. I don't need to tell you what they were doing in the pictures. You can guess. The photos had all been taken in some sort of elaborate building somewhere. There were leathery club-like rooms, and smaller rooms for private sessions and larger rooms for gatherings. There even seemed to be some chapels where there were rituals with costumes involved. Although the costumes were only for the men, of course. The children, the boys and the girls, they were mostly naked, though some had the usual fetishistic outfits on. And there were photographs of all of it. And I imagined there were videos to go with the photographs. The photographs were mostly tokens of the videos, I think.

As I moved from one photograph to the next, an idea came to me. A fear. I began to move faster, look closer, my eyes growing bigger, my heart growing more and more anxious as I searched the faces of all these famous, rich, and powerful men.

"He's not there," said Jerry, reading my mind.

It was a moment before I understood him. A moment before I stopped looking picture to picture. I turned and looked at Jerry instead.

"The Recruiter," I said.

"He's not there. I looked. I even asked Kemal about it. But no, it turns out our chief is exactly what he pretends to be. Kemal was quite disgruntled about it."

I let my breath out. I wasn't aware I had been holding it in.

"But still. Those aren't all the pictures. At least, Kemal claims he has many, many more. He just didn't have space to display them all. So he said at least. But then he is a lying, slaving, whoremongering, child-abusing, drug-dealing, telemarketing monstrosity with a soul made of hellfire and black ashes. I wouldn't believe a word he said about anything. But that is what he said."

I poked a thumb in the direction of the photos. I hoped my face was stony and expressionless. I hoped it hadn't turned as green as I felt inside. "Whatever he is," I said, "he seems to have his hooks in a lot of our people. I mean, this place is like . . ." I gestured at the photos again. I couldn't find the words.

"Like a trophy room," said Jerry softly. "That's what it is, yes. A trophy room. These pictures? They're heads mounted on the walls. Metaphorically speaking."

He went silent then. Stood there, hands in the pockets of his tracksuit trousers. Stood and gazed at the pictures until his eyes grew foggy.

I took advantage of his distraction to study his face for a moment, the marks of his transformation. That was the mystery that had puzzled me since I'd first seen him sitting at the white table in the white courtyard in his white suit: How had the true believer in God and country become this disenchanted mess of a man? In that long quiet pause, some semblance of an answer came to me, some sense of his story.

The Recruiter had sent Jerry to work a hit on the slave-trader Kemal Balkin. Someone—someone back home, someone in our government with a high enough security clearance that he knew about the existence of the Division—had tipped Balkin off that the hit was on. It must have been someone in one of these photographs, someone Balkin controlled because he knew his secrets, served his perversions, and photographed his sexual crimes. So Balkin was ready when Jerry showed himself and made his move. He could have had Jerry killed on the spot. But he hadn't. Instead, he had brought him here, brought him to this room, showed him these trophies.

That was as far as I got before Jerry's eyes cleared, before he turned his gaze on me so that I could see for myself the depths of his disillusionment.

"Why are you here, Jerry?" I asked him. "Why are you still in this house?"

Jerry's lips began to tremble—tremble like a child's. I don't think I'd ever seen anything sadder. I knew what he was going to say seconds before he said it.

"It just . . . did something to me. Seeing these pictures. Seeing this room. I mean, I've killed men, Poetry Boy. By proxy mostly, sure, but face-to-face too, in cold blood. We've all killed people, haven't we? For what?" His lips trembled harder, his chin wrinkled. He gestured at the photographs with a limp hand. "For them!"

I followed his gesture, glanced at the pictures. A fine sampling of our most distinguished citizens. Not at their most dignified, I admit. I could see what he meant. It was hard to miss. That must have been half the leadership of our country up there. They were not an inspiring lot.

"Well . . ." I said. But I couldn't think of anything else to say. Nothing that would help him.

A tear—an actual tear—spilled from Jerry's weak eyes. It coursed down his cheek untouched and dropped onto the Turkish rug, vanishing in its colors. "We work for them, and they work for him, for Kemal, and Kemal's the devil." He sniffled. He gave a miserable laugh. "So he showed me these pictures and then he took me back out to the courtyard. And we sat at the table together, like you and I did, and drank champagne like you and I. And Kemal talked. And I drank. And he talked about all the things that I thought I believed in, and all the pleasures I'd sacrificed for my beliefs and all the things I'd done in service of them. And I drank.

And he asked me: For what? Why had I lived like I'd lived? Why had I killed the people I killed while they . . ."

He gestured to the photographs again.

"Kemal went on talking, and I went on drinking," Jerry said. "I don't even remember when I stumbled off to bed. But when I woke up . . ."

He didn't finish. He didn't have to. I could imagine him waking up to find himself entangled in the naked limbs of his desires. Those girls standing out in the courtyard.

"I suppose he has pictures of me now too," said Jerry, in tears, half laughing in his hollowness and bitterness and despair. "Oh, Poetry Boy! Go away from me. I am a sinful man!"

He laughed again. Then he brought one hand up to cover his face, and he wept. He just stood and wept right there in front of me. Boo hoo hoo. And I . . . well . . . Margaret, the truth is: I was pitiless. I felt nothing for him. Disdain maybe. Not even disdain. He was just another trophy in that trophy room to me. One more head mounted on Kemal Balkin's wall. Maybe that was hard-hearted of me. Probably it was. But you know, those girls outside—they really were just children. Impoverished, kidnapped children. No one to protect them, no one to speak for them. Slaves. And I remembered the way Jerry used to be. With his Bible. Lecturing me and Roy about our nights on the town. And I'm just telling you the truth now: I didn't give a damn how drunk he'd gotten. I didn't give a damn how disappointed in the world he was. How confused he was about what we did or why we did it or who we did it for.

Maybe he was right. Maybe I had become a moralist. Or was in the process of becoming one. Yes. I think there's truth to that. I was changing. My best friend had died at my hands more or less. My lover—I had seen my lover lying dead in a ditch—dead and tortured in a ditch by the side of the road—and that was my fault too, my grievous fault. And a change had come over me. Well, you try it. Try it yourself sometime.

Try to look down at your lover dead in a ditch. Then try to tell yourself there's no such thing as evil.

So anyway. Anyway, I stood there. With Jerry blubbering in front of me. With all these thoughts going through my head. And then . . .

I must have drifted. I must have sunk into one of my reveries, you know. That strange habit of mind I have. Where all my opinions disappear, and it's like the gravity has gone out of the room and all the furniture is floating around and then suddenly it drops down in a new pattern and I see things in a different way. Because suddenly—the next thing I knew—I was running. Running out the door.

"Winter!" I heard Jerry shout behind me.

But I kept on. Racing over the rugs in the hall. Out into the colonnade, the columns flashing past me. Out into the courtyard. Past the half-naked girls. Past the statues of naked girls. Past the plashing fountains. Out into the cul-de-sac in front of the villa on the edge of the woods.

Vaguely, it occurred to me as I ran that the black Caddy—the car that had brought me here—was silent now. Hamza the chauffeur was no longer groaning and pounding on the lid of the trunk. As I ran, I pulled the key fob from my pocket. I pressed the trunk lock. I heard the lock let go with a thunk. I came around the rear of the car and pulled the trunk open all the way. I heard Jerry's footsteps crunching on the gravel. I felt him come up behind me. I heard him let out a moan.

"I didn't know, Winter. I swear! I swear I would never do that to you! I didn't know. I swear."

The chauffeur/thug—Hamza—Hamza was dead in there. It had been a long, painful death by the look of it. Not suffocation. Poison for sure. His body was contorted, his face was blue, frozen in a gaping rictus, foam at the lips, so much foam and the eyes staring and shot through with blood. The drug in the syringe had unleashed some slow-working ruin inside him.

"I didn't know," Jerry kept saying. Sobbing.

I ignored him. I looked down at the dead man. It must have been torture, I thought. I thought: it was meant to be torture.

And I thought: it was meant for me.

15

Margaret didn't have to stop him talking this time. Winter stopped himself, right there, midstory. Margaret took some satisfaction in this. She felt it was the stern expression on her face that did it. The silent scold. He had been staring down at the carpet as he told his tale, and then he glanced up at her and saw that look on her face and his voice trailed off into silence. Mother wasn't pleased with him.

"What," he said. "Why are you looking at me like that?"

"Why do you think?" said Margaret—sounding like a prim hen even to herself.

Winter sighed. "You're a hard woman to entertain, Margaret."

"These are working hours," she told him. "On weekends, I'm a laugh a minute."

Winter did his best to smile at that, but he looked a wreck, an animate disaster area. Face pasty. Hands unsteady. Eyes rheumy. His eyes . . . she thought of his description of Jerry Collins's eyes. Frantic and full of sadness and horror. That was the look in his eyes too.

"Sometimes, you know, my heart grows troubled at the wickedness of the world," he said softly. "You'd think at my age I'd have gotten over it. The things I've seen. But sometimes . . . no."

The room was quiet for several seconds after that. A dull brown quiet in the dull brown room with its dull brown and tan furnishings and decorations. The soft sound of traffic reached them from the street outside. The sunlight and the sense of springtime seemed to beat at the window like a bird trying to get in. Margaret wanted to respond to what he'd said, to say something about the wickedness of the world, how she felt it too, how we all feel it sometimes. She wanted to say something, anyway. Something that might comfort him. But she found she couldn't think of anything to say.

At moments like this, he made her feel small, did Winter. Small and shallow. Inadequate to the task of helping him. Hers was a middle-class practice mostly. The people who came to her were professors; state government workers; professionals; the occasional student. People troubled about relationships, about work, about the usual fears and anxieties. The "worried well." That's what they were called in the therapy business. Ordinary people with ordinary troubles.

But Winter—Winter had done such things—done and seen such things—as she would prefer not to think about. He came to her looking for forgiveness. For acceptance, mercy, motherly love. And she just didn't know if she was up to it. If she had the breadth of experience, the depth of feeling, or the reserves of wisdom that such a job required. People sometimes said that therapists were the new priests. But they weren't, not really. She wasn't, anyway. Priests can give absolution. She didn't think she could.

"Tell me what's happening with Charlotte," she said. Stalling for time, yes, but also—also trying to get at the heart of what he was trying to tell her, to make the connections she needed to make so she could understand him.

Winter was gazing into the middle distance, gazing at something far away inside his own mind. He spoke as from a distance.

"I met the man who's hunting her," he said.

Margaret took a sharp breath in through her nose. He glanced up at the sound.

"You were right," he told her. "I was off my game. He nearly throttled me."

"What does he want?"

"Same as me. He wants to find her."

"Charlotte."

"Yes."

"To kill her?"

"Maybe. Or just to have her. I'm not sure. I just know . . ."

"What?"

"I can't stop thinking about it. It's driving me insane."

Margaret considered this. She still didn't have enough information, she thought. She needed more. "Tell me what you're feeling right now," she said.

Winter gave a mirthless chuckle. "Crazy," he told her. "I'm feeling crazy. You ever see one of those cartoons where the character gets electrocuted, and he shoots up in the air and freezes there and you can see his skeleton? I feel like the mental equivalent of that."

"Frozen. In pain. Your insides exposed."

"It's funnier in the cartoons."

"And you feel if you could just find Charlotte . . ."

"I don't know. Maybe. Maybe it's like you said. Maybe she's a symbol of some sort, a vessel of meaning. I know she's not the girl I loved. But whatever she is, I've got to find her. I've got to find something. I can't go on like this. I'm discombobulating."

"Decompensating."

"Whatever. I'm falling apart."

"Why are you telling me this story about Jerry Collins, do you think? Why do you insist on talking about that instead of this?"

"I don't know. It's part of what happened to me. At the Division. It's part of the story of how I got here."

"Yes, but why now? Why are you telling it to me now?"

Winter considered the question. Margaret watched him—observed him. She could see his eyes moving rapidly this way and that. As if he felt cornered, she thought.

"Late last night, a friend came to see me," he said finally. "He had cheated on his wife. Now he thinks he's in love. He wants to run off with the girl. Destroy his marriage. Leave his son. Desert his wife. It'll ruin the kid. It'll hit the wife like a shovel in the head when he tells her. She's a feminist theorist, poor thing. She has no idea how much she needs him."

"I'm confused, Cam. How is this connected?"

His lips parted as if he would answer her. But he didn't answer her, not right away. Only after a slow struggle did he even try. "It's just—the things we do. You know? The things we all do. Big things but also little things. Everything. Every single thing. None of it matters at all, in some sense, and at the same time, all of it matters. So much. Too much to bear. I make a mistake and my lover dies. Roger sleeps with a girl and his son's life is ruined. Some public official has a thing for little boys and so he's blackmailed into spying for a slave trader and the Division is compromised and all the killing we do just becomes suspect or meaningless. We do these things, these little things. And you tell yourself in the moment there's some room for error, some leeway for sin, but every move you make affects everything else and there's no room, no room for error at all."

"And what's all that got to do with Charlotte?"

"I don't know. Except . . ."

"Except what, Cam?"

He looked at her forlornly. "None of this would have happened if she'd loved me."

Margaret sat back in her chair. She nodded. "And so—what? If you find her, you can put things right?"

"Of course not. I killed people. There's no fixing that. There's no fixing anything. The past is what it is forever. That's the whole point."

"Well, what *are* you looking for then?" Margaret asked him. She swiveled her chair back and forth a little. She steepled her fingers under her chin. "Why are you falling apart like this? What does Charlotte mean to you? What are you trying to find?"

Once again, Winter made to speak, then didn't. He peered at her like a prisoner peering out through the bars of a cage. Trapped inside himself. Trapped in his own history.

Finally, he sighed and sank back in his chair.

"I don't know," he said quietly. "I don't know."

16

Winter looked down at the man in the wheelchair. Larry Moscow—that improbably apt name. A sadly savaged sack of erstwhile humanity. Barely able to turn his head. Barely able to close his mouth or lift his hand to wipe the spittle from his lips. One of his eyes kept fluttering closed. Sometimes his whole body shuddered as if with pain.

Standing over him, Winter thought about *Treachery in the Night*. Was this the man from the novel? Was this the man Moran had lured into the parking lot and beaten bloody?

That moment was a turning point in the story. It bound Moran and Miranda together. There were secrets between them now, for one thing. Their kiss in the woods. The violence in the parking lot. The leader of their cell, Frederick Bernard, would have been furious if he'd found out what Moran was up to. The Phantom of the Zones, luring rioters into brutal ambushes. Frederick Bernard had a plan, a strategy. This was not at all what he wanted.

Somehow—silently, without a promise, without a word—Miranda had agreed not to tell Bernard—not to tell anyone, not even Theo-her-boyfriend—about what had happened.

The secret gave new depth, new meaning, new heat, to the glances that passed between her and Moran.

So there was that, but there was more than that. There was something about their escape from the city, that run together after the violence was over, the thrill of it, the exhilaration. It had linked them together almost physically, almost like an act of love. It made something about them seem inevitable.

And yet still—according to *Treachery in the Night*—Miranda would not give herself to Moran. She would not become unfaithful to Theo. She wanted to leave Theo. She would leave him. She promised Moran she would. She swore it to herself. But day after day went by, and she could not find the courage to do it.

As a result, Moran began to feel like a hungry beast in a cage, pacing back and forth in there, drooling to be fed. He not only wanted Miranda, he needed her, he felt incomplete without her. Every day he couldn't put his hands on her, his lips on her lips, his body inside hers, was like a day spent burning. He was a beast pacing back and forth in a cage and he was a beast in flames. He did not know how long he could stand the fire.

Then there was Theo. Theo knew, of course. He knew that Moran and Miranda were linked together now. He could see the looks that passed between them, feel the change in the atmosphere around them. Some days he felt certain they were already lovers. Some days he thought: Of course they were. Only a fool would refuse to see it. He hated himself for putting up with it, doing nothing. He called himself names. Twisted, crippled, half a man.

Then, at other times, he became convinced it wasn't so. He told himself he was not yet betrayed, not yet, not yet. Then his desire to hold on to the most beautiful woman who had ever loved him became ferocious and ungovernable. He wanted to win her back, to be kind to her, to flatter her and make love to her. He would make a start at it. But at her slightest resistance, his rage broke through, his charm shattered. If she didn't melt at the first compliment he paid her, he became furious. He began to insult her, to carp at her, to curse at her, all but accuse her. Because any fool could see what was happening. But he felt powerless to stop it.

Finally, it was too much. He came into their bedroom one morning and found her standing at the window. He came up behind her with his Dobermans trailing after him. He looked over her shoulder. He saw Moran down below, outside, walking across the field into the trees. Miranda was so mesmerized by the sight of him, she hadn't even noticed Theo, not even with the dogs panting and their claws pattering on the floor, not even now when he was standing right there at her back.

Theo sneered and, seeing him sneer, the dogs growled. Miranda gasped and started, surprised to find him there.

"You can't take your eyes off him, can you?" Theo snapped.

The dogs growled louder.

"Oh my God!" said Miranda. "You scared me."

He grabbed her wrist. The Dobermans started barking. Miranda's eyes went wide with fear.

"Why don't you just do him?" Theo said. "You want him so bad, why don't you just do him?"

"Get the hell off me! Let go! Jesus, those dogs!"

"I ought to set them on you."

With a mighty effort, she yanked her arm free. Rubbing her wrist, she shed tears and cursed him. Theo lost control and smacked her. His malformed arms were thick and powerful, but he was slow. She ducked, and his palm glanced off the side of her head. That made him so furious he struck again, and this time, he hit her on the side of the neck. She reeled back against the window, gagging, clutching the spot. The dogs went wild. They raced back and forth, howling.

"For God's sake, Theo, get them away from me!" Miranda cried out.

For what seemed to her an eternity, he just stood there glaring, sneering, his eyes bright with an insane fury. She did not know if he was going to hit her again or order the dogs to tear her limb from limb or strangle her himself. Any frightful thing seemed possible to her.

He spoke with a voice no different than the growls of the Dobermans.

"Come!" he said.

He pivoted and stalked out of the room. The dogs kept barking at her over their shoulders as they followed after him. In the quiet that followed, Miranda sank to the floor, weeping.

When Winter read this scene, he felt he had swallowed the pages and was choking on them. It wasn't anger he felt. It was beyond that, beyond anything so simple. It was more a kind of wild nausea of despair. What a swimmer must feel in the moment he realizes he cannot beat the riptide that is carrying him out to sea.

This was a story that could have no happy ending—not for him anyway.

"Who are you?" asked the man in the wheelchair. Larry Moscow's voice was slack and hollow. His words were slurred because he couldn't move his mouth properly. That was a hell of a beating Moran had given him, Winter thought.

"I'm an English professor," Winter said.

"How did you find me?"

"Gerald Dinh gave me your name."

Crumpled up in his wheelchair as he was, Moscow's scowl looked like a spasm of pain. "That fascist! Are you one of them?"

Winter shook his head. "No. I'm not here about the politics. I don't care anything about that."

"You don't care?" said Moscow, gaping.

"Whether socialists or fascists win a street fight? Believe me, no. I'm just looking for a girl, that's all."

Moscow went on gaping for a few more seconds, but as this had no effect on Winter he finally gave it up. With an effort, he lifted the back of his hand so he could wipe his mouth. "You said you might know who did this to me."

"I might. I don't know his name yet, but I think I can find him."

"Are you a Fed?"

"No. I told you. I'm an English professor."

"Looking for a girl."

"That's right."

"The girl who was with him. With the man who did this to me."

"I think so. Yes."

Moscow made a noise Winter could not interpret. Maybe it was a groan of pain, or a grunt of anger. Maybe it was something else: a murmur of hope and expectation. The man who had beaten him had never been caught and clearly this tormented him. Moscow worked to turn his wheelchair toward the middle of the room. He made a vague, sloppy gesture with one limp hand. It took a moment before Winter realized he was pointing him toward the sofa.

Winter sat down. He looked around him as Moscow labored to maneuver his chair into position across from him. It was a small living room in the small house, not expensive but not shabby either. The chairs and the sofa looked old—their upholstery faded—but clean. Everything was clean: the floor swept, the mantelpiece dusted, the end tables polished to a shine. Moscow lived here with his parents. Winter guessed his mother kept the place tidy for her crippled son.

There were photographs on all the tables, but he couldn't get much of a story out of them. A family. Larry Moscow and his two sisters, one older, one younger. Their mother, chubby and blandly cheerful. Their father, thick and squat, a workingman. He was smiling in the pictures, but he seemed to have to put some effort into it. The living room window looked out on the small front lawn and the street, a street of other houses like this one, small with small lawns, but respectable, clean. They were on the side of the city opposite from Charlotte's house, that last house, where Winter had seen her all those years ago. A strange breeding ground for would-be revolutionaries. Or maybe not, he thought.

"Why?" Moscow said. He was still curled and crumpled in his chair, still scowling as if he couldn't unfreeze his face.

"Sorry?" said Winter.

"Why are you looking for the girl who was . . ." He had to pause here to swallow. It looked like an unpleasant process. ". . . who was with the man who attacked me?"

"I think I used to know her. I think she may be in danger."

"And you're going to rescue her?"

"I'd like to warn her."

"Because you're an English professor."

Winter smiled distantly. "Have you ever heard of a novel called *Treachery in the Night*?" he asked.

Moscow grunted and shook his head.

"You probably wouldn't have. It's self-published, sort of an underground thing. The story is set during the riots. Not the last ones, the ones before. There's a scene in it where a man enters one of the zones with his girl. Lures a . . ." Winter had to search his mind for an inoffensive word, not the one he would have used. ". . . a paramilitary man . . ."

"Security."

"Leads a security man into a parking lot . . ."

"It was a park."

"It's a parking lot in the novel. He lures him there and attacks him. Like what happened to you."

For several seconds after that, Moscow nodded, his one good eye gazing at nothing, or into the past perhaps. He spoke a word but Winter couldn't understand it.

"Sorry," Winter said. "What was that?"

"Beautiful," said Moscow more clearly. "She was beautiful. The girl who was with him. Is that why you want to find her?"

"It's a long story," said Winter with another small smile.

Moscow turned his head a little. He stared into space. That way he sat, with his body slack and folded in on itself—it made Winter feel sorry for him. He remembered what Gerald Dinh had told him: how Moscow was a sadist who would look for excuses to berate and lash the women in his charge. That might not have been true, but Winter suspected it was, and it made him despise Moscow: a punk in a mask with a stick in his hand. Still, he felt sorry for him all the same. He couldn't help himself. He could still feel Moran's arm snaking around his own neck. What if the Phantom had choked him unconscious? How would Moran have tortured him then? It might be Winter in a wheelchair now, just like this kid. Or dead like Susannah Woods. So yes, he felt sorry for Moscow, punk that he was, whatever he was.

"The police didn't care," Moscow said then. His voice was mournful, a hollow knell. His bad eye fluttered shut and open. "It was days before I could even talk to them. They laughed at me. Not out loud, but I could see it. The way they looked at each other. They came to the hospital. Stood over my bed. They looked down at me. It hurt to talk, but I did it. They looked at each other. I could see them laughing."

Winter remembered how the rioters had harried embattled police out of their own buildings. Covered the building with anti-police graffiti. Thrown firecrackers and bottles at officers. Put some of them in the hospital. It was easy for him to imagine the cops had not been altogether sympathetic to rioters who got hurt themselves during the chaos.

"I said to them," Moscow went on. "To the cops. I yelled at them. 'Stop laughing at me, you bastards.' I said, 'You fascist bastards.' I said, 'You want them to win, don't you?' They just looked at each other. There were two of them. Two detectives. They looked at each other with these knowing looks, these sneers. Laughing eyes. One of them—Suskind, his name was—I still remember—he said to the other—Brown—that was his name—Suskind said to Brown, he said, 'Oh, take it from me, kid, they're not winning anything.' He was talking to me but looking at Brown and Brown was looking at Suskind. And they laughed, the two of them. With me lying there. I couldn't move. The doctors say I'll never walk again. Never have sex anymore. I'm twenty-four. This is what that fascist thug did to me. And the cops laughed."

Winter nodded. He could imagine all this. The boy shattered and desolate. The unsympathetic police. He could picture the cops glancing at each other, smirking.

And he could see Moran—whatever his real name was—Moran and Charlotte racing from the scene, running through the thrilling dark together, hand in hand.

Take it from me, kid, they're not winning anything.

17

That night, Winter walked through the city. It had never recovered from the riots, neither the first wave nor the second. The stores were still shut, the windows still boarded. The outer walls of empty buildings were covered with swirling graffiti designs and radical slogans—like painted shouts that had faded to echoes years before. There were only homeless shadows here, trudging through the dark of night like the wandering dead. Once, as he himself wandered, a carload of child gangsters sped by, their engine roaring. When they saw Winter, they shouted at him through the car windows.

He remembered Jerry Collins weeping. *I've killed men. For what?*

Oh, he was sick at heart, Winter was. Sick at heart altogether. The more he and Margaret probed the depths of his mind, the more he suspected there was nothing down there but static and blur. Who was he anyway? This empty man in this ravaged city, weary to his soul? What was he trying to find?

Just before he returned to his Jeep, he stood motionless at a crossroads, right out in the center of the street, no traffic passing, no streetlamps anywhere. The traffic light clunked and changed color above him, bathing him in green then yellow then red.

Unseen thoroughfares vanished into shadow before and behind him, to left and right.

Who could free him from the weight of his past? he wondered. How could anyone wash the blood off his hands?

He thought back to that moment two days later as he hiked through the spring forest to the lakeshore. It was one of those April days that are so full of life they are almost melancholy, glorious and melancholy both at once. The new leaves, pale green, seemed transparent in the light of the clear sky, pale blue. The tangled, unseen forest depths were so loud with birdsong, he couldn't keep himself from wondering what the hell they were singing about. In his sad, half-crazy state of mind, he wished he could be part of it all, just fade, free of himself, into the life and death of the planet. But at the same time, he felt like one of the homeless he had seen on the streets of the broken city: like a zombie; like a ghost.

He trudged on through the woods along an overgrown path that barely seemed a path at all. He thought of Larry Moscow in his wheelchair, and the detectives who had laughed silently when they saw the ruin of him.

Take it from me, kid, they're not winning anything.

He thought of Charlotte who, in his mind, was now one with Miranda in *Treachery in the Night*.

After the scene in the novel when Theo hit her, the story had returned to where it had begun: the prologue.

That was the next morning. Moran had come back from one of his mysterious outings into the Zone. He had found Miranda alone in the kitchen. She was standing at the window, staring blankly out. She was still wearing her long nightshirt. The bruise on her neck where Theo had hit her was plain to see.

Moran stood too close, towering over her. "Miranda," he said in a low growl.

He reached out with one big hand and gently touched the purple bruise with his fingertips.

She drew away. She put her hand up. "Don't," she said.

But there had been a moment's lag before she moved, before she spoke. There had been a moment when she'd let his fingers linger on her. When she finally did move away, she looked up at him. Their eyes met.

Then there followed the scene when Theo and Moran and the Dobermans had gone off hunting into the woods together—those gunshots—and only Moran had returned. With Theo gone, there was nothing to stop him and Miranda from becoming lovers, and they did.

Again, Winter might have read the scenes of their affair with any number of normal emotions. Jealousy. Anger. Disapproval. Even voyeuristic excitement. But none of those words described what he felt. It was more like that moment in the ruined city, standing at the crossroads in the dark of night. Standing in the green then yellow then red glow—that's how he felt when he read those love scenes: alone, with shadows on every side of him.

At the same time, in that cool, distant portion of his mind where he was a professional interpreter of literature, he could see that these scenes were deeply symbolic to their author. The late Susannah Woods had clearly envisioned Moran as the Über-mensch, the one man honest enough to understand the great truths of the ruined world, and the one man strong enough to do the merciless violence that would bring it back to health. At the same time, in Ivy Swansag's imagination, Miranda's womanly weakness was a danger to him. Her softness threatened to seduce Moran away from the purity of his hatred and cruelty. The sex between them foreshadowed Moran's downfall.

The Übermensch, Winter repeated grimly to himself now. What thoughts, he wondered—what thoughts had gone through Susannah Woods's mind when her fictional Übermensch suddenly came to life and tied her to a chair in her shed and tortured her to death? What was it the French philosopher had said? Imaginary evil is romantic. Real evil—not so much. Words to that effect.

As it played out in the novel, Miranda soon found herself overwhelmed by the Übermensch-y power of Moran's sexual passion. He was too much for her, a force of nature, an almost inhuman torrent of desire sweeping her very selfhood away. And so on. As much as her natural womanhood wanted him to dominate and overcome her, her bourgeois ego resisted him. She soon began to want to be free of Moran, just as she had wanted to be free of Theo.

This portion of the narrative culminated in a feverishly detailed sex scene written from Miranda's point of view. Winter skimmed these pages. He didn't have the heart to read the scene more closely. He looked it over until he got the idea: much moaning, many body parts described in detail, many juicy adjectives and spasmodic orgasms. And when it was over—after God alone knew how many breathless, throbbing, rippling, fiery paragraphs—Miranda, wearing nothing but one of Moran's gigantic T-shirts, came downstairs with him and walked him to the Farmhouse door.

It was late evening, dark falling, dusk filling the unlit living room behind them. It was the time when Moran went out to hunt his prey. The lovers pressed together in the open doorway. Miranda stood on tiptoe to kiss him goodbye. Then came a minute description of Miranda's afterglow, which, again, Winter skimmed. The way Ivy Swansag saw it: Miranda (the living symbol of corrupt society) almost succumbed to her healthy desire to surrender to Moran's tumescent Aryan masculinity, but her weak and treacherous female heart rebelled. She whispered to him, "Be careful." But secretly, she was already plotting how to get free.

Moran, however, suspected nothing. As the darkness gathered outside, he swept Miranda up into his arms and kissed her deeply. She all but dangled from his lips, lifted and pressed against him by his powerful arms, her toes barely scraping the jamb.

With that, he was gone, hulking into the dusk. She waited until the red taillights of his truck had vanished up the driveway. Then she shut the door and turned back into the living room.

She gasped loudly as a match flared, making the dusky interior blaze. All her after-passion was washed away in the light of that fire. For an instant, all she could do was stand and stare.

At last, the bright blaze resolved itself into the flame of a match. Frederick Bernard was sitting in an armchair by the cold grate, lighting a cigarette. His pale, thoughtful face, his childishly jagged hair, his intellectual eyes—all glowed in the red halo of the fire for a moment, then faded into the twilight as he waved the match out and tossed it into the dead hearth.

"I thought you were gone for the evening," Miranda said. She shivered and hugged herself, feeling exposed, naked under Moran's T-shirt.

Bernard took his time, leisurely inhaling smoke, blowing it out in a long stream, before he answered. "The others are at a meeting. I stayed behind. I wanted to talk to you."

"To me?"

"You should sit down," said Frederick Bernard in his nasal, nerdy voice. "You should listen carefully to what I have to say."

Miranda did not sit down. She went on hugging herself. The Farmhouse felt vast and cold. "I should go up and get dressed," she said. But she didn't move from the spot. She sensed she shouldn't. She sensed something important was coming and she had to wait for it.

Bernard leaned forward, the cigarette glowing in his hands. "Where's Theo, Miranda?" he said.

"I told you," she said in a small voice. "He left. We had a fight and he left." It sounded unconvincing even to her.

"Without his truck?" said Bernard quietly. "Without his clothes or his laptop? I don't think he did, Miranda. I don't think he left, not at all."

She wished she could have answered strongly. Somehow her voice would not do what she wanted. It continued to come out of her small and unconvincing. "What do you think then?"

Bernard let out a weary groan. He got to his feet—not quickly, not suddenly, and yet even his slow rise made Miranda start as if he'd leaped at her.

"Miranda," he said. "Miranda." He came toward her, shadowy, but with the cigarette glowing as he took another draw. He exhaled and the smell of the smoke was all around her in the thickening darkness. "What have you done?"

He stood before her. She hugged herself tighter. She wanted to back away from him, but didn't, couldn't. She felt he had somehow pinned her there, that she was in his power.

"What do you mean? I didn't do anything," she said.

Bernard gave a glum laugh. "No. I don't expect you did. You're not the doer of things, are you? You're the cause of things being done. But what do you think it looks like? What do you think it will look like to the police?"

"The police," she said. Now her voice was not just small but also numb and toneless.

Frederick Bernard turned aside—turned but did not move away. He was still close and Miranda still felt impaled by his presence, helpless to escape. She felt everything slowly changing. She was becoming afraid. "I sat down here and waited for you." Bernard went on. "I could hear the two of you upstairs. Ha, anyone could've heard you even the next state over."

"Shut up. That's gross. That's disgusting," said Miranda, hugging herself.

"It is disgusting," Bernard said. "Just thinking about you with that gorilla. Christ, Miranda. Don't you know how beautiful you are? You could have anyone."

"It's none of your business who I have or don't have. Leave me alone," she said.

He laughed. Flicked an ash into the unseen spaces. Took another aggressive puff and breathed the smoke out at her. "Don't be stupid, Miranda. You're not a stupid girl. Don't act like one. They'll be here soon."

"Who?"

"Who do you think? I told you. The police."

"The police?" Miranda was about to say, but the words turned to dust in her mouth. In what was now the dark, with the shape of Bernard sinking into silhouette, with his cigarette glowing bright red and his eyes flashing with the light of it as he took a last draw, the conversation was dreamlike to her, like that moment when a dream goes bad, and the images shift into nightmarish monstrosity, and the dreamer is suddenly full of fear and then awake, her heart pounding—that was what this was like as she began to understand what Bernard was telling her.

"What do you think it will look like to them?" he asked again. He dropped the cigarette to the wooden floor and crushed it out under his shoe. "How long do you think it will take them to find the body? Do you think they'll believe you when you say you didn't know? Would anyone believe you? Would anyone . . . ?"

"Don't!" Miranda clapped her hands over her mouth as if to hold the scream in. This really was a nightmare, wasn't it? She felt as if she'd been asleep—asleep in dreams and in desire—and yes, she was wide awake now, her heart pounding.

Bernard gave another laugh, a nasty chuckle, and moved even closer to her. He was a small man, only a little taller than she was, but she felt completely overwhelmed by him.

"Yeah," he said. "Yeah. Now you begin to get it, don't you? The police will wait—at least I think they'll wait—until everyone's here. Mayhew, Andrea, Dolan, Fiona, Moran too—I think they'll wait for all of them so they can take all of them at once. But they will come, Miranda, you better believe it. Guns blazing, I wouldn't be surprised."

She had to make an effort to drag her hands down from her mouth so she could speak. Even then she could only speak in that same small whisper. "How do you know? Who are you?"

"Exactly," he said cruelly. "Now you're asking the right question. And I'll tell you. I'll tell you who I am. I'm the only one who can help you. Not Moran. Moran! Jesus! 'Oh, oh, oh, you big strong gorilla,' " he said, mimicking her passion in a high-pitched voice. "He's nothing now. He was always nothing. Less than nothing. He's helpless. He's going away forever, like any other brainless thug. And so are you, beautiful. So are you, if you don't do everything I tell you."

Miranda was still in the cold clutches of her nightmare awakening, but the sudden reality of the danger she faced propelled her into the moment like a car propelled into a wall. The police were coming. The police, guns blazing, any second now. She felt she had only this one second in which to decide what to do. All the considerations, practical and emotional and even moral, were cascading behind her forehead like digital rain. Theo had been an emotional prison. Moran had set her free but so completely overwhelmed her that she felt as if she were disappearing into him. Now it turned out that Frederick Bernard was a traitor—a police informant. The police were coming and, Bernard was right, they would think she had helped him murder Theo. But what if . . . ? What if this was also her chance to escape? To be free?

What was the price? What would Bernard ask of her? How would she answer him? What should she decide?

Her hands fell from her face. They slowly wafted to her side. She gazed dully at Bernard in the blackness. Only his eyes were visible. His bright eyes and the teeth bared by his triumphant smile.

"All right," she said—and still she could only whisper. "All right. What do you want me to do?"

Winter emerged from the forest onto an isolated spot at the edge of the vast lake. He was dressed for hiking in khaki cargo pants, and a red shell over a navy sweatshirt. Once he was out of the shady woods, the sun spilled down on him. It felt warm and good. The long walk had worked some of the agitation out of him, but he knew he was still sick inside, nervy and fragmented. Whatever had been shaking him to pieces, he knew it would not stop until he found Charlotte, and maybe not even then.

For a few seconds, he surveyed the scene. At first, he thought he was alone here, but then he caught sight of the figure he'd come looking for. A fisherman. He was standing a little ways down the coast, just offshore, knee-deep in the lake. Even from where he was, twenty yards off and around a bend, Winter could see he was a hearty outdoorsman. Broad and sturdy in his black waders and utility vest. His face obscured by large sunglasses and a bushy white Hemingway beard, a baseball cap over his shaggy hair. He was expertly lashing the air with a fly rod, dropping his fly in the shaded places where the trout and steelhead were hiding. His movements were so practiced and casual that Winter could only shake his head in wonder. He was lost once again in admiration of the chameleonlike transformational powers of Stan "Stan-Stan" Stankowski.

Stan-Stan was an undercover federal agent and so, by profession, completely insane. In his mind, he was the star of a TV series in which he played the part of an undercover federal agent playing the part of whoever he was pretending to be in this week's exciting episode. Thus he approached each assignment like an actor approaching a role. He could so completely reshape himself into his cover identity that the real Stan-Stan, if there actually was such a person, seemed to disappear. Winter found it unnerving sometimes. It was like talking to a lunatic who was very convincingly playing the part of an undercover federal agent who was a lunatic portraying a federal agent portraying somebody else, and so on, world without end.

Currently, as Winter understood it, Stan-Stan was pretending to be a fishing guide in the hopes of gaining the confidence of some high-level drug traders who were in the habit of hiring such guides between moving product back and forth over the Canadian border. Winter snorted and shook his head again as a fish hit Stan-Stan's fly like an undersea mine exploding. With flamboyant expertise, the crazy agent proceeded to land a trout approximately the size of a small submarine. How did he learn to do this stuff on such short notice?

"Why, bless my robust suntanned soul!" said the fisherman, sloshing through the water toward him. He held the line looped over his hand so that the trout thrashed on the hook, throwing rainbowed spray into the bright air. "If it isn't that pretty-as-a-picture college professor who's constantly blowing my cover so he can play detective while I get my enormous testicles vivisected by some South American gangster and he goes back to reading poetry to eighteen-year-old coeds." Even his voice was different from the last time Winter had seen him. He had been a homeless schizophrenic then, his words a long, mad mutter. Now his voice was deeper, bolder, more robust: the voice of an ebullient mountain man.

"It's good to see you too, Stan-Stan," Winter said.

"I'm gratified to find you looking like a walking garbage fire. My God, your eyes, man! You look like you're having a nervous breakdown. What the hell's going on, boyo?"

"Nervous breakdown is close enough. Do I really look that bad?"

"I was being polite."

Winter gazed out over the glittering water. He sighed. "I'm going through a bad patch, I guess. It happens."

"So does suicide. I can dream anyway. I sometimes wonder what it would be like for me to get through an entire assignment without you giving me away to the murderous enemies of everything good and decent or at least not forbidden by federal law."

The trout on his line thrashed again. Water flew off its tail and Winter felt it patter against his cheeks. "Oh, throw it back, would you?" he said. "Or bite its head off or whatever you're going to do. Don't torture the poor creature."

Stan-Stan's bushy white beard spread over his wide grin. "Squeamish, huh? Like a woman," he said. With a single deft move he curled the hook out of the fish's mouth and dropped it in the water. It rippled like a wave, then sped away into the murky depths. "All right. Now, talk fast, you gorgeous Kewpie doll, before my overdone manly façade crumbles and I sweep you into my arms."

"*Treachery in the Night,*" said Winter. "It's a novel."

Stan-Stan gave an overdone manly guffaw. "Novel. It's Nazi porn is what it is."

"You've read it?"

"Let's say I have."

"It's true, isn't it? It's based on a true story."

"I couldn't say."

"Sure, you could. Why couldn't you?"

Stan-Stan pinned him with the eyeless hunter-green dark of his sunglasses. "Because I'm a duly appointed federal agent with a security clearance and you're a poetry pansy who probably drinks chardonnay."

"You really are attracted to me, aren't you?"

"I could be if I weren't this much man."

A great heron rose off a log on the lakeshore and climbed toward the sky with balletic majesty. The two men watched it: a graceful blue beauty moving against the green backdrop of the trees.

"Should've brought my rifle," murmured Stan-Stan.

"You've heard of the Phantom of the Zones, right?" Winter asked him.

Stan-Stan peered through his shades into the middle distance. "I haven't heard about a single classified thing. Not while I'm talking to a low-level academic from a second-rate university."

Winter pressed on: "I talked to a man who was badly beaten by him. By the Phantom, I mean. He'd been one of these red thugs in black bloc during the riots and this brownshirt thug had caught him alone. He said the police acted as if whoever had done it was going to be caught. 'They're not winning anything.' That's what the police said about the Phantom and his friends. I took that to mean that someone of your federal ilk was planted in their ranks, or at least you had an informant in there. I took it to mean that you'd infiltrated their organization."

"Ilk?" said Stan-Stan. "Federal ilk? You disgust me, Winter. Ilk is a vagina word."

"Am I right or not?"

"I can't help you, Winter. This is not like the barely concealed homosexuality beneath my hypermasculinity. This is serious. It's not something I can talk about."

"Look, I don't care about your operations. The fall of the republic is nothing to me. I'm just looking for a girl. Someone I used to know. She's in danger."

"Sorry. I've got to get back to asphyxiating fish. It's not like studying literature. It's the sort of thing men do. If they're real men."

With that, he turned away. Sloshed deeper into the water as Winter stood on shore watching him, frustrated.

"How about this?" Winter called after him. "How about I tell you what I think, and if I'm right, you don't have to say anything. If I'm wrong, maybe you could give me some sort of indication, set me on the right path."

Stan-Stan didn't answer. He had now positioned himself a few yards away with his back to Winter. He began whipping his rod in the air, the line moving against the blue sky, as graceful as the heron's wings.

"At the end of the novel," Winter told him. "The supposed leader of one of the extremist cells turns out to be a federal informant. With his help, the feds stage a raid on the farmhouse where the extremists are hiding out, part of a coordinated series of raids on all the extremist cells set up around the city. The hero of the piece, this blond beast named Moran, has a chance to get away, but he heroically returns to rescue his girlfriend, Miranda. There's a gun battle with the feds, and Moran is riddled with bullets. Before he dies, he delivers a fifty-page-long stream-of-consciousness riff during which he imagines a sort of Valhalla for white men who have defended the values of the master race. It's very stirring stuff, if you happen to be a Nazi. But the tragic irony is that Miranda—the girl he died for—has made a deal with the informant, Frederick Bernard. They escape together and she essentially becomes his prisoner because any time he wants he can turn her in for murder. In the epilogue, we see that she's been forced to become a wife and mother, producing more bourgeois offspring to feed the decadent multiracial capitalist machine in the crumbling ruins of a mongrel society."

He paused and listened for a response from Stan-Stan. Nothing. Only the rippling water and whispering leaves and birdsong. Stan-Stan went on whipping his weightless fly through the air and landing it in various perfect spots offshore.

Winter continued. "But I don't think that's what happened. In real life, I mean. In real life, I think the whole gunfight and monologue and so on is just fascist romanticism. I think Moran—whatever his actual name is—I think he got away."

Again, he gave Stan-Stan a chance to reply. Stan-Stan merely drew back his fly and began to cast again.

Winter pressed on. "I think Moran escaped the feds and disappeared. Maybe Miranda tipped him off to the coming raid, I don't know. But whatever, he was gone. Underground. Maybe out of the country somewhere. But anyway, gone—gone for years."

Another pause. No response. Stan-Stan went on fishing as if Winter weren't there. Winter couldn't tell if the agent was following his instructions or ignoring him.

"Except now," said Winter. "Now he's back. And he wants his Miranda. Maybe to take revenge and kill her. Or maybe to carry her off and bang her into orgasmic Nazi paradise. I don't know. I just know he's dangerous. He found the author of *Treachery in the Night* and tried to torture Miranda's location out of her. He killed her in the process. Then in New York, he tried to kill me in the same way for the same reason. If he does find Miranda, keep or kill, it's not going to be pleasant for her. And the thing is: She matters to me. So I want to find her before he does."

Stan-Stan lofted his fly just wide of a mayfly hatch, the sort of shimmering black blur of insects that hovers above the water, inviting the fish to leap and feed.

"I'm figuring if Frederick Bernard, or whatever his name is, was an informant, you might know where he is, where he's gone to. And if he really did take Miranda as his prisoner wife, that would mean you know where she is too."

Stan-Stan drew the fly back and this time sent it straight into the thick of the hovering hatch. But again, it dropped wide of the mark.

"Eh, that's not going to work," he muttered to himself.

Winter held his breath. Was that an answer? A clue? Was Stan-Stan telling Winter he had gotten something wrong?

"All right," Winter said. He gazed off across the water toward the far trees, thinking. A hawk cried somewhere: *scree, scree!* A warbler of brilliant yellow fluttered down out of the sunlight and vanished among the leaves. "All right," he repeated. "Then if you don't know where the informant is—if you don't know what happened to Frederick Bernard—he must have found another way to relocate."

Stan-Stan went on fishing.

"Let's look at this from a different angle," Winter said. "What if Frederick Bernard was playing both ends? What if he really loved Miranda? He turned the extremists in to take Moran out of the picture. But then he went to his extremist contacts to get a new identity and go somewhere where the feds couldn't find him, and take Miranda down for murder? How about that?"

There was a long sloshing splash as Stan-Stan turned around to face him, thigh-deep in the water. "Are you still here?" he said. "I thought you'd left because you realized it was impossible to get any classified information out of me and also because you understood that if in fact an escaped homicidal fugitive has returned to the country looking to do murder, then a federal police agency of one sort or another has probably been on his trail ever since he butchered the fascist bitch who wrote that stupid novel in the first place. It might also occur to you that said federal agency would have so many lines into the internet communications of these Nazi creeps that the minute said murderer tries to contact one of his old friends to find out his girl's new identity, we'll come pouring down on his head like the bricks of a Philistine temple and should therefore be allowed to do our jobs and hunt this soulless killer down without being interfered with by some pretty-boy intellectual dandy who should be at home explaining rhyme schemes to barely legal college girls."

Winter opened his mouth to answer. But he didn't answer. Because there was no answer. Because, nutty as he was, Stankowski was basically right about this.

The dramatic blood and thunder conclusion to *Treachery in the Night* had clearly been pure fiction. There had been no citywide raids on the extremist cells. No shoot-outs with the police. If there had been, it would have made the news and Winter would have discovered it in the course of his research. It was the violent lunatic Moran the feds had been after from the beginning. And when Frederick Bernard had tipped them off to Moran's whereabouts, they had come for him and he had escaped. Maybe Miranda—Charlotte—had tipped him off. Or maybe not. But in any case, he got out. He lay low for years. And then came back for the love of his life—or for revenge—one or the other. He had killed Susannah Woods in the belief that she had arranged Charlotte's escape. He had come after Winter believing he knew where she'd gone. And—Stan-Stan was right about this too—the murder of Susannah Woods would have tipped the feds off to his return.

Winter felt he should have known all this. He felt he would have known it if he'd been thinking straight. But he'd been in such a haze of emotional pain ever since Charlotte had shown up at his apartment—and even before—he was lucky he was able to walk, let alone think.

He lifted his eyes to Stan-Stan's sunglasses. Was it possible the undercover man had actually grown taller and huskier specifically for this assignment? In any case, Stan-Stan's expression behind his white beard was unreadable. The dark lenses of his shades reflected the dragon-toothed disk of the sun, now risen above the trees. Winter could only gesture helplessly, no argument to make, nothing to say.

"Go home, Winter," Stan-Stan told him. "I say this with all due respect—which, OK, is no respect—but it's true: You look like crap. And when you come to think of it, you are crap. Everything about you is useless and ridiculous, especially in this mental breakdown state you're in. Go home and read poetry and let us do our jobs. We'll get the guy and save the girl, and if that makes you feel inadequate as a man, you can rest assured it's only because inadequate-as-a-man is obviously what you so totally are. Go home."

Winter let out a breath. He blinked as if awaking. As if awaking, he looked around him. Yes, he thought. Yes. Stan-Stan was right. What was he doing here? In the middle of nowhere. This wood. This lake. With nothing to contribute to the case but nostalgic puppy love and mind-rattling neurosis. He nodded. He turned to go.

Then he paused.

"Oh, don't pause," said Stan-Stan in the water behind him. "And don't turn around."

Winter turned around. "Just tell me his name. Moran. Tell me his real name so at least I'll know when it's over, when she's safe. I won't interfere. Do your thing. Just tell me."

Stan-Stan showed Winter his back again. He lifted his rod and began casting his fly again.

"Madigan," he said to the wide-open water. "His name is Henry Madigan. And yes, he's a killer to the bone."

18

Winter returned to campus dragging a sense of failure behind him like it was the corpse of a fat man: useless weight but how do you get rid of it? It had been a long drive down from the north and it was late afternoon when he parked his Jeep in the garage beneath his apartment building. He came out and headed straight for his office in the Gothic without stopping to change out of his hiking clothes.

There was no reason to go to his office really. He'd taught his last class for now, given his last exam. The spring break had started. He had test papers to grade but he could do that from home if he wanted to.

But he didn't feel like going home, like sitting home alone. There was nothing for him to do in the hunt for Charlotte now except wait for news that the feds had tracked down Moran—Madigan—and busted him or killed him. It shouldn't be hard for them to do, he thought. Somebody in the movement must have helped "Frederick Bernard" and Charlotte disappear into thin air as they had. That man—the Identity Man—that's who Madigan would be looking for now. And with the feds tracking the extremists' every move on the internet, the minute he found the guy who'd given Charlotte her new identity, they would know about it.

The campus was all but empty now, the university all but closed. The day was growing cooler as the sun arced down. And as the day dimmed, the atmosphere grew melancholy.

Winter zipped up his shell as he walked. As he came within the shadow of the great castle-like monstrosity that housed his office, he noticed a fairly sizable group of people moving along the sidewalk at the edge of the campus. It looked as if there were a march of some kind going on. Some sort of gathering anyway. He paused outside the Gothic's enormous arched entryway to watch, wondering what it was about.

"Cameron," came a familiar voice behind him.

He turned and was surprised to see Adele Sexton—Reinhold, he reminded himself—Adele Reinhold, Roger Sexton's wife. Something about the look on her face made him hesitate, made him examine her. She must be one of those women who got cold easily, he thought, since she was huddled inside a brown woolen overcoat with a slouchy hat covering her light hair, and yet she was still shivering. He studied her face, wan and tense behind those big glasses of hers.

"Adele," he said uncertainly. "Fancy meeting you here."

"Well. It is the English Department," she said with a faint, sad smile. "I do work here."

"Isn't it the break though?"

She tilted her head. "You're here. And I have papers to grade."

He nodded. He felt certain that Adele had come to her office for the same reason he was heading to his. She didn't want to go home. Why not? he wondered. Had she found out about Roger's affair with young Barbara? Or did he just think that because he knew about it? He wasn't sure. He would have to be careful what he said to her.

She was looking past him at the crowd moving along the sidewalk. He followed her gaze.

"What do you suppose they're up to?" Winter asked her.

"They're going to church," she said. "It's Good Friday."

"Is it?"

They stood together watching the procession a moment. Winter would rather not have spoken, would rather not have asked, but he felt he had to, as a friend. He faced her.

"But that's not why you look so sad, is it?"

"No." She managed a faint smile. "Not a believer. I have enough troubles without worrying about my sins."

"Would you like to take a walk?"

With a sinking heart, he saw her eyes fill behind the distorting lenses. She pressed her lips together hard and quickly slipped her arm in his, an old-fashioned gesture that pleased him.

They walked along the path beside the great building, in the shade of the spring trees. They said nothing for a long time. With Winter carrying his burden of failure and she some sadness of her own, it was enough for them to keep each other company.

After a while, though, she said, "You won't feel sorry for me, will you? I'd hate that. I couldn't stand it, really. I mean, I already know you don't respect me."

"No, no, don't say that, Adele. I respect you a great deal. And I like you a great deal. Truly."

She gave a soggy and unhappy laugh. She leaned her head against his shoulder as they walked. "Oh, you're an old patriarchal relic, and you like me because I keep a good house and enjoy being a mother and I can cook. I know all about you, Cameron Winter."

"You are a wonderful cook," he said.

She laughed, but he could hear the tears at the edge of her voice. He kept his eyes averted out of politeness.

"I meant you don't respect my work," she said. He felt her glance at him, but still looked away. "I wish you did, you know. It would mean a lot to me."

Winter was desperate to come up with a response but found himself completely stymied. He thought Adele's work on Jane Austen was nonsense. Claptrap theories muddied with pseudo-scientific verbiage—completely antithetical to the author's sensible genius and clarity. He silently urged himself to lie but just couldn't make the words come. Another failure to drag around behind him.

"Now it seems I'm not even very good at—" Adele started. That was as far as she got before her voice broke.

Winter walked on, still mired in silence. He wanted to tell her Roger was an idiot to have betrayed her with that dopey piece of fluff. How could he say that though? He still didn't know how much she knew. She might be sad about something else entirely and then he'd have given the game away. On the other hand, if he remained tongue-tied like this, wouldn't that give it away too? This stupid situation was like a web with him fly-like.

Finally, he found a way out. "Tell me what's the matter, Adele," he said.

She sniffed. "You've heard the news, right?"

He did glance at her now. The big glasses magnified the sorrow in her eyes. It made his heart hurt to see how deep it went. "I haven't. No. I've been away. Hiking up north. What's happened?"

"A student has disappeared."

"What? Oh no."

"A girl named Barbara Finley. She'd taken a class from Roger."

Winter opened his mouth, but his mind had rushed ahead of him, trying to compute the ramifications. Barbara had disappeared? Literary man though he was, he had no word to describe what that made him feel. *Terror* was the best he could come up with. He felt as if some deep well of terror had opened up inside him. He was terrified for Adele and Arthur—and for Roger too.

"Apparently, she and her roommate were getting ready to leave for the holiday," Adele went on. "Then Barbara got a frantic call from her mother. She didn't say what it was about. She just rushed out and drove away. That was two days ago, and she hasn't been seen since. Her mother says she doesn't know anything about it. She's worried sick."

Since in Winter's interior world, it was always the year 1795, he did not like to curse in front of a lady, so he swallowed his first reaction and said, "That's awful."

"No one noticed she was gone for a whole day," Adele went on. "Her friends thought she was home. Her parents thought she was here."

They were still walking together, arm in arm—walking in that slow, automatic way people do when they're barely paying attention.

"Awful," Winter murmured again. "I know her."

"Do you?"

"I met her once, yeah."

"Yes, apparently she's *met* a lot of the faculty."

It was a second before he caught her tone. Then he stopped walking. So did she. Her arm slipped from his as he turned to her. They were standing in a pleasant little grove of red maples. The leaves hung down around them on every side, green with spring but growing golden with the falling of the sun.

"No," he said to her earnestly. "It was nothing like that."

Adele gave a bitter little laugh. "Why on earth not? It seems to have been like that for every other male on campus."

"Well, not me. It just wasn't. She was a student . . . I don't know. It just wasn't."

"According to the police, it was a sort of sport with her. Running up a body count, the girls call it now. We used to call it sleeping around, back when it mattered."

"The police," said Winter flatly. That dark well inside him grew deeper, darker.

"Oh yes. Oh yes. They came to our house." The look of anguish and disgust that passed over her features cut right through him. "Oh, Cam, it was so *dreadful!* These two detectives. With these fake . . . pleasant . . . insinuating smiles. Asking these fake, pleasant, insinuating questions. Like we were all just talking about some local tag sale or the weather. When it hit me what they were really asking about . . . this missing girl and whether Roger had . . . *met* her! Poor Roger. I almost pitied him. Standing there with this stupid look on his face, like a boy covered with jam who says he never went near the jam jar. 'Oh, no, she was just a student of mine. I didn't know her that well.' Those awful detectives grinning and nodding. Pretending they believed him. As if anybody could."

"Look, you never know. He might have been telling the truth." The deception came out of Winter's mouth before he even thought about it. He was appalled at how easy it was.

Adele's reaction only made him feel worse. She lifted her big glasses to him, her big, miserable magnified eyes pleading with him. "Please don't. Please. Respect my intelligence at least, Cam."

"Adele . . ."

"I do my little best, but I know I'm not anyone's dream girl."

"Oh, nonsense. You're lovely. Anyway, that's not the only reason a man is faithful to his wife."

"Not in your world maybe, but in the twenty-first century where the rest of us live, that's about the size of it." She went on looking up at him. "Look, I'm a grown woman. I know what men are. If it was just some piece of midlife stupidity, I'll take my pound of flesh out of him and forgive him eventually. But the police seem to think . . . I don't know what they think, but they acted like . . . like this was serious. Like this girl is in danger if she hasn't already been . . . Cam, you don't think Roger would do anything . . . anything terrible, do you?"

Some bluster came out of Winter's mouth, but it didn't quite form itself into words. He stopped making noise and thought about it. His gaze rose over Adele's slouchy hat and into the green and golden leaves around them. What exactly would Roger do when it came down to it? What was he capable of? After all, the man had actually been planning to leave his wife and child over this girl. He had gone to her and told her he loved her and she had laughed at him. He had come to Winter for comfort and advice and Winter, in a bad mood, had mocked and lectured him. Who knew what rage he might have flown into, what atrocity he might have committed in a fit of humiliated passion?

As Adele looked up at him, as he continued to stare at nothing, the expression in her eyes changed from one of pleading to one of fear, as if she also felt that well of terror inside herself.

"Oh my God," she whispered. "How serious was he about this girl?"

Winter didn't answer. He had slipped into a fugue state, that strange habit of mind he sometimes had. It was another moment before Adele's question got through to him. It brought him back to himself. What was it she had asked him? How serious was Roger about Barbara?

He looked down into her frightened face. He remembered how kind she had been to him in his melancholy. A fierce affection for her washed over him—and a fierce sense that he was a man and she was a woman and, this being 1795, he was obligated to protect her from blackguards and cads.

"Do you trust me, Adele?" he asked.

Behind the big glasses, her eyes traveled over his face, trying to read him, trying to decide whether, in fact, she trusted him.

"I don't know. Yes. I mean, there's something hidden, something secret about you, like a whole other Cameron who's nothing like the one I know but . . . yes, in the bigger sense. In fact, I don't think I know anyone I trust more."

"OK. Good. Then listen. This is going to be all right."

She made a strange choking sound and suddenly began to cry. "Is it? Is it?"

"Yes. I promise. Go home to your family. You're a wonderful friend, Adele. A wonderful wife, mother—a wonderful person altogether, and I think the world of you. I really do. And listen. I know I'm not part of your set and everything, but take my advice, all right? The next time Roger lies to you about this, believe him. Forget the pound of flesh. The quality of mercy is not strained. Just believe him. Eventually, he will come to kiss the ground you walk on. As he damned well should."

19

Winter had never been a technical man. He didn't favor a lot of gizmos. Even during his time in the Division, there had been support staff to handle that sort of thing. But there was one device he had recently acquired for his own innocent purposes: a tracker. He found it incredibly useful. He kept it in his computer case so he could track the case whenever he forgot it somewhere, which he often did. So when he left Adele, it was no trouble at all for him to take the tracker out of the case and attach it to a car before dark fell. Then he went back to his apartment and waited for the car to move.

It happened when he thought it would: near nine o'clock, about an hour after nightfall. The blip on his tracking app started to flash and travel. A few moments later, Winter was in his Jeep SUV again, following the signal out of town.

It wasn't a long drive. He hadn't expected it would be. Thirty minutes of two-lane north and he entered a drab main street of a small village. A couple of traffic signals and a mall created an island of dim light in the surrounding darkness. He was past the island in a moment, and out on the shadowy curling lanes of a tidy suburb, one gray house after another, one lawn after another, all within sight of a small lake, a patch of blackness reflecting a sliver of moon.

The signal led him on. Soon, he had left the suburban village behind. He was in a nest of scraggly trees. The houses here were no longer gray, no longer trim. They were neglected vacation cabins, each standing slanted and ragged in a little nowhere of its own. It was by one of these cabins, in a shadowy and secluded spot, that his signal came to rest.

Winter shut his headlights off and coasted slowly through the darkness. He parked a hundred yards away from his destination and slipped from his car. He walked quietly along the edge of the pavement. The spring night had turned cool. He had changed into jeans and a sweater beneath his windbreaker. His ivy cap was perched on his head. His dark clothing blended with the night.

One dim yellow light guided him to the cabin he wanted. In the glow, he made out the Prius parked in the dirt drive amid a cluster of bedraggled trees. As he neared, he heard the cabin door open. He saw the light spill out from within. He stopped where he was to keep the shadows wrapped around him. He stood with his hands in his jacket pockets and watched as Roger Sexton's department chairman, Devesh Khan, came outside.

The shape of the scrawny, ugly little man was enlarged by his clothing: a padded autumn jacket and a watch cap on his head. He left the cabin door open, only the screen door in place. He moved over a short dirt path to his car, opened the rear door, and stuck his head in. When he emerged from the Prius, he was holding a brown paper supermarket bag. He carried it back to the house.

Winter moved quickly then. He angled off the road and onto the sparse grass to muffle his footsteps. He was under the trees as Devesh reached the front door. When Devesh pulled open the front screen, Winter was right behind him, so quietly he never knew. Only when they were both inside, when Winter caught the closing door, when Devesh noticed that he hadn't heard the door swing shut behind him—only then did Devesh spin around and see him.

His shocked reaction would have been comical slapstick if it hadn't been for what followed. Devesh let out a high-pitched womanish cry and staggered backward, his bag dropping to the floor as his arms pinwheeled wildly.

Winter tried to rush him, but a collection of fruits and vegetables spilled out of the bag and blocked his path. A grapefruit, two apples, and four tomatoes all came rolling toward him, slowing his forward progress.

Devesh, meanwhile, was frantically unzipping his coat and reaching inside. He tripped over the edge of a coffee table and fell backward, sitting down hard on a dumpy sofa. At last, he managed to wrangle an automatic pistol out of his belt. He leaped up off the sofa and stuck the gun out in the direction of Winter's heart.

"Get out! Get out!" he cried. His voice was still high-pitched with panic.

There was a small dining table over by the living room window. There was a small lamp on the table. The lamp was lit—the only light in the place. It cast a dim, shadow-riddled glow over everything.

"Get out or I'll kill you, Cameron," Devesh shouted at him. The two men were close together, barely a foot apart. The gun was a Beretta .45. At that distance, with a slug that big, Winter judged Devesh might actually hit him if he pulled the trigger.

"Put that down, Devesh," said Winter. "You're not going to kill me."

"You think I won't? I could lose everything. I have to kill you."

"Really? How are you going to get rid of my body?"

Taken aback by the question, Devesh tried to think: How *would* he get rid of the body? As he thought about it, his eyes shifted down and to the left. Winter seized the opportunity to snap the pistol out of his hand and hit him in the head with the butt end.

Devesh was no great beauty at even the best of times, but when his eyes flew up in his head and his tongue jutted out of his mouth, the sight of him was downright painful to look upon. He dropped back onto the sofa and rolled off onto the floor. He lay there face down, groaning in pain.

Winter, annoyed, stalked angrily across the room to a doorway. He reached along the wall and flicked on the light. Here was the kitchen, cramped and grimy. There was another door here, a cellar door. It was locked with a keypad lock.

Winter marched back into the living room. Devesh was struggling to get up. Clutching his head with one hand, he grabbed hold of the coffee table with the other and pulled himself to a sitting position, his back against the couch.

"What's the keypad code?" Winter asked him.

"Listen to me. Listen to me, Cameron," Devesh said. He closed his eyes tightly as he rubbed the bruise on his temple. "You have to understand. She's the love of my life. She means everything to me. I'm willing to do anything to keep her."

Winter laughed.

Devesh could only open his eyes slightly. He flinched with pain when he moved his head so he could look up at where Winter stood above him. "Just listen. Seriously. Taka2. It's going to be worth billions. You understand? You can have a piece of that. A big piece. You'll be rich. All you have to do is walk away and you will be a rich man forever."

"Walk away? You mean, you want me to leave a girl locked up in your cellar so you can rape her?" Winter asked him. "Let me explain something to you, Devesh: No. Now what's the keypad number?"

"I won't tell you! I won't tell you! She's mine!"

Winter grew even more annoyed. He sneered. He grabbed the coffee table with one hand and flung it across the room, exposing

Devesh's legs. "She's not yours. That doesn't even make any sense. Tell me the number or I will shoot you in the kneecap. I've seen this done, Devesh. It's incredibly painful. What's the keypad number?"

"Please! Please! Let me keep her! She's the love of my life!"

Winter pulled the trigger. The sound of the gunshot was so loud it seemed as if the entire house had exploded. The bullet struck the base of the sofa about two inches from Devesh's shoulder. Devesh let out a babbling, hysterical shriek. He covered his head with his hands for some reason.

"The number," said Winter.

"Seven eight six three." Devesh began to sob.

"Is she chained up or something? Do I need keys?"

Devesh cried uncontrollably. Winter gestured angrily with the pistol. Cowering, Devesh fished his key ring out of his pocket. He held it out weakly. Winter snatched it from him.

"Please. Please. Please. Let me keep her," Devesh sobbed. "She is the love of my life. Please."

Winter strode back into the kitchen. He was wild eyed. He was muttering to himself: " 'Let me keep her.' She's not a pony, you jackass. She's a person. You can't keep a person. That's what the word *person* means. What is it you computer geeks don't understand about the English language?"

He keyed the code into the pad and pulled the basement door open. The smell of fear and feces wafted out of the darkness to him. Angry as he was, his heart nonetheless softened with sorrow for the suffering of the girl down there.

He found a light switch. Flicked it. The lights went on downstairs. Immediately, he heard the girl trying to cry out. By the sound of her muffled squeals, he could tell that Devesh had gagged her. He briefly considered going back into the living room and shooting Devesh in the face. But as appealing as that idea was, he had to get this girl out of her makeshift prison first. He stomped down the rickety wooden stairs.

It was a bad scene. Barbara was naked and chained to the iron frame of the bed. Her hands were cuffed behind her. There was just enough length of chain to allow her to reach the latrine bucket in the corner. Every wall of the room had been covered in concrete in order to seal her in.

The look in the girl's white eyes went well beyond terror into mad frenzy. She continued to let out pitiful muffled shrieks behind the duct tape. Devesh had put the tape over her mouth and then wrapped it around her head.

"It's all right," Winter said. "It's me. I'm going to help you."

He unlocked the cuffs. She flung them off into the corner as if they were on fire. She scrabbled wildly at the duct tape, trying to get it off her mouth. Winter knelt at her feet and unlocked the shackle on her ankle to free her from the chain. She unwound the duct tape and threw it after the cuffs. She started to scream and babble. Nonsense words poured out of her as if she were a toddler.

Winter stood up. He turned his back to her and stripped off his windbreaker. He handed it to her while still turned away so as not to look at her nakedness.

"Put that on, Barbara," he said. "Tell me when you're dressed and I'll get you out of here."

He heard the tenor of her cries change. She began to weep in anguish as any woman might. Winter thought again about shooting Devesh. He was dangerously close to being serious this time. He was no amateur in such matters. He knew exactly how he'd dispose of Devesh's body. The bastard's disappearance would remain one of those mysteries they make TV shows about.

"All right," Barbara managed to say.

Winter turned and found her looking tiny and fragile under the tent of his jacket. He lay a hand softly on her shoulder. "Come on," he said.

He helped the sobbing girl up the stairs. When she saw Devesh sitting on the floor, still forlorn, still sobbing himself, she went wild and leaped at him in a tigerish rage. Winter only just managed to get his arm around her middle and hold her back before she tore the man to pieces. She fought against his grip, screaming the foulest curses. Winter wasn't entirely sure he shouldn't let her go, but he judged this to be the sort of situation where it was best to follow the established order of things. He wasn't thinking so clearly that he could trust his own creative choices.

Eventually Barbara's strength gave out. She collapsed against Winter's arm. He held her to him and stroked her hair while she cried. He drew her over to the table and gently sat her down in one of the chairs.

"Don't you understand: you're the love of my life," Devesh cried out to her.

"Devesh," said Winter. "Stop talking. I'm this close to shooting you. Don't talk anymore."

"But I . . ."

"Devesh. I mean it now."

Devesh fell silent, crying and sniveling. The girl slumped in the chair, her head hung down. She shook as she wept.

Winter took out his phone and punched in 911.

Devesh reacted with shock and fear. "You're calling the police?"

"Of course I'm calling the police," said Winter. "You abducted and raped this woman. The police are who you call when that happens. That's what the word *police* means."

He reached a state trooper and gave him the location.

"My life is ruined," Devesh wailed.

"Devesh, I'm not going to tell you again," Winter said.

Barbara lifted her head. Her features contorted with savage rage. "I hope they rape him to death in prison," she snarled.

"Well, you can put on a happy face because they probably will," said Winter.

"You hear that? They're going to rape you to death," Barbara told Devesh.

Devesh raised his eyes in appeal to Winter. Winter gave him a warning look. If the man said he loved Barbara again, or complained about his miserable fate, he really was going to blow his brains out.

But what Devesh said was: "I planned so carefully. How did you even find me?"

Winter snorted. He nodded toward Barbara. "She told her roommate she got a call from her mother. She'd recognize her mother's voice. She's not going to get that wrong. So I figured it was your stupid AI thing doing an imitation, like you had it doing at the Sextons' dinner party. That meant it was either you or Roger who called her away. I didn't think either of you would kill her, not in cold blood like that, so that made it an abduction. That would take time and planning, somewhere to hide her. Your wife said she was going to see her mother for spring break, so this would be the perfect opportunity for you to make your move. So I put a tracker on your car and waited."

That reminded him: he had to retrieve the tracker and stow it in his glove compartment before the police found it. He could hear their sirens in the distance now. They were growing louder quickly.

"They're going to put me in prison!" Devesh wailed.

"You're going to die there!" said Barbara.

"Give me the gun, Cameron. I will kill myself. Please," said Devesh.

"Don't give it to him," cried Barbara. "Don't give it to him. I want him to suffer before he dies."

"Don't worry," Winter told her.

To his great relief, victim and criminal both fell silent then. They all three sat still and listened to the sirens come. Winter glanced at the girl. She was hugging his windbreaker tightly around her. She was staring into space, her whole body trembling violently.

Winter felt the sight of her in that condition would break his heart. At the same time, he had an urge to say something stern and paternal to her. Something on the order of *Let this be a lesson to you, young lady*. But even in his discombobulated state, he was pretty certain this was a very bad idea. Anyway, he didn't have the first clue what the lesson would be.

He was glad to see the red lights of the patrol cars flashing at the window.

PART FOUR

THE IMAGE OF A FEELING SOUL

*B*ear with me. I'm almost at the end of this story. It matters. It explains some things. It's part of how I got here.

So where was I? Hamza. The chauffeur, remember? We found him dead in the trunk of the car. Poisoned with poison that was meant for me. So there he was and there was Jerry standing next to me sobbing like a child.

I turned to him—Jerry, not the chauffeur obviously, the chauffeur was dead—I turned to Jerry and roughed him up a little. Nothing dramatic. I grabbed the front of his stupid white tracksuit in my fist and shook him.

"Pull yourself together," I told him.

"I didn't mean for this to happen, Winter, I swear," he said again. "They wanted to know the chief's favorite agent. That's all I told them."

I shook him again. "Shut up and pull yourself together."

That was it. I released him after that. I couldn't very well beat the sense back into him.

"We've got to get out of here," I said.

"What? I can't. Where would I go?"

"What do you mean where? We've got to get home. Back to DC. We've got to report to the chief. Tell him what we found."

"But . . ." He gestured back toward the villa, back toward the hidden trophy room with its lurid photographs. "The chief might be part of it. I'm part of it now."

I shook my head. "The chief's not part of any of that."

"How do you know?"

"I just know," I said. "And you—well . . . you might go to prison, Jerry. And given the people in those photographs and how powerful they

are, you might never get out of prison alive. So you might as well get used to being dead because if you stay here they're going to kill you too. In fact, they're probably on their way here to kill you right now. So all in all, you'll live longer if you get in the car."

He continued to stand where he was, red eyed, gaping at me stupidly. I got tired of trying to explain it to him. I turned back to the trunk instead. I reached down and grabbed Hamza's corpse by his jacket lapels. I dragged the body out of the car and dumped it on the ground where it sent up a cloud of dust.

"Get in the car, Jerry," I said again. Jerry just stood there, staring at me. "Last chance. Because I'm getting out of here."

I slammed the trunk lid. Walked to the driver's door. Got in behind the wheel and started the engine. For a second, I thought Jerry would stay behind. I thought: Let him. But finally the passenger door opened and he dropped into the seat beside mine. I hit the gas and took off.

We descended the mountain through the forest. I remember the blue sky and the sun coming down through the leaves in beams. It looked like columns of light standing all around us, like we were driving through the gleaming ghost of an ancient temple. I drove in silence, trying to think things through. What had happened here? What did they want? And who were they? Jerry stared ahead through the windshield, dazed, like he'd been smacked in the forehead with a shovel.

"I don't know what to think anymore, Winter. I swear I don't," he said after a while. "All those people in those pictures. They're important. Powerful people. Do you think Kemal controls all of them?"

I shook my head. "Not Kemal. Kemal Balkin's no international player. He's just a fat businessman, raking in coin. He's a middleman for someone else."

"You mean someone else controls those people, but not him?"

"That's my guess."

"Someone outside the US?"

"I don't know. Or inside. I don't know."

He turned his face to me. I glanced at it. His thousand-yard stare: that empty look soldiers get when they've seen more battle than a man's mind can stand.

"All those men—you think they'd sell out their country just to keep people from finding out the sex stuff they do?"

I snorted. "Did you see those pictures?" I asked him. "To keep those pictures secret, I think those bastards would burn down the world."

He nodded, still staring that stare. "When you're doing it, it's like it isn't real. You think it won't be real if no one else sees."

I didn't answer. I left him alone with his thoughts.

"It's not true though," he went on. "It's not true no one sees. God sees. Doesn't he?"

I still didn't answer. But he asked me again: "Doesn't he?"

"I don't know. How the hell do I know what God does?"

"He sees, Winter. He sees all the terrible things we do."

I sighed. "It'd be pretty hard for him to miss them."

He was staring ahead now, staring at nothing as far as I could tell. "You know what's funny?"

I did not know what was funny and I said so.

"What's funny," said Jerry, "is I don't even know why I did it."

"Why you did what? Banged some kids? That's the thing about sex crimes," I said. "Everyone has a motive."

"I mean, what could I believe in after what I'd seen? Those pictures in the trophy room. And if you can't believe in anything, what difference does it make what you do?"

He went quiet again and so did I. The car wound down the long hill. My eyes scanned the woods around us, peering through the columns of sunlight. I don't know what I was looking for exactly. I kept thinking someone would be coming after us, but I didn't know how or when. Might be in secret or out in the open. Might be any minute or it might be a while.

I might be wrong too. It might never happen. But at that moment, I wouldn't have bet a dollar on our chances of getting out of the country alive.

"It's the chief they want, isn't it?" Jerry Collins murmured then. "That's why they tried to kill you. They knew the chief would send you—send someone he trusts—and they wanted him to understand: They were inside the Division. They wanted to let him know he was not protected. There was no one he could trust."

"Whoever's behind Kemal," I said. "Maybe the Division is the only thing left he doesn't control."

Jerry's mouth opened as if he were about to respond, but he didn't say anything, not at first. At first, he just gave a small puff of air and kind of—I don't know what to call it. He smirked, I guess. I guess that's what it was. I remember thinking it looked strange on that boyish all-American face of his.

"Or maybe not," he said. "Maybe they do control it. Maybe this was the chief's way of getting rid of you. A masterpiece hit. Sure. Maybe you can't trust the chief either."

"I can trust him."

"Maybe. But maybe not. I mean, what are you going to do when he sends you out to do a hit on some American, some senator or some journalist. Someone he thinks has gone rogue. Will you do it because you believe he's fighting back? How will you know he isn't working for the bad guys?"

I didn't answer. I didn't have an answer.

We got down the hill. We drove through the wilderness. We expected to see assassins in our rearview any minute. But we didn't. All the same, we ditched the car just to be safe. We made our way on foot to a nameless little cluster of houses that looked like it had been there since Jesus's days. We stocked up on supplies and made our way to the coast, and from there, to Athens.

Or I did anyway. Not Jerry.

I don't know when it happened exactly. We were on the last leg of the journey, in the cargo hold of a freighter in the Dardanelles. There's a city there right at the narrowest point, a place called Çanakkale. It's close to Troy—the site of Troy, you know, where the war was. I don't know why, but I had this sort of mystic urge to see the place. The place where everything began, I guess, if you care about the stuff I care about.

Anyway, at that point, we were about to reach the Aegean, so I figured we had lost anyone who was chasing us if anyone was. I came up on deck and looked over the side. There was this huge Trojan horse on display, right in front of me. I found it touching after our journey, after what I'd seen in the trophy room, after what had happened to Jerry and his faith and patriotism. It gave me the sense—the sentimental sense—that nothing is ever lost, you know, not really, that we still might go back to the beginning of things and start fresh.

I found out later the horse was a life-size prop from a movie. Such is life.

Anyway, I was standing there, looking out at the scene, and I spotted a movement down below, a figure moving through the small crowd of tourists—and damned if it didn't look to me for all the world like Jerry Collins. He'd been with me, we'd been having a conversation, not half an hour before. But now, when I went back down into the hold to find him, he was nowhere in sight. He was gone—gone completely.

I went on to Athens alone and caught a plane from there back to the States.

I was in my apartment exactly ten minutes—I didn't even have time to change my shirt—when I was summoned to meet the Recruiter again. Same place as our last meeting, out on the path by the Potomac. Same time even, just around dusk with the autumn light dying.

It was cold that night, I remember—cold and damp. There'd been rain in the morning and we had to skirt puddles all along the way. The Recruiter and I walked side by side, heading toward Mount Vernon. I told him everything that had happened. All of it, step by step, just like I've told you. I recited the name of every man in those pictures in Kemal Balkin's trophy room. Now and then, after mentioning one name or another, I glanced over at him to check his reaction. Which was a waste of time, of course. With that deadpan expression of his, how could I ever know what he was thinking about anything?

So we kept walking, side by side. Not a word did we speak and the dark folded over us.

What the Recruiter finally said was: "So Jerry Collins lost his faith, did he?"

"Seems that way," I said.

"He lost his faith and now he thinks there's no God."

"Yes."

He puffed a curt laugh out of one side of his mouth. "It's a good thing he didn't lose his faith in France. Where would we get our merlot?"

Weary as I was, I laughed.

"Yes, you can afford to laugh," the Recruiter said with a sigh. "Your mindless unbelief protects you from the pain of disillusionment. You're like a chimpanzee who's in no danger of losing his faith in science simply because some scientists are found to be corrupt. Or to put it another way, the conformist stupidity of your materialism is like a condom over your head: it may suffocate you, but at least nothing will get in there that might cause labor pains."

"Gee, thanks, chief," I muttered. "I'm a chimpanzee with a condom on his head. Keep flattering me like that, and I'll follow you anywhere."

"I don't see what else you can do. If the most powerful men in our country are potentially compromised by enemies either foreign or domestic or some combination of the two, you're left with nothing to believe in besides me, aren't you? It's lucky for you your inchoate pseudophilosophy of life leaves you with no reasonable grounds for self-respect, or you'd find yourself pathetic when you weren't ridiculous."

I nodded into the dark of night. "Funnily enough, Jerry said pretty much the same thing before he disappeared on me. He said you might start sending me out on hits against senators or journalists on the excuse that they were enemies within the gates, and I'd have no way of knowing whether you were telling the truth or simply protecting your own position, whether I was still fighting for my country or just committing cold-blooded murder."

"Well, he was right about that anyway," said the Recruiter quietly. "It's a good thing you have no logical basis on which to build the foundation of a moral outlook, otherwise you might find yourself in the sort of dilemma that could drag a thinking man into a bottomless vortex of suicidal madness."

"Well, thanks for saying so, but that's actually less reassuring than you might think."

I glanced his way again, but he wasn't there anymore. Startled, I stopped. I cursed. Had he vanished again? No. When I searched the night, I found him standing on the path a few yards behind me. With his hands in the pockets of his overcoat, he was gazing through the trees at the river. The water was dark and the woods were dark. The rain clouds beyond the trees were silver with moonlight. The Recruiter's face was obscure in the new-fallen night, but then, it would have been obscure in broad daylight too. Who could ever know the man?

After a few seconds, he drew a deep breath and faced me.

"Kemal Balkin owns some very powerful people in our government," he said quietly. "And someone, somewhere, here or abroad, owns Kemal. Is that pretty much the long and short of it?"

"Pretty much, yes, sir," I said.

"Well then," he answered with a sigh. "It seems we have our work cut out for us, don't we, Poetry Boy?"

What happened next, the way I remember it—to be honest, I'm not sure if it really happened or not. Memory can do that. Rewrite things. But if it happened any other way, it's not in my mind anymore. There's just the memory now.

What I remember is that I was looking right at him when he said that, that thing about having work to do. I was looking straight at his silhouette there on the path beneath the trees. One moment, there was his distinctive shape before me in the darkness.

The next moment, there was nothing there. Nothing but the night.

20

Once again, Margaret let Winter talk himself into silence. It was frustrating for her. She was a patient woman. Being patient was part of her job. But he could push her to her limits. She had read the news stories over the Easter weekend. About the girl tied up in the cellar. About the head of the university's prestigious artificial intelligence project in jail, charged with kidnapping and rape. The story had topped the local and state news shows and was even featured on some of the national sites during the slow holidays. And this time, Winter hadn't managed to keep himself out of the picture. He had done his best to minimize his role in the affair. He avoided interviews. He said only that he had grown suspicious of his friend Devesh Khan and had followed him to the cabin where he found a poor young woman trussed up and hysterical. But the police report added some stirring details to the story: the fact that Khan had pulled a gun on the English professor, that the two men had wrestled for the weapon, that a shot was fired before the struggle ended. Margaret doubted that had been much of a wrestling match. Still, it made Winter the hero of the tale.

So the fact that Winter could come in here and plunk himself down in her office chair and start talking about . . . Turkey! Well, it was irksome, to use a polite word for it. It made the therapist want to take him by the shoulders and shake him until he stopped droning on about the Trojan horse and whatever else he was prattling about. Only the instincts formed over forty years of therapeutic practice allowed her to hold her tongue and wait until he exhausted himself.

Finally, he sat quiet, slumped in the armchair. He looked quite awful, she thought. His posture was collapsed in on itself. His gaze was blank and faraway. His stare—what had he called it?—that thousand-yard stare—when a man has seen more battle than he can stand—how could she not feel some tenderness and compassion for him, frustrated as she was.

"I read about you in the news," she said gently from the height of her therapist's swivel chair.

He gave a small, unhappy grunt. "That's it? You don't want to find out more about how the entire leadership class of your country has been compromised by a fat Turk and his shadowy masters?"

"I thought you were very brave," she went on. "I was very proud of you."

She was gratified to see that he had to struggle to keep from smiling at that. "Beating up computer geeks is not that difficult, Margaret. In fact, it's a regular part of my workout routine."

"I'm curious," Margaret said. "Was this man, this artificial intelligence man, Devesh, was he the friend you told me about? The one who was going to leave his wife for a younger woman?"

Winter massaged his eyes, bringing himself out of his memories. "No. No. It was the same girl, but a different geek."

"Oh my. Sounds like she got around."

He made a quiet noise. "Yeah, you could say that. I do imagine I'll hear from my friend sooner or later. No idea what effect this'll have on him."

"Oh, I think it'll wake him right up most likely."

"Do you? I would be glad of that. I hate to think he might still leave his wife. She's the best thing about him."

"Well, there are no guarantees. But my guess is if she'd like to remodel her kitchen this would be a good time to ask."

Margaret was gratified again, because now Winter straightened a little, brightened just a little.

"That would be good," he said, nodding to himself. "That would be something almost like a happy ending."

"Good," said Margaret. "Now—tell me what's happening with Charlotte."

He shook his head ruefully. "God, you're relentless. It's like having a bloodhound for a therapist."

"Somehow I'm going to find a way to take that as a compliment."

He made a distracted gesture. "I'm off the Charlotte case. I met with a contact of mine in federal law enforcement. He says they're on top of it. This bad guy who's after her—Madigan—they've apparently been hunting him for years. The way they figure it, he'll eventually contact whoever gave Charlotte her new identity, someone he knows, part of the movement he's in. And since the feds are hooked into the extremist computer networks every which way, as soon as the bad guy tries to contact them, they'll round him up. Another happy ending, such as it is."

"Not very happy to have your old flame involved with people like that, though, is it?"

He shrugged. Margaret did not find that very convincing. "One extreme was evil so she went to the other. 'Turning and turning in the widening gyre . . . mere anarchy is loosed upon the world.'"

"And where does that leave our sad and solitary hero Cameron Winter?"

He managed a small smile, but she did not find that very convincing either. "You're a wonderful therapist, Margaret, but you can't fix everything."

Margaret took a moment before responding to that. She steepled her fingers under her chin. She swiveled slightly back and forth in her chair. She felt painfully aware of her love for the man, all its motherly depths and inappropriate jags of desire, the whole messy business. It was just the sort of thing that might muddy her motives and lead her into a stupid mistake. At the same time, she could feel—and she could see by the ruined look of him—that his soul, if that was the word she wanted, was so near the surface right now that she could almost hold it in her hands. He was right, of course. She couldn't fix everything. But she could do a great deal of damage trying to fix whatever she could. She knew she had to seize this moment of emotional crisis—but softly, softly.

"What?" said Winter. He could tell she was working toward something. Some strategy of approach.

Margaret let out a steadying breath. "I was thinking . . ." she said. "As you were telling your story—about Turkey and the trophy room and so on—I was thinking how that story and this story about the girl in the basement and the story about Charlotte too—about how they all had the same sorts of underlying themes in a way. They're all stories about desire, aren't they? Obsessive desire. Desire for youth particularly. They're stories about the way passion adheres to the past—or to lost time, that might be a better way to say it. Like Gatsby looking at the green light."

She watched as Winter's eyes flicked left then right, as if she had cornered him somehow. Maybe she had.

"Doesn't everything have those themes?" he asked her. "Desire. Obsession. Lost time. Aren't those the only themes there are?"

"Oh no. Not at all. There are many other themes in life. Many that are more important too. But not in your life. You're like a passenger in a train on a circular track. You keep looking out the window and seeing the same scenery go by and you think that's the only scenery there is."

"I don't know. It doesn't really make sense," he muttered glumly. "I didn't make Devesh kidnap that girl. How can all the things that happen to me have the same themes?"

"Because you're the organizing principle. You're the one telling the story. Either that or you're a character in a novel being written by God."

Winter snorted. "God."

"Yes. You remember God. Large Jewish fellow? Long white beard? Lives in the clouds?"

That got a laugh out of him—and Margaret laughed, pleased to see him look almost like himself for a moment. It gave her hope for him, and for the work she was doing.

He waved his hand in front of his face, as if to clear his vision. "All right, Margaret. I give up. What's your point here?"

"Well . . . do you remember what I told you about Charlotte?"

Already, he had slumped again. Weary, forlorn, staring that thousand-yard stare. He nodded heavily. "Yes, yes. You told me it wasn't that I couldn't find love because I was obsessed with her, but that I was obsessed with her because I couldn't find love."

"That's right. And what else?"

"That it wasn't really her I was obsessed with. That she—her image in my mind—had become a vessel for all kinds of meaning."

"Any thoughts about what that meaning might be?"

"Oh. Oh, I see where you're going. Lost time and the past and all that."

"Yes. But try to be more specific. It's your lost time after all, not just anyone's."

He sighed heavily. Wearily. Forlornly. "All right." He looked into the space between them, avoiding her gaze. "Charlotte, you know, was practically a child when I knew her. And I was even more of a child. And she was kind to me. And I loved her. And I . . . I gave her something of myself. Something I gave to no one else. I trusted her to keep it safe. And when she left, I guess, she took it with her. And now that she's come back . . ." He hesitated on the brink.

"What?" said Margaret.

"I'm afraid," said Winter.

"Yes. You are afraid, aren't you?"

"I'm afraid of finding that thing again. That thing I gave her."

"What thing? What thing is it, Cam?"

Now he did raise his eyes. He met her gaze with his. As long as she'd been doing this, as much experience as she had, there was still something shocking about the naked feelings of a man like this. She saw his lip tremble, and she felt it, she felt a tightening in her throat.

"My soul," he said. "There's no sense mincing words. I gave her my soul for safekeeping. My feeling soul."

"Yes. Yes, I think that's right," Margaret said.

"And she became the thing I gave her. In my mind. She became the image of my feeling soul, and when she left . . ."

"She took it with her. Or that is, her image carried it down into the darkness of your inner self."

"I stopped feeling anything. Because I couldn't stand the pain of losing her. Which, after all, was just the pain of moving on, the pain of life, the pain of simply living in the world."

"Yes."

"And that's how I made myself a killer. Not how, but why. So I could test the coldness of my heart on death. So I could truly become this stony thing I've made myself. All dead inside."

"Not dead, sweetheart. Buried, yes, but not dead."

His mouth twisted convulsively. "No, no, no. Whatever soul I ever had, I don't think I could bear to bring it back now. I really don't. To come to life and see myself, so drenched in blood. To feel, to really feel, the things I've done. Or to let someone else see me or . . ."

"Love you," said Margaret. "If you can't stand to see yourself or love yourself how could you ever let someone else see you or love you or accept your love. Someone, say, like Gwendolyn Lord."

"I don't think I could bear it."

"Oh, but you can though. You will. Bear it, I mean. I know you, Cam. You were built to live, or you would not be here. You were not made to go loveless into oblivion, or you would not be in this room with me, looking for what you lost. Looking for Charlotte. But . . ."

The look he gave her then . . . later that day, when she had time to consider it, she thought that expression of his might have been the single most poignant thing she had ever seen. He looked so lost, almost childlike, so desperate for any direction from her, any hint of a direction out of the petrified forest of his heart.

"But what?" he said to her—so quietly she could barely hear him. "I was made to live, but what?"

"But first you have to find her."

"Find her?" he said, as if in a daze—in a fog—in a dark wood.

"Charlotte. The real woman. So you can separate your soul from her image. Break the vessel of the image, so to speak, and set yourself free to feel . . . well, everything. Shame, guilt, loss, love, life, the whole disaster."

She watched, heartsore, as the meaning of her words slowly seeped into his mind. He blinked, then blinked again.

"Oh my God," he whispered. "Oh my God, Margaret, what have I done?"

"Well, yes. I mean, really, Cam," Margaret said. "Some crazy federal agent friend of yours tells you to stop looking for her, and you just do it, just give up, just stop? That's not like you at all."

"He said they were on it," he murmured in a tone of dull amazement. "Stan-Stan. He said there was an Identity Man among the extremists. That this killer, Moran—Madigan—he would go to the Identity Man and then the feds would be waiting."

"And you just believed him."

"I . . ." said Winter.

The pain of watching him struggle through his own defenses was intense—like watching a small child struggle through an illness. "Well, this sort of thing isn't in my line, you know," Margaret went on. "Spies and killers and extremists and so on. I mostly deal with the minor neuroses of the middle class. But it just seems to me—if the police knew who this so-called Identity Man was, they would know where Charlotte was, wouldn't they? And if they thought Charlotte had been complicit in the murder of Eddie-her-boyfriend and they knew where she was, wouldn't they have arrested her already?"

"Oh my God," Winter whispered again. "You're right. They have no idea where she is. Which means they don't know who the Identity Man is. Which means Madigan could find him first, and they would never know. And then Charlotte would be unprotected. Oh my God, Margaret. What have I done?" he repeated.

"It's all right, dear. You've been under the weather, psychologically speaking. I'm sure you would have seen it yourself if you'd been at your best."

Winter raised both his hands and pushed his long golden hair back from his face. The hair, the face, Margaret had always thought, of an angel in a Renaissance painting. She could not take her eyes off it.

"But . . ." he murmured. "But you said . . . you said I shouldn't . . . you told me I wasn't up to it. You said I was . . . I don't remember. Some stupid therapy word."

"Decompensating."

"Yes. And my skills would be eroded, that I would be no match for a ruthless killer like Madigan. You said, Margaret . . ."

Margaret managed a smile. It was meant to be both tender and encouraging, something he could remember if the worse should come to the worst and he should reach Charlotte too late. She spoke to him very gently.

She said: "Since when does a big, strong man like you take advice from a nervous old biddy like me?"

21

Winter was frantic now. He told himself he had to think. But he couldn't think. How could anyone think with his head jammed like rush hour? A bottleneck of specters and fears. The uprising past, and the oncoming Madigan, and his own shuddering state of mind were all gridlocked together in a chaos of interior noise. How could he think at all when he was so busy going mad?

He hurried from Margaret's office and up the main street toward campus. The weather was pale and fine. With the university closed for the break, and the state government on hiatus, the sidewalks were all but empty. The happy bunnies and the colored eggs and the other blue and white Easter decorations watched him from the shop windows as he rushed past, like ghosts themselves now that the holiday had come and gone.

"Winter!"

Winter started at the sound of his name. A colleague named Brad Halliday had blocked his way. A smallish, baldish man, with a grayish goatee. A professor of comp lit. A Marxist theorist. He had managed to write an entire book about *Paradise Lost* without making a single honest observation. Winter had almost admired the purity of it.

Winter stopped and stared at him as if he had just awoken from a deep sleep.

"Well, that was quite a thing!" said Halliday with a brittle grin. The lenses of his glasses flashed in the soft spring sunlight. "Good for you for putting a stop to it. Real Boy's Adventure stuff. I didn't know you had it in you."

Winter didn't understand at first—then he realized the man was talking about Devesh and Barbara, the story in the news. He knew Halliday despised him. His congratulations were bristling with hostility.

"Oh. Oh, yes," Winter said in a poor imitation of normal conversation. "Crazy, right?"

"Not as crazy as the lawsuit the family will bring against us. The dean must be apoplectic. You'll be lucky if you don't lose your job, my friend. It's not like you have tenure, remember."

Winter stared at him stupidly. The image of Barbara in Devesh's cellar—the gut-clenching pathos of the sight of her there, and the smell—were still vivid in his mind, awful, nauseating.

"What the hell was Devesh thinking?" said Halliday.

Winter nodded blandly. He gave Halliday what he hoped was a collegial slap on the shoulder. Then he hurried away as fast as he could, afraid he might start to rave like the lunatic he felt he was on the verge of becoming.

He was stopped twice more before he reached campus. A woman he did not even know recognized him from the news. She was very small and old. She stood in front of him and wagged her finger up at him as if she were scolding him, as if it were he who had chained a woman in his cellar, not Devesh. Her puckered mouth moved, but he had no idea what she was saying. He just kept answering her, "Yes, yes, yes," until he could break free.

After that, the bartender from the Nomad Tavern saw him go past and came out onto the sidewalk and called after him. The bartender was a ponytailed hipster in his forties. He shook his head like a man of the world as he mused upon the staggering seductive powers of women and the puttylike brains of men. The dazed and frantic Winter also shook his head like a man of the world, though not perhaps of this world. Once again, he seized the first break in the conversation to hurry off.

He reached the campus. Headed up the main path, majestic buildings lining either side beyond the slender trees. Again and again, he told himself he had to get to someplace quiet, someplace where he could be alone and think. But how could anyplace be quiet when all the noise was inside his mind. And how could he think with Madigan closing in on Charlotte and the clock ticking, ticking . . .

He reached the Gothic, thick stoned and castle-like. He charged through the arched doorway as if he were rushing in out of a thunderstorm instead of a bright, mild morning. With the holiday on, the building felt blessedly hollow, like a ruin. Hoping to avoid any more human obstacles, he kept his eyes on his shoes as he hurried up the stairs. Even so, an eight-shaped blond with some administrative title or other stood in his way and stopped him in his tracks. She was shocked, she said, shocked that such a thing could happen right here at their university.

"You're a hero," she said to him. "Wrestling for that gun! We're all very proud of you."

Even Winter didn't know what he muttered in response. As far as he was concerned, the only thing heroic about him was the heroic restraint that had kept him from shooting Devesh in various sensitive locations before blowing his head off. Again, he told himself he had to get away and think. He finally did manage to get away from the woman and continue up the stairs. Up the stairs with phantoms crowding his mind, and the clock ticking, and Madigan on the move, all of which made thinking impossible.

He came into his cubbyhole of an office. Flicked on the lights. He squeezed between the bookshelf and the desk, cursing helplessly as his shoulder brushed against *Critique of Pure Reason* and the book fell to the floor in a splatter of dense, Germanic prose. His trailing foot kicked the volume as he went past. He nearly tripped and fell before he managed to wedge himself into his chair.

Think, he told himself. But all he could think was: How could he have listened to Stan-Stan? He must be cracking up. He was cracking up.

"Cameron!"

Winter nearly groaned aloud when he raised his eyes and saw Roger Sexton lumbering through the door. Huge, disheveled. Jacket wrinkled; shirt half-untucked. His mouth was moving as he muttered to himself. His eyes were wandering in confusion.

This was awful, Winter thought. The clock was ticking. Madigan was looking for Charlotte. Getting closer by the second. Why had he listened to Stan-Stan, like a fool? He had to think. But he could not think.

Roger shut the door behind him. He was so huge he seemed to fill the room like a parade float in an outhouse. He waved his big mitts in front of him. It was the first time he and Winter had seen each other since Winter had pulled Barbara out of that basement.

"God, Cam, I feel like Hiroshima," Roger said.

Winter put a hand to his forehead. He felt his sanity was held together by clothespins and force of will.

"Roger," he said. "Look, I'm sorry. But I can't do this right now."

"I feel . . ." said Roger. He searched for the right word in the air before him, as if it were one of a swarm of words buzzing before his eyes. "I feel just devastated. Utterly devastated. I'm in ashes. Radioactive ashes."

"Roger, listen," Winter said. "I'm kind of having a personal crisis here. I need some time. I need . . ." His voice trailed off.

"Devesh . . . Barbara . . ." Roger said. "I mean, how could he? And she? Who the hell even was she, man? I mean, I offered to give up everything for her. And there she was with Devesh. I just keep thinking of them together. I feel . . . I feel . . . I don't know. I don't know."

Winter stared at the big man. The shock of Roger's indifference to him stilled the frantic noise in his brain for a moment. For about the sixteenth or twenty-seventh time that morning, the image of Barbara in the cellar returned to him, the image and the smell. What the hell was Roger talking about? *I keep thinking of them together.* As if Devesh and Barbara had been rowing on the lake, her twirling a parasol above her head and him plinking a ukulele . . .

Winter, who a moment before had been truly worried he was losing his mind, was now wondering if he was the last sane man on earth. So often he struggled with the fact that he had killed people. But just now he was wondering if maybe he hadn't killed enough of them. Maybe he should have killed them all.

"I was sitting at home when the news came in," said Roger. He stood enormous in the tiny space and gazed into the ether ethereally. "We were about to have breakfast. I was in my chair at the table, you know. Reading on my device. And a group email came in. First one and then all these others right after that, colleagues reacting to the news. And I guess I just went into a kind of shock. Reading about . . . you know. Devesh. Barbara. You. You! I mean, what were you doing there?"

"Well, I . . ."

"It was such a horror," Roger said. "Such a horror. And I . . . I lowered the device, you know, and looked around me. Around the kitchen. We were in the kitchen. Adele was at the stove making omelets for us. Arthur was sitting at the island, playing one of those games of his. And suddenly I saw . . . Christ, Cam! Christ, I thought: I have everything. You know? I have everything a man could want, everything that matters in the world. Adele and Arthur and omelets and a kitchen. It was just like you told me, Cam. You told me and I didn't listen. And now . . ."

He raised a pudgy hand in the air and his eyes filled. It looked absurd to Winter: a circus bear the size of a parade float with swimming eyes.

"Now there'll be a trial," said Roger, in a choked voice. "News stories. Investigations. A lawsuit against the university probably. It will all come out. I mean, won't it? Of course it will. I know it will. There's no stopping it. Everything will come out and . . . and I'll lose her. Them. Adele. Arthur. The kitchen. Won't I? Of course. Adele will never stand for it. It'll all come out and she'll leave me and I'll lose everything!"

Squeezed into his chair between the desk and the window, Winter stared at his enormous friend where he filled the tiny room.

"Oh God," cried the tearful circus bear parade float in anguish. "Everything!"

Winter gaped at him for a few more seconds and then managed to say: "Oh, I don't know, Roger. There may not be a trial and anyway . . . I don't think any of us knows, really, how much forgiveness might be available if we only had the courage to go looking for it." He dragged his hand down over his face and sighed. "Maybe that's what you should do, you know. Maybe you should just go looking for it. Go home. You know? Go home, Roger, and look for forgiveness. That's what the word *home* means."

But Roger did not go home. Not right away, at least. He had many other things he wanted—or maybe needed—to discuss. Strategies; possibilities; hopes; fears. Anxieties. Philosophical meditations. And so on. He must have been there in that little office another half an hour, or even forty-five minutes. So it seemed to Winter anyway, later, after he blinked and found that Roger was leaving and he was finally going to be alone. For a moment, he wondered what Roger had said to him during all that missing time when he wasn't paying attention. But only for a moment. He didn't really care.

Because, in fact, while Roger was talking, Winter had gone into that weird, silent, weightless state of being in which all things seemed to float in air, untethered to his personal point of view. He had been telling himself to think, think, think, but he could not think and, as it turned out, he didn't have to.

When he returned to himself, he saw Roger, snuffling, shuffling shamefaced to the office door.

"Thank you, thank you, my friend," Roger kept muttering. "Thank you so much."

Winter could only gesture—only vaguely—because he had no idea what the man was thanking him for.

Roger left and shut the door behind him. Winter turned in the cramped space behind his desk—turned as much as he could—and looked out the window at the pale green trees under the pale blue day. It came as only a mild surprise to him that all his questions had been answered during his fugue state. He knew where he had to go now. He knew what he had to do.

Margaret was right, he thought. She was always right, always about everything. He was not meant for loveless oblivion. He was made to live, but first . . .

First, he had to find Charlotte.

22

He had forgotten how much he loved the smell of old books. The smell and the silent presence of them. On their shelves in place and in their piles as if abandoned. Standing or lying or splayed on their faces. Stately and self-sufficient and yet eager somehow to be lifted, opened, read. Words calling out to him through time. Lonely minds drifting through lost centuries. What they'd felt and what they'd known. Better now than in their lives because the flesh was gone from them and all that it was heir to. Just the inner man remained, the inner man or woman, of its time and yet eternal. The soul, as it were. The image of God, as it were. Large Jewish fellow; long white beard; lives in the clouds, he thought.

Speaking of long white beards, here now was the spindly old man coming into the bookshop, long white beard first, the cat bell on the door jingling as he came. Hunched, dwindled, and slow, yet wiry and muscular, he turned in a half circle stiffly and shut the door and locked it.

"I wondered which one of you it would be," he said.

His back was still to Winter—Winter, sitting in the shop's deep shadows, sitting on a small wooden chair amid piles of books, like

Mother Goose sitting among children. Winter smiled quietly. "You should be glad it's me, Old Bill. Me and not Madigan."

"Oh, I don't suppose it makes much difference," the bookseller replied. He turned again, still stiffly. Glanced at Winter once, but only briefly. Then, hunched and slow, he shuffled through the silent chaos of books to his long table and settled into the chair behind it with a weary sigh.

Winter stood and hooked his own chair by the back and carried it toward him.

"Both of you were bound to get here sooner or later," the old man went on. Stroking his beard, studying the tabletop and the books tossed all aslant across its surface. "Only difference is, with you coming first, I'll still be alive when he turns up. Not sure whether that's a good thing or a dad-blamed catastrophe."

Winter set his chair down on the opposite side of the table. Settled into it, sitting just where he'd sat during their first conversation.

"Your friend, Susannah Woods. Ivy Swansag," Winter said. He gave the name a German tilt, *Svantsag.*

The bookseller's beard moved as if he were smiling behind it. "Figured that one out, did you?"

"Hitler's birthday!" Winter said. "You should be ashamed of yourself, you old fool. I thought you were a Christian."

"I am. Some days. Other days, I just want to flush the whole damn planet down the toilet. Don't you?"

Winter didn't answer. "She had guts anyway, your friend Susannah," he said instead. "I'll give her that."

"She did," said the bookseller. "She had guts aplenty."

"Madigan worked her over pretty hard, but she didn't give you up."

"Yeah. The way I imagine it, he didn't know to ask the right questions. Still, it was gritty of her. She was a game old girl, Susannah was. A true soldier of the cause."

Winter shook his head.

"You don't think so, huh," said the old man. He leaned forward, his arms resting on his knees, his hands sinking beneath the table, unseen. "You don't think we're in a fight for the soul of the nation? You think we ought to just put our faith in the powers that be?"

Winter laughed. "Faith in the powers that be. No. I don't think that would describe my state of mind."

"Well, what's your big idea then? You think we should just sit here? Just take it? While they burn down our cities? Make a mess of a white man's country?"

Winter rolled his eyes. "I don't have a big idea. I'm just looking for a girl, that's all."

"Yeah. Yeah, well . . ." said the bookseller grimly.

With that, he brought his right hand up from under the table. He was gripping that titanic gun of his, that Old West cannon. There was just enough open space between the books on the table for him to clunk the gun down on top of it. He did clunk it down—clunked it down and let it go with a snarl of disgust.

"You're not going to pull the trigger then?" Winter asked mildly.

"Not much point, is there? Since you took the bullets out. You think I wouldn't notice the missing weight? I'll be damned if I give you the satisfaction of watching me go click click click like some kind of idiot fifteen-year-old."

"There's no outsmarting you, Old Bill."

The old man's spindly body dropped back in his chair. His beard hid a quirked expression of chagrin. "I fooled you for a while though, didn't I? Took you some time before you come back here."

"Maybe," said Winter. "To be fair, I haven't been operating at top capacity." He waggled a finger at the side of his own head.

"Yeah," said the bookseller. "Crazy, huh. Girl crazy. I could tell that. The fems—they will do that to you."

"Tell me something," Winter said. "The way I see it now, you were the only one Susannah trusted. You bringing her groceries, checking up on her, her with no phone and you with no computer. I figure you must've been out to her house a lot more than you let on before. You must've heard more of Charlotte's story than you let on."

"Maybe. Maybe a little more," the old man allowed.

"Well, tell me this then. How did it end? Charlotte's story, the real story. There was no big shoot-'em-up with Madigan dying a hero's death like in the novel, was there?"

Old Bill snorted. "No, nothing like that. Susannah—well, she had a writer's imagination. Poetic license and all. Plus all she had to go on was what Charlotte told her."

"Right. So what did she tell her? Was she really Madigan's lover, like Susannah wrote in the novel?"

He gave another phlegmy snort. "Hell, I wouldn't think so, no. Madigan—Moran—the way Susannah wrote him—sort of a hero, a force of nature and like that—that was just her again, just Susannah and her imagination. Madigan—he was, you know, what you'd imagine he was. Another lost man in a lost country. Too angry to think straight. More violence in him than sense. What did he ever do but lure a couple of those red fools into the darkness and beat 'em half to death? Not that they didn't deserve it, mind, but so what? Where does that get us? And all the kissy-kissy stuff in the book—that was Susannah too. That's not the way Charlotte told it. She was never with Madigan. She was in love with Emmanuel James from the beginning."

"Emmanuel James. The leader. The man who's called Frederick Bernard in the novel."

"That's right," said the old man, his long white beard flowing as he nodded. "Charlotte saw him in the bookstore that time and fell for him on the spot. That's why she agreed to join the others. Madigan didn't even come into it until later. Susannah just liked the thought of him, you know. She thought all that violence was romantic. Women!"

Winter considered this for a few silent seconds. "So—just to get this straight—the way Charlotte told it to Susannah: She joined the movement for love of Emmanuel James. And then what? Was it James who killed Eddie-her-boyfriend? Was Eddie killed at all?"

"Oh, he was killed, all right, and Madigan killed him. That's what Charlotte said. Charlotte didn't love Madigan but Madigan loved her and he couldn't stand to see the way this Eddie fellow treated her, giving her the hard hand and so forth. Then, of course, once Madigan did him in, Charlotte figured it was only a matter of time before he killed Emmanuel too. So they got the hell out of Dodge. That's the whole story."

"And Madigan?"

The bookseller shrugged. "The feds moved in on him and he got away. That's all I know."

"And the whole love triangle, and the federal informant . . ."

"That Susannah—she had an imagination, all right. She loved the cause. She had her theories—theories about everything. That's why she wrote the book. To make her ideas known. That's what the story is really about. That's all there is to it."

For a long few seconds, the two men sat without speaking, surrounded by the books everywhere.

"Now I told you something," said the old man then. "You tell me something."

"All right," said Winter.

"What put you on to me finally? What brought you back here?"

Winter smiled. "A friend of mine—one of those G-men you're so fond of . . ."

The old man gave another of his guttural snorts.

"He told me not to worry," Winter went on. "He said the feds had the extremists well under surveillance on the internet. He said the minute Madigan tried to contact someone in the movement, they'd be on his case. But the first words you ever said to me were: Never use computers. Right? No phone. Nothing to trace. Nothing to link into. Nothing left behind."

"That's the beautiful thing about this modern world of ours, son. It can't find you if you hide in the past."

"I wish that were true," Winter said. "I think the world finds all of us eventually. But you did slow me down, I'll give you that. And you seem to have fooled the feds entirely."

The old man's head went up and down. He gave a chuckle of self-satisfaction.

"The only one who could have given Charlotte her new identity is you," Winter went on. "Handcrafted, the old-fashioned way. That's why no one can find her. They're following every electric clue, but the only place she left a trail is in your head."

"Yup," said Old Bill, still self-satisfied. "That's about the size of it."

"Well, look," said Winter, with another sigh. "I'm not going to torture her location out of you."

"Why not? Madigan will, when he gets here. What are you, soft?"

"A little. I'm a little soft, yeah. But give me about twenty minutes and I can flood this place with federal agents. Or maybe you'd like that. A spell behind bars would beat Madigan cutting you to pieces anyway."

"Ah!" said the old man. He waved his wrinkled hand in the air like swatting at mosquitoes. "I'm too old to get cut to pieces. The minute Madigan walks in here, I'll tell him what he wants to know before the bell on the door stops tinkling. Then again, I'm too old to go to prison either, so I'm gonna tell you, too, no disassembly required. Man, this Charlotte, she must be something special, if any woman is. The way you two can't leave her be. You love her, do you?"

Winter frowned, thinking it over. "I don't know, Old Bill. Yes. No. Maybe. I don't know. I loved her once, that's for sure. Now? Well. You might say I left something in her keeping and I want it back, that's all."

"Fair enough, I guess. The fems, am I right?"

The old man moved surprisingly quickly—quickly enough to make Winter tense, even with the bullets safe in his pants pocket. But all the bookseller did was wrestle a pad and a pencil stub out from under a mess of books. With speed and with a flourish, he scribbled Charlotte's new name and her address. Tore the page out and handed it across the table to Winter. Winter folded the page and slipped it into the inside pocket of his windbreaker.

"You gonna give her to the *federales*?" the bookseller asked.

Winter shook his head. "No," he said. "No, I don't think I will."

"Good. Never did like those scummy bastards."

"All the same, you might want to consider giving them a call. They could come in handy. Because he will be here—Madigan. He might not figure it out like I did, but he'll try everything else until you're all that's left, and then up he'll show."

"Yeah," said Old Bill, sucking one cheek in. "That's the way I see it too. Like I said, I'm not gonna argue with him."

"He still might kill you. Just for the fun of it."

"Well." The old man shrugged. "I'm too old to die young. I guess I'll just take what comes."

Winter lumbered to his feet. Gave a one-finger salute by way of a goodbye. He was at the bookstore door—had his hand on the knob, ready to make his exit—when Old Bill spoke again and stopped him.

"You know," the bookseller said. "There's something I like about you, professor. I can't put my finger on it. Not exactly. But I wouldn't want you to lay too heavy a load of judgment on me. Not if you can help it, anyway. I did used to believe in all this. I really did."

Winter had glanced back over his shoulder and saw the old man waving his hand to indicate the books around the room, all the old books everywhere.

"Truth and liberty and justice and the American way and like that," the old man said. "I used to believe in all of it. Just sort of lost my faith, I guess."

"Well," said Winter. "I guess it's a good thing you didn't lose your faith in France. Where would we get our merlot?"

Whatever the old man answered, the cat bell rang over it and Winter was on his way.

23

It was hard for Winter to describe his feelings even to himself. Words, he found, weren't up to the task. *Sorrow* and *fear* were the ones that came to him. They weren't exactly right, but they were as close as he could get to describing what was in his heart.

He drove his Jeep SUV onto a covered bridge of ancient wood. The tires rumbled on the planks as he crossed the winding river. The river ran through a deep forest, then plummeted over a cliff into a gorge. Winter saw the waterfall—the cataract—as he emerged from under the bridge's roof. Being who he was, he thought of Wordsworth, the poet mourning his lost youth and its unburdened sense of splendor.

> *The sounding cataract*
> *Haunted me like a passion: the tall rock,*
> *The mountain, and the deep and gloomy wood,*
> *Their colours and their forms, were then to me*
> *An appetite; a feeling and a love . . .*
> *That time is past,*
> *And all its aching joys are now no more,*
> *And all its dizzy raptures.*

Winter had not had a youth of aching joys and dizzy raptures. He had been a poor little rich kid, friendless and neglected. Still, there had been Charlotte and he had loved her so, loved her as only a boy can love. And he had lost her. So that accounted for the sorrow.

As for the fear . . . well, here he was, driving toward a reckoning. What would it mean to him to see her again, the real woman who had somehow become the image of his feeling soul, its image and its living tomb? What would it be like if he could finally let her go and take that soul back into himself? Could he live in full again, knowing who he was and the things he had done?

He did not know the answer. And with every mile that rolled away beneath him, every minute that brought him closer to her, his fear, his sorrow, those feelings, whatever words he used for them, filled him more completely.

Go home, he had said to Roger. *Go home and look for forgiveness. That's what the word* home *means.*

But he—Winter—had never had a home. Not really. Only his memory of this girl, this long-gone girl, his long-gone soul.

He drove on. The forest never really ended. The town just sort of grew up amid the trees, two church steeples and a baseball field, and maybe a thousand rooftops breathing up out of the greenery.

It was now just morning. The town was waking. Cars rolled out of garages. Men walked their dogs under the trees, and women were at the kitchen windows. Kids rode bikes. He drove down a main street of old-fashioned brick shops. Jewelry and ice cream stores and a dry cleaner. In the winter, thought Winter, tourists would come here to ski. Now? It looked like a village lost in time. What was it the old man had told him? The modern world can't find you if you hide in the past. Maybe Charlotte had believed that too. Maybe that's why she had come here.

Her house was at the end of a little lane that ended where the woods gathered again into hills of pines. There were only three houses on the block, two old clapboards, sagging in on themselves, and the last one, a neat little stone-faced cottage with a couple of gables on its pitched roof. That was hers.

He slowed the Jeep and brought it to the curb in the shade beneath a broad pine. He gazed at the cottage across the street and felt a pang of longing. For days, he had been haunted by the smell of the girl chained in Devesh's basement prison. Her slop bucket and her terror and her despair. But now, those aromas faded and were replaced by an older memory. The musty Old World smell of Charlotte's house when they were children. The cookies baking there. Her sweet strawberry perfume.

He sat and waited, but not for long. Only a few minutes, and then the garage door rolled up and a dusty recreation vehicle rolled out from inside it, a man driving.

Winter heard his own breath catch as Charlotte stepped out of the garage shadows. He sat and watched her as she waved goodbye.

She had a baby on her hip, and a little boy was standing by her side, also waving. She was rounder than in the old days, the girlish figure gone. But she was elegantly shaped nonetheless under a flowing pale orange top, with jeans below. Her hair was at once darker than it had been, and paler—there must have been some silver in it creating the effect, though he couldn't be sure at that distance. He could make out the face he remembered, though, just as delicate, just as solemn, just as sweet. He could not put words to the feeling of seeing her. There were too many layers of complexity.

The dusty RAV came down the drive into the street and backed into a turn. It went forward then. It passed him quickly. He caught only a glimpse of the driver. A gaunt, balding man, but good-looking. A sensitive face under black hair sprinkled with gray, and a black beard. Emmanuel James: the intellectual leader of the extremist cell, the model for Frederick Bernard in *Treachery in the Night*, Charlotte's husband now, the father of her children.

Charlotte went on waving and as her eyes followed the car down to the corner, she spotted Winter's Jeep. The expression on her face changed, but he couldn't read it. He could see she had stopped smiling though.

The RAV turned the corner and traveled out of sight. Charlotte lingered another second, then sank back into the shadows of the garage with her children. The garage door came down and she was gone. Winter felt her going like waking from a dream.

Winter had a momentary urge, a boyishly bashful urge, to hit the gas and drive away. He smiled at that. He shouldered the door open and got out of the Jeep.

It was a cool day up here in the eastern mountains. The forest smell was rich and liquid, dark and green. There were big white clouds passing overhead, but mostly blue sky and the sun shining. It seemed a long walk from the Jeep to the front path. He wished he could put words to his feelings so he would be prepared to meet her. But there were no words.

He stood at the front door and rang the bell, nervous as a boy on his first date.

He heard a dog bark and quick little footsteps within. Charlotte's little boy came to the sidelight and peered out through the glass. Winter got a glimpse of Germanic pug features on a face as round as a plate. The dog kept barking.

Charlotte appeared at the sidelight next, her and the baby standing over the boy, three heads on a vertical like a totem pole. This time, Winter was close enough to read her features. She drew back slightly, startled at the sight of him. Then she smiled with delight and, to him at least, she was as beautiful ever.

She pulled the door open quickly. "Oh!" she said. A flood of warmth filled the syllable. "Oh! It's you! What are you doing here? How did you . . . ? This is such a surprise. Come in. Come in, sweet." *Sweet.* It was what she had called him when he was little.

It was as strange an experience as he could have imagined. Stranger. He had thought about her so long, her actual presence felt unreal to him. But the boy he had once been—that boy felt real suddenly—a vulnerable, childish consciousness stirring to fresh life within him—the ghost of himself in the haunted dungeon of his heart.

"Come, come. Come into the kitchen, sweet. Oh, it's so good to see you," Charlotte went on. "How did you find me? What are you doing here? Such a surprise. Come to the kitchen. I can feed the baby in there and we can sit, and Gert, you will make pictures while I talk to Mr. Winter . . ."

She had that way of talking he had always remembered, a foreign rhythm she'd picked up from her father as a child, as if she had his accent, though she never did. In fact, much of what he remembered about her was there again. That last time he had seen her, she had been half-mad, totally different from the girl he knew originally. But now he could see her madness was gone and she was something like her old self, her child self, grown. Serious and self-controlled and focused and competent. The homemaker's magic mastery of infinite detail. She had been made to be a homemaker and wife and mother, and now she was, he thought.

As he came into the cottage, he felt swathed in a cloud of unreality and the past. He sat at the kitchen table while she fussed about. Stuffing the baby into her high chair, setting some cereal and a juice cup in front of her. Settling the boy at a child-sized table where he could draw with colored markers. Making coffee and chatting all the while. Winter gazed at her, his lips slightly parted. The kitchen was full of windows. The windows were full of forest. The light that poured in was green and golden. It was, Winter realized, a sort of vision for him: a vision of the life he would have had if she had only loved him. He wished—or half wished—he could break free of it. He wished he could return to the world as it truly was. He couldn't though. The vision held him within itself as by a fairy-tale spell.

"How are you, sweet?" she said. "You look wonderful. You haven't aged at all. It's so good to see you. It's been so long."

He answered her, but barely knew what he said. The scene was too uncanny. It overwhelmed him. The baby in the high chair. The boy at his little table. Charlotte fetching mugs, pouring coffee, taking charge of half a dozen objects like a juggler. He felt as if he were standing outside himself, standing at the cottage window, peering in at his own living daydream.

She set a mug of coffee in front of him, and the scent of it was like her scent, the coffee and vanilla scent that wafted over him as she drew near.

She sat across from him and put her hands over her mouth, her eyes glistening. "Look at you. Look at you," she said. "I can't believe it has been so long. My old sweet. My little sweet from the old days."

He smiled. He couldn't help it. It was as if his life, the life he'd really lived, the work he'd done, the men he'd killed—as if that were the dream, and he had awakened into this, the life he'd really wanted, the home he'd never had. "Yes," he said softly.

"And you are a professor now, yes? I saw this online once. At a university. How impressive!"

He nodded vaguely, still swathed within his vision. The fact that they were talking so casually, as if this were no more than an old friend's visit—the fact that they were not talking about the Farmhouse or Eddie's murder or Madigan coming closer step by step—all this was only a faint intrusion on his fantasy, sparrows pecking at the window of the house of dreams.

"Yes," he said distantly. "Yes, and look at you—your children. They're so beautiful. But I suppose that was to be expected."

"Ah. Thank you. Thank you. Yes. They are everything to me."

"And I take it that was your husband I saw driving off," he said in that same faraway tone.

She said yes—yes, it was. She said Emmanuel was the assistant manager of a ski resort at the edge of town. It was slow now with only the summer visitors but in the winter, it was very busy, she said. He had his hands full then. He worked very hard.

"But why are you here?" she asked, as if he might just have been passing through. "Why have you come? How did you ever find me?"

Winter slowly blinked. For a moment, he couldn't remember—why had he come? How had he found her? "Well . . . you came to see me, Charlotte. Didn't you? I thought—I thought you needed my help."

For a moment, she stiffened—stiffened and paled—her gaze turning inward. "But—how did you know? I never reached you. How did you know I'd been there? Or where I was . . . ?"

"I traced you," he said. His voice was thick, sluggish. As if he'd been drugged by the sight of her and was just coming around. "I saw your picture in the building's security video. The book under your arm. I read the book. I know your story."

He saw her catch her breath. He saw a fiery spark of fear in her eyes. Her glance shifted to her little boy. He was drawing a house, a standing rectangle with a triangle on top. A stick figure family under the lollipop tree outside.

Charlotte dropped her voice. "He will go to his camp in half an hour, and we can talk about it then," she said quietly.

With that, she arose from her chair. She went back to fussing about the kitchen. Wiping the baby's face. Telling her son to clean up his drawing desk. She and Winter continued their strange, dreamy chitchat. What is it like to be a professor? Poetry, how wonderful.

How did you ever find this little town here? How are the schools for the children? As if he had just dropped by for a visit. Two old friends.

Then, after a short while, Charlotte said she had to get her son ready for the bus. She plucked the baby from the high chair and took the boy by the hand and off the three of them went, a little family in their morning routine. Winter sat alone at the kitchen table. Now and then, he lifted his mug to his lips, though the coffee had gone cold. His mind was blank. He had no words to describe what was happening inside him. The unreality continued to envelop him. He thought he ought to break free of it, but it was too sweet, too soft, too still. This life he hadn't lived. These children that were not his. This woman who had not loved him.

The bus arrived to take the boy to camp. Charlotte and her children went outside. Winter stood at the kitchen window and watched them. The yellow bus pulled up to the curb and stopped. The boy climbed aboard. Charlotte stood on the verge of grass, looking on, holding the baby on her hip. The boy passed behind the bus windows to sit with his friends inside. Charlotte moved the baby's hand to make her wave goodbye.

Thought was slowly returning to Winter's mind now. He thought of Roger Sexton coming to his senses in his kitchen. He thought of Jerry Collins in the courtyard of the villa near Istanbul. Margaret was right, he thought, right again, right about everything: It was all one story, one story of desire and obsession, obsession with the past. It was all so terribly sad.

He moved from the kitchen to the living room. He was there when Charlotte came back inside. She shut the door behind her. She stood for a moment, holding the baby. Their eyes met. Winter caught the scent of her again, coffee and vanilla.

"Let me put the baby down and we can talk while she is sleeping," she said.

She carried the baby up the stairs to the nursery. Winter stood alone in the living room. He could hear her upstairs singing a lullaby in German. Winter's nanny, Charlotte's aunt, had sung that song to him sometimes when he was a child. He recited more Wordsworth to himself: *Whither is fled the visionary gleam? Where is it now, the glory and the dream?*

And just as suddenly as that, he awoke into reality. It was like coming out of one of his fugue states, that strange habit of mind. As if the gravity had left the room for a moment and all at once returned, the furniture falling down to the floor in a completely new arrangement.

Oh God, he thought. *Oh God, oh God, my heart is breaking. My heart is breaking.*

What was it? What was happening to him? The lullaby from his childhood. The children who were not his. The woman who was not his. The love, the past, the life that was not his. *Oh God*, he thought again. It was agony, worse even than this last long bout of depression and madness. What was it?

Her perfume, he thought. Of course. The scent of her. It had given her away. It had told him everything.

The lullaby upstairs was over now. Charlotte had stopped singing. But she did not come down. Seconds passed and more seconds. Still, she did not come down. Maybe she was gently laying her child in the crib. Maybe she was hovering near, a loving mother making sure her baby was really asleep.

But Winter didn't think so.

Winter thought she was on the phone, arranging his murder.

A floorboard creaked. He lifted his eyes. There she was, standing on the stairs, halfway down, in a pool of that strangely golden light from the forest outside. Gazing down at him as he gazed up at her. They remained like that a long moment, and he thought of how much he had loved her.

Then she hurried down the stairs and across the room and came into his arms.

He held her close, tight. He felt her soft form pressed against him. He drew in the scent of her, the scent that gave her away. He knew his time was short, his killer was coming for him, but he could not release her. When he was a boy, he would have given anything to hold her like this, and he could not release her now.

It was she who let go finally. He was relieved. Grateful. He had been about to make a fool of himself. He had been about to try to kiss her.

"Come," she said. "I will tell you everything."

They returned to the kitchen. They sat at the table again. She told him her story.

"I never wanted to go to that house," she said. "It was Eddie who took me. All that politics. I never cared. It was only my anger at my father. How he had betrayed his friends to the Stasi back in Communist days. I am so glad all that is over now. I never cared about any of it. Not really."

He watched her as she spoke. His eyes went tenderly over her features. He couldn't help himself. She was no longer the porcelain doll of a girl he'd known. She was a little plump now and pie-faced. But he could still see the girl she'd been, that delicate beauty that was almost too ethereal to be real. He watched her and he pretended to listen. But he did not listen. He was done with stories. Done with lies.

How many had there been? How many layers of deceit? There was the story Charlotte told Susannah Woods after she had escaped the federal raid on the Farmhouse. There was the story Susannah Woods wrote in *Treachery of the Night*, full of sentimental violence and romance. There was the story Winter had told himself, of how Charlotte was swept from passion to passion, from man to man. Her father, Eddie, Madigan, her husband now, Emmanuel James.

But none of those stories was true, least of all the one he told himself. It wasn't the men who controlled Charlotte, it was Charlotte who controlled the men. Because of who she was. Because of what she believed.

"I was afraid of Eddie," she told Winter now. "That's why I went to the Farmhouse. I wanted to leave him but he was violent. He would never have let me go."

No, Winter thought. Maybe she had come to Eddie in anger at her father. Maybe the ideas had been Eddie's before they were hers. But she was the stronger character of the two. Serious and self-controlled and focused and competent. With the homemaker's magic mastery of infinite detail. Left to his own devices, Eddie would have moldered away, grumbling, into the bitter muck of his own theories. It was she who took action. It was she who brought them to the Farmhouse and to Emmanuel James.

"Madigan was mad. He loved me. He hated Eddie. I didn't know what he was planning," she said.

No, thought Winter. She had used Madigan. She had led him on until he would do anything for her. She had shown him the bruises Eddie had left on her. *He will never let me go*, she told him. She knew exactly what mad Madigan would do—would do for her.

Madigan had murdered Eddie in a dream of love, as Charlotte knew he would. Then she and Emmanuel James handed Madigan to the feds. Because he was out of control, violent, ungovernable—a threat to their movement. They probably thought he would die in a gunfight with the law. But he had escaped.

"When I heard he had come back from South America," she told him, "I did not know where to turn. I was done with all that. All I wanted was to live my life, raise my children."

No, Winter thought. Hiding out in this small town, she would never have known about Madigan's return unless her fellow travelers in the movement were still in touch with her, unless they had told her he was looking for her. Because she was one of them. She and Emmanuel were the leaders of the remnant that was left.

"I came to you for help, but then I did not want to put you in danger," she told him.

No, Winter thought. She needed someone to get rid of Madigan for her as Madigan had gotten rid of Eddie. But how could she find an assassin who was not connected to the movement, who would not give her location away?

Winter was not sure how much Charlotte knew about his government work, but he suspected she knew more than she should. Maybe some government contact had told her, maybe some disaffected exile from the Division had joined her crowd. Winter had felt her following him for days before she made her approach. It was only at the last second that she had changed her mind. Some sixth sense must have warned her that he was not the man for the job, that he would find out about her and betray her to the law. She had reached the very door of his apartment before her doubts stopped her and she changed her plan. She had walked away. But she had left that scent in his hallway. That perfume.

It was the scent of the past, his obsession. The sense of smell and memory are linked in the mind. She knew that, so she wore the childhood perfume when she came to him. So he would remember. So she could wrap him in the old dream. So she could get him to do her killing for her, as Madigan had. That was why she was wearing the coffee and vanilla scent now, the scent that was mentioned in the prologue to *Treachery in the Night*. It was because she had been expecting Madigan. That's why she was surprised when she saw him—Winter—at the door instead.

"I thought of coming to you for help because I had read about you online and your adventures. But at the last minute I realized. I could not hide the truth from my dear husband," she said. "I went to Emmanuel and, yes, he saved me. He arranged a meeting with Madigan. He told him that we were together. That we had children, a family. He told him that he would do anything to protect us. So he had written out our story, including Eddie's murder. Everything he knew. He had made sure that, if anything happened to us, the story would be given to the police. If he hurt us, they would know it was him, and they would have him for murder. He even offered Madigan money. Not very much, but it was all we had. In the end, Madigan—he did not take the money. But he realized there was nothing for him here, only danger. Arrest. Prison. He went away. Back to Colombia, I think. Back to his trafficking business there. Maybe he will come again, I don't know. He is not a rational man. He does not think in straight lines. The world is not the world for him. It is all a story he tells himself inside his head. Even his love for me, you know. I think he was following some kind of dream of who he thought I was, not who I was really. I think the truth is: he is happier where he is. And I think we are safe for now. I will never stop being afraid for my children but I think—I think for now we are safe."

No, Winter thought. Madigan was here. Maybe waiting outside for him even now. He would not come in. He would not bring the violence into her home where her baby was sleeping. He would take him in his car or follow him out of town and kill him there. Just as Charlotte had told him to.

Winter went on nodding, pretending to listen. But her words were now no more to him than an aural blur. Her voice, her lies, had become a sort of music. It was a moment before he realized she had stopped speaking. She had come to the end of her story.

It was time for him to go. Time to face Madigan. Still, he lingered another moment. There in the kitchen. With the coffee cups. With the forest light. With Charlotte's face before him. She had been very kind to him when he was little. Very kind when he was lonely and afraid. An isolated and rejected boy, he had put all his feeling into her, and all his capacity to feel. And now—now, he thought . . .

Now, he was never going to see her again. This—this very moment—was the last moment he would ever be with her. He understood it had to be that way. There was no other way for it to be. He even understood that it was the best thing for him in many ways. This pain he felt, this agonizing heartbreak, what was it but the vessel breaking, the image shattering that held his feeling soul, his soul and all its suffering returning to him, where it belonged?

"I should go," he tried to say. He had to clear his throat before he could speak more clearly: "I should go."

Charlotte's eyes filled. She reached across the table. She took his hand where it lay there still. She clasped his hand with both of hers and all his sense of what might have happened but had not happened washed over him in a fresh wave of longing.

He did kiss her finally. They were in the doorway saying goodbye and he couldn't help himself. It was a swift, soft, stolen kiss, but his whole dream life was in it. How lost, he thought, how lost are the things that are lost. Lost forever.

Then he drove away from the little stone-faced house on the little lane that ended at the forest. Charlotte stood in the doorway and waved goodbye to him. Winter watched her in the rearview mirror. How lost, he thought.

Then he faced forward, faced the road ahead. He did not need to keep looking behind him.

He already knew that Madigan was there.

24

He could not see the killer at first. All the same, he was sure he was there somewhere behind him. He was also sure that he'd be carrying a gun this time. He did not need to torture Winter for information. He had already found Charlotte. She must have reached out to him, through the movement, through their network. *Come back to me, my love,* she must have said. Or words to that effect. So this time, Madigan simply wanted Winter dead. He would hold him at gunpoint, take him into the woods, shoot him, and bury him. Just as he had done with Eddie. For her.

Winter, though, was making other plans.

He drove through the little town again, down the main street where the locals greeted one another on the sidewalks as they walked to lunch. The early afternoon sunshine glinted brightly on his windshield as he drove past the brick stores and into the residential area, past the houses among the trees.

The houses grew fewer, farther apart. The trees grew denser. As the hills of forest closed in on either side of him, he got his first glimpse of Madigan in the rearview mirror. He was driving a pickup, bright blue by the look of it. He was still too far away for Winter to identify the make or model.

Winter drove on. He returned to the waterfall and the covered bridge. He went rumbling over the boards and crossed the river. Now there was nothing but deep woods all around him. No traffic, no houses.

It was a good place to make his stand.

He could have called the cops. He knew that. He could have called the feds, either the bureau or one of his friends in intelligence. But he wasn't going to do that. He wasn't going to call anyone. He wasn't sure why not. He still wasn't thinking all that clearly. He told himself he was trying to arrange a happy ending. But even he suspected he was lying to himself. There was not going to be any happy ending. Deep down, below the level of consciousness, he knew he was simply acting out of a muddled mixture of honor and pride. On his honor, he did not want to be the one to bring the law down on Charlotte, bad as she might have been. And in his pride, he remembered how Madigan had nearly choked him out last time they met and he wanted a rematch. He wanted to bring the bastard to the earth himself.

He drew near the spot he was looking for. He remembered it from when he passed it on his way into town. It was a little grassy turnoff. A patch of brown grass on the verge of the forest. It was large enough for a couple of trucks or maybe three. Beyond it, there was a narrow trail dropping sharply down into the woods. There was probably a fishing spot down there, he thought, a clearing by the river where it wound through the bottom of the gorge.

Winter parked his Jeep on the brown grass. He stepped out into the spring air. His nerves were strung tight, keyed up—too high, he thought. He was too ready, too eager to unleash all his pent-up inner turmoil in an explosion of violence. He tried to breathe more steadily as he walked around to the back of his SUV. He opened the hatch. Lifted the lid of the spare tire compartment. Wrested the tire iron free from its alcove. He liked the feel of its weight in his hand.

He headed down into the woods on the narrow trail.

Quickly, the trees were thick around him, mostly maples, hickories, and sycamores. Their leaves were large and blocked the high sun. The light filtered down through the foliage so that it seemed to infuse the underbrush. It was as if, instead of falling from the sky, the light was rising from the earth like steam. All the wood around him glowed green and golden.

He paused. He heard the river rushing somewhere out of sight. The birds were singing brightly. Ahead of him, like a magical locale in a fairy tale, there stood a little clearing surrounded by conifers. Sunbeams fell through the needles and striped the air. The spot reminded him of the Hemlock Cathedral where he had trained for his work in the Division. The Recruiter had set his men against one another there as if in an arena and he had taught them how to kill with their bare hands. In his high-strung, agitated state, Winter felt that a locale like this, so rife with memories and meaning, must be somehow inevitable. This was where this battle had to end.

Madigan, meanwhile, seemed to have slowed his truck down and dropped back. There was only one road out of town in this direction. There were no turnoffs, not for miles. There was no chance he could lose Winter here, so he must have thought it best to stay out of sight. In any case, it took him a full five minutes to reach the place where Winter's Jeep was parked. He pulled his bright blue truck in behind it. The truck was a Ford Raptor F-150, as it turned out.

Madigan stepped down from the cab and yes, he had a pistol in his hand, just as Winter had predicted he would: a Glock 9. He tucked the blocky weapon in his belt and pulled his black shirt out to cover it. He was dressed all in black: black shirt, black jeans, black track shoes. For a moment, he stood there, enormous, studying the terrain, smiling slightly.

Did he appreciate the setup? Did it occur to him how well Winter had understood his psychology and how cleverly he had arranged their meeting? The Recruiter had taught his people that too: how to get their targets to do what they wanted. As the Phantom of the Zones, Madigan had drawn his prey into solitary places where he could attack out of nowhere. And here was Winter, drawing him into the woods in the same way. It was like a dare. How could he not accept the challenge? Being who he was, it was impossible for him to resist.

He headed down the little path, following Winter's footprints where they were still visible in the dust and duff.

Madigan came down the slope and reached the clearing. He slowed as he stepped into the ring of evergreens and the columns of sun. Maybe he saw the inevitability of the place too: a place like an arena. That may have been why he grinned to himself as he drew the gun from his belt.

Winter had watched all this, crouched low, holding the tire iron ready. He had circled back from the clearing in time to see Madigan's truck arrive. He had waited in hiding while Madigan stepped out and headed down the trail. When the time was right, he followed after him, moving silently through the trees beside the path.

Madigan edged deeper into the clearing. He scanned the forest, holding his gun steady. Winter came up behind him, the tire iron angled to his side. He planned a whiplike strike to the other man's temple. He knew such a blow could kill him. He also knew he was not in complete control of himself. He would not be able to gauge or limit the force of his attack. It was even possible he was intending to kill the man. He wasn't sure. He didn't care.

In any case, he never got the chance.

The ground of the clearing was covered with old conifer needles. They were brown and damp and soft. They muffled Winter's foot-steps so he could approach silently. But the needles also hid a small dent in the earth. Just as Winter was about to strike, his foot sank suddenly, his ankle turning. He grunted. Madigan heard him.

Madigan swung around with the gun. Off-balance, Winter couldn't strike at his head. He'd have been shot before he con-nected. Instinctively, he struck out clumsily at Madigan's wrist. The Glock fired. There was a gout of flame and the explosion echoed through the forest as the shot went wild. Madigan lost his grip and the pistol dropped out of his hand.

Winter tried to strike again, the head shot this time. But he was still unsteady. Madigan, still turning, blocked the blow with his left arm and threw a right-hand punch. He was off-balance too and startled too and Winter threw his arm up to block the blow. The fist, aimed at Winter's face, hit him instead on the shoulder and drove him back.

Both men leaped away to regain their footing. They faced off, bright-eyed and vicious. Winter brandished the iron.

"Come on, come on," Madigan said.

Winter hesitated. He did not want to grapple with the much bigger man. And Madigan hesitated. He did not want to get clubbed with that iron. Each juked, circling, trying to read each other's motions.

Winter saw Madigan's eyes shift toward the gun where it lay on the bed of brown needles. Madigan made a dodge toward the weapon. Winter attacked, swinging the silver bar, the bar glinting. It was a mistake. Madigan's move was a feint. When Winter charged, Madigan stepped in fast. He blocked his arm and grabbed him and drove him to the ground.

They hit with a thud, Madigan on top. Winter grunted as the breath was knocked out of him. He knew he had to act fast and he did, driving his left thumb into Madigan's throat. Madigan gagged. Big as Madigan was, Winter threw him off and rolled away, scrambling to his feet. Madigan was on his feet too, coughing and furious. In his rage, he rushed the smaller man, repaying one mistake with another.

Winter vanished from his path like a magic trick. He ducked to the side and elbowed him in the temple as he passed, then hammered his fist into the back of his neck. Winter felt the ground shake when the big man fell face-first into the duff. But Madigan fell near the gun and grabbed it. He rolled onto his back, bringing the barrel to bear.

Winter kicked the weapon out of his hand. This time, the Glock flew almost to the clearing's perimeter.

Madigan tried to rise, but the blow to his neck had hurt him and he was slow. Winter kicked him in the face. Madigan, seemingly unstoppable, still managed to roll with the kick and leap to his feet. His mouth was pouring blood.

The two men came together, murder in their hearts. Madigan wanted to get his hands on the smaller man and kill him with his superior size and strength, but Winter wouldn't let him near. The bigger man's punches were swift and powerful, the mighty thrusting of a great machine. But Winter dodged and danced, kicked at him low and high and would not approach him. Here was something at last Margaret had been wrong about. Winter's skills had not deteriorated, not these skills, not now. His heartbreak and his loss, his fury and his thirst for vengeance were coursing through him like blood. All the killing tricks the Recruiter had taught him in his youth—all these his body remembered in his rage. Madigan roared in wild frustration as he swung again at Winter's head and found Winter had darted away once more before the blow landed.

The two men broke apart. They circled. Both were panting now. Each stared at the other with eyes that were gleaming and glassy, animal eyes. Madigan's chin was streaked with blood. Winter's cheek was scratched and bleeding where the duff had cut him when he fell.

Madigan moved in first. He knew he had to get close to finish it. Winter's speed and skill had countered the greater reach of his arms, but his legs were longer too and pile-driver powerful. A kick would bring him in, and then he'd break Winter's neck with a single move.

He kicked, low, toward Winter's knee. Wild, reckless, and expert, Winter spun. He twisted around out of Madigan's way, got behind him and elbowed him hard in the kidney. He turned, quick as light, and punched him in the same kidney then punched him in the floating rib and punched him in the floating rib again.

Anyone but a monster of the imagination would have dropped to the ground, but not Madigan. Amazingly he struck back, planting a gigantic fist in the side of Winter's mouth.

Winter's world turned black, the blackness streaked with jagged yellow light. He staggered backward and fell. Madigan had him. But now, Winter's blows took effect. Madigan staggered also—staggered to the side like a wounded bull, and also—finally—went down.

Battered as they were, both men tried to rise. Madigan sat up and swayed, sick and gasping. Winter sat up, wiping the blood from his chin, gasping too. Madigan let out a raw curse. Winter echoed him. Madigan turned to the side and gagged as if he would vomit. Grunting, Winter pushed himself to his feet by force of will. Bent so low he touched the ground with his fingers, he stumbled a few steps to the edge of the clearing and dropped down next to the gun. He grabbed hold of the pistol. He dragged himself to a nearby pine and sat exhausted with his back against the trunk. His face hurt and his head ached horribly.

Madigan sat on the bed of needles with his legs bent up in front of him. He leaned forward, his arms resting on his knees. Breathing hard, he looked at Winter where Winter sat with one leg lifted, his arm resting on his knee, the Glock dangling from his hand. He was also breathing hard.

"You're gonna have to shoot me to keep me here," said Madigan. His voice was a croak. "I'm leaving now unless I'm dead."

"All right, I'll shoot you then," said Winter.

"No, you won't."

"You don't think so?"

"You're not the type."

Winter considered shooting him then and there just to prove him wrong. But it was true. He wasn't the type, not in these circumstances, not in cold blood.

"All right," he said. "So what then?"

Madigan made a gesture with his head, a sort of shrug. "As soon as I can stand up . . ." He straightened and groaned and rubbed at his torso where Winter had punched him. "As soon as I can stand up, I'm gonna walk out of here."

"Back to Charlotte's."

"She's mine. I tried to stay away from her. That was no good. She's coming home with me."

"And you think I'll just sit and watch you go?"

"That's right. That's right. It's that or shoot me. And like I said, you're not the type."

A lightning bolt of pain went through Winter's head and his whole face contorted so that his bleeding mouth ached and he moaned. He gave a snort that was almost laughter and considered Madigan who considered him back and also gave something like a laugh.

Winter remembered what Charlotte had said about the man.

The world is not the world for him. It is all a story he tells himself inside his head. Even his love for me, you know. I think he was following some kind of dream of who he thought I was, not who I was really.

Literary fellow that he was, Winter could not miss the irony. Charlotte's words could have described him just as well as Madigan. As if he and Madigan were the same somehow, two sides of the same person. And with Madigan all dressed in black as he was, he could easily serve as Winter's Dark Other, an archetype from a myth or fairy tale. It was as Margaret said: it was as if—really eerily as if—he was in a story being written by God.

"So what do you think?" said Madigan.

Winter made a helpless little gesture with the Glock 9. "Ah, to be honest, I think you're right. I think you're going to get up and walk away and I'm too badly injured to stop you and I'm not the type to shoot you. Not anymore, anyway."

Madigan nodded. He clearly intended to stand, but it took him a long moment to work out how exactly he would do it. Finally, he gave it a try. He groaned again as he planted a hand in the brown needles and pushed himself to one knee. He groaned even louder as he rose to his feet and stood towering darkly amid the trees. Even this early in the afternoon, his shadow, falling on the ground in front of him, was so enormous it nearly touched Winter's outstretched leg.

"I don't want you to get me wrong," Madigan said.

"I don't have you wrong, Madigan, believe me," said Winter.

"I will come back. I will come back and kill you."

"Yeah, yeah, yeah. Whatever."

"You won't know where, you won't know when, you won't even see it coming, but it will happen."

Winter waved him off with his free hand. "If you're going, go," he said. "Don't push your luck."

Massaging the spot on his side where Winter had hit him, Madigan began shuffling slowly and painfully toward the far edge of the clearing. Winter sat and watched him go. Once again, he considered shooting him, but this time he wasn't serious. What would be the point? He knew exactly how this story was going to end. In some sense, it was already over. There was nothing left for him to do.

Madigan reached the head of the trail. Winter heard him groan again as he began the slow climb, bent over and holding his side. Winter sat where he was and watched as the big figure blended with the tree trunks and the tangled branches and the tangled vines. Finally, the hulking black shape blended with all the black shapes of the deep woods, and Madigan was gone.

Good riddance, Dark Other, Winter thought.

The story was over. He smiled to himself.

It hurt like hell to smile.

EPILOGUE

"Well?" said Margaret Whitaker. "For goodness' sake, you can't just end it there. What happened next?"

When Winter hesitated, she went on: "So help me, Cam, if you sit there with those cuts and bruises on your face and lapse into some story of the long ago past, I will get out of this chair and knock you sideways."

Winter laughed—and flinched with the pain. Margaret smiled nonetheless. There was something in that laugh, some fresh energy, that she found encouraging. His eyes were brighter too than they had been recently. Yes, the bruise on his mouth and the scrapes on his cheek were ugly. She couldn't help fretting over that. But he had a habit of coming to her all banged up in one way or another. It was just one of those things about him she had had to get used to. All in all, though, she thought, he looked like he was doing better, psychologically speaking. His depression—his emotional crisis—seemed to have passed.

"Well," he said. "After Madigan left, I waited there in the forest. To let my head clear, for one thing. But also to give the man time to drive away. Then I went back toward town, found a small hotel, and checked myself in."

"A hotel? Really? You were that certain about what was going to happen."

He shrugged with one shoulder. "The future is never certain. That's what the word *future* means. But there are times when the facts and the personalities involved only leave so many options open. In this case, the options seemed pretty much limited to one."

Margaret swiveled back and forth in her high leather chair. She went on smiling at him fondly. She liked the wry, confident tone that had returned to his voice. She liked having the old Cam back.

"You're too clever. You've gotten ahead of me," she told him. "How did you know all this?"

He chuckled once. She liked the sound of that too. She enjoyed watching him enjoy himself. There were times when it troubled her to realize how much she loved him. This was not one of those times.

"Look," he said. "Madigan thought Charlotte was going to run away with him. That was never going to happen. She had come to me in the first place hoping I'd kill him. When her instincts told her I was not that guy, what would she do?"

"Go home to her husband. Solve her problems on her own."

"It was more dangerous. That's why she didn't do it in the first place. But in the end, if you want something done well . . ."

"Do it yourself."

Winter nodded. Then he drifted away for a moment. Margaret could see all that fresh energy go out of him. For long seconds, he sat there silent, peering wistfully at some invisible something in the space between them. His dream of the past, she thought. The life he had not lived.

"You know, trauma really does leave scars on a person," she said gently. She hoped the idea would comfort him. "Discovering the truth about her father and the Communists—it really did change Charlotte—change her from the girl you knew at first. All that manipulating of men, controlling them, getting them to act for her, do what she wanted. I think it must have been a reaction. Her father was everything to her. When she found out what he was, she became angry and frightened. She couldn't trust men anymore. She needed to have them dancing on her string in order to feel safe."

Slowly, Winter closed and opened his eyes. Blinking away his fantasies of what might have been, Margaret thought. Another moment and he had come back to himself and back to her. "Anyway," he murmured. "Where was I?"

"What happened next, after Madigan left," she said.

"Right. Right." But still he was quiet for another few seconds. Quiet and far away. Margaret sat still and studied him. That face of his, which she found lovely. Which sometimes made her rue her own long, gray marriage. Which sometimes made her wistful for her scholarly youth. He had the face of a poet—the face of an assassin and a poet both. In some sense, she supposed, it was her job to teach those two how to live with each other.

"So," she prompted him. "You drew Madigan into the woods and fought him to a draw. Then off he went, and off you went and checked into a hotel."

"Yes. It was a small ski lodge actually. Very homey. They were happy to have my business during the offseason." Winter's bruised mouth turned up slightly. The mischievous light went on in his eyes again. "I ordered a hamburger and a bottle of wine from room service. Some fries. I had lunch."

"You didn't. Did you?"

"I did. All that fighting made me hungry."

"And you just let events play out."

"Well, no. Not exactly. You remember that tracker gizmo I have? The one I used to track Devesh to his lair?"

"Oh yes, I remember."

"Well, I had it with me in the glove compartment of my Jeep. So before I followed Madigan into the woods, I stuck it on that bright blue truck of his. You know, just in case he got away from me."

"You are just a walking bag of tricks."

This time, Winter's bruised mouth turned up into a grin. His eyes grew even brighter and yes, she thought, with a flood of warmth, yes, his crisis was over. He had come through. She had helped him through. He was going to be all right.

"And so what did you do then, young Cameron Winter?"

"I ate my burger. I drank my wine. And I watched Madigan's truck moving about on the tracker app on my phone."

"And you saw him return to Charlotte's house?"

"No, in fact. Not to her house. And not right away either. He waited until evening came. Then he drove into the hills—to an abandoned ruin of an old house high up in the hills."

"To meet her there, you mean. To meet Charlotte."

"So he thought."

"Aha."

"I mean, she was there waiting for him. I'm sure of it. She must have been. I think the plan required the two of them, her and Emmanuel both."

"That way all Madigan's attention would have been on her."

"Exactly. And Emmanuel would have come up behind him. Anyway, when I drove up to the ruined house the next morning, there was no sign of any of them. The truck was gone and so was Madigan."

"Gone," said Margaret, keeping her voice as toneless as possible.

"Yes, I had tracked all that with my gizmo. They—Charlotte, Emmanuel—one of them—probably both—had driven the truck down to a lookout above a reservoir in a hidden valley. They rolled it off the edge and sank it in the water."

"With Madigan's body still in it, I presume."

"No, I think they buried Madigan up in the hills by the abandoned house. I'm pretty sure I found traces of his grave in the forest. In any case, I think it's clear: his reunion with his old girlfriend wasn't all he hoped it would be."

"So she used Madigan to get rid of Eddie for her, then tried to use Madigan to get rid of you, then used Emmanuel James to get rid of Madigan."

"That's a cynical way to look at it. I think it's nice to see a husband and wife working well together."

His tone was light. His body was relaxed in the chair. His bruised mouth was quirked upward in a small smile. All his pain was in his eyes. That would be there for a while, Margaret thought. Probably quite a long while.

"You know," she said. "I can't help noticing that you haven't called the police about all this. Or at least you haven't mentioned it, if you did call them."

"No. No, I haven't called them."

"That's a bit dangerous for you, isn't it? I mean, you're a bit of a loose end in all this."

"I'm not worried."

"No. You wouldn't be, would you?"

He smiled again.

"So you're just going to let her get away with all this?" Margaret said. "For old times' sake."

"Well, Margaret. I'll tell you something interesting."

"Oh, do."

"At this offseason ski lodge I was telling you about? Where I had lunch? There were two other guests. I saw them in the lobby when I checked in. They were all dressed up in brand-new fishing outfits. Vests with lots of pockets, and waterproof pants and whatnot. Except their shoes. They were wearing loafers. Totally useless on a fishing trip. Loafers and white socks. Margaret, if these guys weren't a pair of federal agents, the world is a very different place than I think it is."

Margaret opened her mouth again in mock surprise. "You think they're onto her," she said in a tone of wonder. "All that contact between the extremists and Madigan, Madigan and Charlotte. You think it was like Stan-Stan said: the feds were tracking all that."

"That's why she came to me first."

"And now you think the law has found her. They're finally on her trail."

"It would not surprise me if they were."

"And yet . . . yet still . . ."

Winter raised his eyebrows at her.

She went on: "I mean . . . you're really not going to do anything? Anything at all? You're not going to warn Charlotte about the feds? Or help the feds with their investigation? Or offer to adopt those two poor children who'll be left all alone if Mommy and Daddy go to prison? You're just going to let it all unfold as it will?"

Winter ran one hand up through his long light hair. He worked his jaw to get the stiffness out of it. "You know, in the old days, when I was in the Division, the Recruiter—he taught us how to manipulate people. How to discern their characters, their desires, their needs—and how to use all that to move them into a situation where their scope of action narrowed to a point and they were all but helpless to do anything but what we wanted them to do. Our targets thought they were making decisions on their own, but really, we were guiding them exactly where we wanted them to go."

"But you didn't do any of that here. Or am I missing something?"

"No. You're not missing anything. You're right. I didn't do any of that. And yet, the effect was kind of the same, wasn't it? It was really as if someone else had done all that manipulation work for me. And in the end, for Charlotte, for Emmanuel, for Madigan too—given their characters, given their desires—their options had become so limited, it was easy for me to see what they were going to do."

"Hence the burger and fries and wine, while Emmanuel and Charlotte lured Madigan into their trap," said Margaret.

"Hence the burger and wine and fries, that's right," Winter said. "No other action from me was required. It really was as if the three of them—Charlotte and Emmanuel and Madigan—as if they were all living in a story being written by an invisible hand."

"Oh, my goodness, Cam," said Margaret drily. "Don't tell me you're starting to believe in God. My heart couldn't stand the shock."

This time, Winter's smile—damaged by bruising as it was—was yet broad and warm and full of affection. "Let's not get carried away," he said. "No. No, all I'm saying is that—that Charlotte's story—well, it's not my story. Not anymore."

"Ah, I think I see," said Margaret. "Her story is not your story, and so you're staying out of it. The feds will catch her or they won't. It will be as it will be. There's nothing more for you to do."

"Well . . ." Winter made a face, waggled his head a little. "I wouldn't say that exactly. I wouldn't say there's nothing more. I mean, I still have a story of my own to live out, don't I?"

"You do. You do indeed."

"So, you know, I was thinking—I was thinking I might go home this evening and call Gwendolyn Lord."

Margaret lifted her chin. *Yes*, she thought. *Yes, of course*. Suppressing a pang of foolish jealousy, she managed to manufacture an approving smile. "So it seems the Great Author of your story has maneuvered you into a position where you, too, have only one possible path of action," she said wryly.

"Well, not one. Not only one. I mean, I could not call her."

"Could you not?"

"I think so."

"But you will, won't you?"

"Well. To be honest, I don't think it will matter much what I do. I don't think Gwendolyn will want to talk to me anyway. I've waited too long. I don't think she'll forgive me for that."

"Oh, Cameron," Margaret said, not without feeling, and not entirely without a sense of loss. "I will bet you a dollar that forgive you is exactly what she'll do."

He straightened slowly in the armchair. His lips slowly parted. "Would you?" he said. "Would you bet on that, really?"

"I really would, yes."

"You think she'll forgive me."

"I do," she said. "I have, haven't I? You've told me all the worst things about yourself. The worst things you've ever done."

"I have. Yes."

"And I'm still here, aren't I? I'm still right here with you."

"Yes. Yes, you are. And . . ." He looked around him with a sort of wonder, as if surprised to find himself where he was. "Actually, I find that . . . I find that very encouraging," he said.

From the authority of her therapist's throne, Margaret beamed down on him benevolently. It was a bittersweet victory for her—a little—but it was a victory all the same. He was her client, after all, first and foremost, and she had done for him what she was trained to do, what she had promised him she would. There was still more work for them ahead. Hard work. Winter didn't know it yet, but she did. Removing the fantasy of Charlotte from his mind was only a way of opening the path into the true hurts and traumas of his childhood and his youth. For now, however, that was enough. Margaret had guided him through the maelstrom in the darkest part of his heart and she had brought him to that good place where the water began to run clear. That was not nothing. That was her job. She was proud of herself.

"You think she'll forgive me," Winter repeated softly. He was still thinking about Gwendolyn Lord. There was a slight hitch in his voice, but he smiled at her. "That really is very encouraging. Very encouraging. Because I would very much like to see her again. And you are always right about everything, Margaret."

"Not always, dear. And not about everything," said Margaret Whitaker. She steepled her fingers beneath her chin and swiveled slightly back and forth in her chair. "But there are some things I know."